MORE PRAISE FOR
FIRE AND BONES

"Kathy Reichs is the master of the propulsive thriller. Combing through ashes, bones, and a dark bootlegging past, Temperance Brennan races to thwart an incendiary conspiracy before it all goes up in flames. A special treat!"

—Daniel Kalla, bestselling author of *High Society*

"Reichs is blazing hot—handle with care!"

—Candice Fox, *New York Times* bestselling coauthor of *Never Never*

. . . AND FOR KATHY REICHS

"I love Kathy Reichs—always scary, always suspenseful, and I always learn something."

—Lee Child

"One of my favorite writers."

—Karin Slaughter

"[She has] thrilled readers with pacy, mazey tales grounded in real science. . . . We readers are truly grateful."

—Ian Rankin

"Kathy Reichs writes smart—no, make that brilliant—mysteries."

—James Patterson

FIRE AND BONES

A TEMPERANCE BRENNAN NOVEL

KATHY REICHS

SCRIBNER

NEW YORK   LONDON   TORONTO   SYDNEY   NEW DELHI

Scribner
An Imprint of Simon & Schuster, LLC
1230 Avenue of the Americas
New York, NY 10020

First Scribner hardcover edition August 2024

SCRIBNER and design are trademarks
of Simon & Schuster, LLC

Simon & Schuster: Celebrating 100 Years of Publishing in 2024

For information about special discounts for bulk purchases, please contact Simon & Schuster Special Sales at 1-866-506-1949 or business@simonandschuster.com.

The Simon & Schuster Speakers Bureau can bring authors to your live event. For more information or to book an event, contact the Simon & Schuster Speakers Bureau at 1-866-248-3049 or visit our website at www.simonspeakers.com.

Interior design by Erika R. Genova

Manufactured in the United States of America

1 3 5 7 9 10 8 6 4 2

Library of Congress Control Number: 2024937767

ISBN 978-1-6680-5092-7
ISBN 978-1-6680-5094-1 (ebook)

For the brave men and women who risk their lives safeguarding our homes, forests, and loved ones—for every firefighter everywhere

The right to search for truth implies also a duty; one must not conceal any part of what one has recognized to be true.

—**Albert Einstein**

PROLOGUE

H er nose prickled.
Her throat itched.

She coughed.

Old buildings are musty, she told herself, groggy with sleep.

But why the acrid smell? And what was that bitter taste on her tongue?

Had her instincts been correct? Should she have fled upon seeing the nightmare warren of jerry-rigged rooms? The windowless space her fifty bucks had secured?

She opened her eyes.

To total darkness.

Dust. It's only dust.

Not convinced of that explanation, her hypothalamus ordered up a precautionary round of adrenaline.

Her olfactory lobe IDed the pillow, dank and mildewed from decades spent cushioning the heads of down-in-the-heels travelers. She raised up from it. Slid her phone from beneath it.

The screen came to life, illuminating her hand and the frayed ribbon bordering the ratty polyester blanket. The cast-off glow revealed little else of her surroundings.

Swinging her legs over the side of the mattress, she sat up, scrolled left, and tapped the flashlight app. Sent the plucky little beam looping around her.

Shadows bounced from the room's sparse furnishings in a jumble of cascading angles and shapes. A bureau held level with an ancient keyboard jammed under one corner. A rusty brass floor lamp. A wheeled metal clothing rack holding four hangers.

Nothing alarming.

Until the narrow white shaft landed on the door.

Black smoke was oozing through the gap where the bottom failed to meet the floor. Beyond the gap, orange-and-yellow light danced fitfully.

Flames?

Barely breathing, she tiptoe ran across the carpet and placed a palm on one panel.

The wood felt warm.

She touched the knob.

Hot!

Using the hem of her tee, she turned the handle and inched open a peephole. Flames twisted around the bed and curled the drapes at the window in the adjacent room.

Her breath froze.

She slammed the door.

Ohgodohgodohgod!

She listened. Heard no alarm. No sirens.

What to do!? What to do!?

She called out.

"Help! Please! I'm in here!"

Nothing.

She yelled again and again until her throat screamed.

Catching her breath, she strained for any sign of another human being.

Heard no voice. No movement.

Make a run for it? Somehow that seemed wrong. There were flames just beyond her door. She had no idea of the safest route out of the building.

Heart hammering, she retrieved her mobile and jabbed at digits with one trembling finger. Missed. Tried again.

A woman answered on the first ring.

Nine one one. What's your emergency?

The building I'm in is on fire!

Ma'am. Please stay calm.

Oh, God!

Give me your location.

I don't know the address. It's a rented room.

Okay. I've alerted the fire department. A team will arrive shortly.

I'm going to die!

No. You're not. I'll stay on the line with you. Do you understand?

Yes.

She coughed.

Ma'am, are you injured?

It's getting hard to breathe.

Does the room have a fire escape?

No!

Her eyes felt like smoldering embers. Tears ran down her cheeks.

A window?

No!

A door?

Yes! It feels hot!

Do not open the door. Can you wet a towel or pillowcase and place it over your face?

There's no water in here.

Choking black smoke was slowly filling the room. She coughed until her belly ached and she tasted blood in her mouth.

What's your name?

What?

What's your name?

Skylar.

Skylar, I want you to keep low and move away from the door.

Did the woman sound angry? At her? Was this predicament her fault?

I'm sorry. I didn't mean for this to happen.

Her gut heaved. She gagged.

Skylar. Move away from the door.

Nausea and terror were taking their toll. She could barely hear. Barely think.

Skylar! Move back!

The barked command made her flinch. And spurred her into action.

Covering her mouth with one shaky hand, she crawled into the narrow space between the bureau and a back corner of the room. Pressed her shoulders to one wall. Shot forward upon feeling the heat through the thin cotton.

Arm-wrapping her drawn-up legs, she gulped a series of shallow breaths. Leaned sideways to vomit. Swallowed to wash the bitter bile from her mouth.

Where was the 911 woman? Had she been abandoned? Left alone to die?

Where was her phone? Had she dropped it when the woman's shout caused her to jump? Had she really *had* a mobile? Or only imagined one?

The blaze sizzled and popped on the far side of the door, barely visible through the thick dark smoke. Her ears took in the sounds, detached now, incurious.

Beyond her tiny room, something went *whoosh*. Flames sent tentacles licking through the cracks around the jamb, painting her body in swimmy amber tones. She watched the plastic sign hanging from the knob twist, blacken, and melt. *Shh! Quiet!* it ordered.

She thought hypnotically: *I'm going to die. I'm going to die. I'm going to die.*

The mantra calmed her some. Or maybe her brain was succumbing to the lack of oxygen.

Images skittered through her mind. Her dog, Peaky. Her sister, Mellie. The bridal dress she'd worn less than a year earlier.

Had he found her?

She lowered her lids.

Black dots swirled behind them.

She rested her forehead on her upraised knees.

The room began to recede.

The dots congealed into solid black.

CHAPTER 1

The collection of tiny, gnawed fragments had once been a man. I'd known that right off.

But was that man Norbert Mirek?

I glanced at the wall clock. Eight p.m. I should have left hours ago. But here I was with Norbert. Possibly Norbert.

I was in autopsy room four. The stinky room. My usual haunt.

The whiz-bang ventilation was having little impact on the stench rising from the mix spread out before me. A mix of soil-crusted scat containing vegetation, hair, bone, and sundry unidentifiable inclusions.

The bony bits weren't the olfactive offenders. They'd long since parted ways with any soft tissue that bound them together. The culprit was the poop.

I'm a forensic anthropologist. I regularly handle decomposed, burned, mummified, mutilated, dismembered, and skeletal remains. Putrefied flesh does not gross me out. But digging through shit has never topped my list of preferred tasks. This case was reinforcing that aversion.

Unsorted droppings lay in piles to my left, findings of interest on a blue plastic sheet to my right. Additional bags lined a counter at my back.

Here's the story as I learned it from CMPD homicide detective Skinny Slidell. Though officially retired, due to budget cuts and personnel shortages, Slidell was stepping in occasionally to help resolve low-profile cases.

Always a treat. Skinny has all the charm of dripping snot.

Norbert Mirek, age sixty-eight, owned Lost Foot Pastures, a forty-acre tract of woods and farmland in rural Mecklenburg County, North Carolina. For decades Mirek lived alone on the property, his only companions the pack of rescue dogs he allowed to roam freely. Some thirty of them.

One year ago, Mirek went missing. Two days ago, while hunting turkey at Lost Foot, Mirek's nephew, Halsey Banks, noted coyotes acting oddly beside a road skirting an overgrown field. Curious, Banks walked the area and found several bleached hunks he thought could be bone. And glasses he thought belonged to his uncle.

CMPD cops had run cadaver dogs over the property and collected the motherlode of canine poop. That poop now lay on the stainless-steel table over which I was bending.

Mirek's family wanted answers. Mirek's family's *lawyers* wanted answers.

Skinny was nagging.

That's why I was still at the lab.

Yet, I was finding it hard to focus. It wasn't just the late hour. Or the organic bouquet invading my nostrils and permeating my clothing and hair. My mind kept looping to the upcoming Memorial Day weekend. To a rendezvous with Ryan and a leisurely three days in Savannah.

We'd booked a room at a small B&B called The Tumble Inn. Ryan would fly to Charlotte the next day. I'd pick him up at the airport and we'd head to Georgia. Four-hour drive. Easy-peasy.

Ryan, you ask?

An astute question.

Andrew Ryan, *Lieutenant-détective, Section de Crimes contra la Personne, Sûreté du Québec. Retraité.*

Translation: For decades, Ryan was a cop with the Quebec provincial police. Now retired, he works as a private investigator. A sort of bilingual, trans-border Philip Marlowe.

Ryan is also my longtime partner, both romantic and professional. More on that later.

Concentrate, Brennan!

I tweezed free another fragment. The round edge and large pit told me it was a chunk of femoral head. The tooth marks told me it had been doggy lunch.

I placed the chunk with the others.

Returned to Mount Turd.

"Hey, big guy." Tossing my purse onto the kitchen counter and setting the pizza beside it. "Sorry I'm late."

No feline.

Anticipating a long day, I'd filled Birdie's bowl with kibble before leaving that morning. Instead of his usual ankle-wrapping welcome, the cat was ignoring me. His way of saying he did *not* like the dry chow. Or my long absence.

Bird had a point. It was going on ten. I'd been away almost fourteen hours. But I'd managed to finish sorting through the poop.

Satisfied that some of the bony remnants retrieved from the scat were human, I'd bagged samples to send off for DNA testing. I'd also packaged several gifts for the hair and fiber guys. Then, too exhausted to compose a report, I'd dictated a few sketchy notes before heading home.

To a cranky cat.

Who'd soon learn he'd be staying with a neighbor for three days.

Whatever.

All I wanted was a hot shower, the pizza, then bed.

I got my three wishes. Was down and out when Ray Charles burst into song on my bedside table. "Georgia on My Mind." My current ringtone. You get it, right?

At that moment, I didn't. My brain was too groggy.

Blinking, I grabbed the phone and checked the screen.

The digits on top said 3:02 a.m. The sequence below announced Katy's number.

Sweet Jesus!

A veteran of far too many wee-hour calls, I'm convinced that none ever brings good news.

Suddenly rigid with apprehension, I answered.

"What's wrong, Katy? Where are you?"

"I'm fine. Will you just chill?"

"It's the middle of the night."

"I often call in the middle of the night."

That was true.

"Can you please snap to?" she said.

I sat up and scooched back against the headboard. Took a beat. Then,

"How goes it, Katy Matey?"

"Do you know how dorky that sounds?"

"You used to like it."

"When I was six."

"Aren't *we* in a mood."

"I am *not* in a mood."

First the cat, now my daughter.

"What's up?" At three a.m.? I didn't add that.

"Taxes and Chinese balloons."

"And you say I'm a dork?"

"I have a favor to ask."

"Sure," I said. Automatic.

"You're not going to like it."

Great.

"Do you remember my speaking of Ivy Doyle?"

"Sorry, I don't."

"Ivy's a reporter. She was embedded with my unit during my second deployment to Afghanistan. Now she works for a television news station in Washington, DC."

A TV journalist. Katy was right. I didn't like where this was heading.

"I want you to do an interview with her. About a fire she's covering."

"You know I don't do interviews."

"Why not?"

"Nothing good ever comes from talking to the press." Same category as late-night calls. I didn't say that, either.

"Jesus, Mom. That's so close-minded."

"Let's just say I've been burned."

"No pun intended."

"Hilarious."

I heard the whoosh of a pop-top. Gulping.

"Can you just speak with her?"

"Sweetie, I—"

"I *owe* Ivy." A new tension edged Katy's plea. "Big-time."

My daughter rarely spoke of her time in the military. Of the combat she'd seen. The back-to-back war zone tours that had changed her forever. The nightmares that still haunted her sleep.

"I wouldn't lay this on you if it wasn't important." Katy's voice told me this was a hard ask for her. "To me."

I waited.

Katy drew a taut breath. "Ivy saved my life."

I remained very still, picturing my daughter's army-cropped blond hair. Her intense green eyes. The scar on her cheek.

The scar about which she'd never spoken.

"Do you want to discuss it?"

"No. I want you to help Ivy. She really needs this."

"Why?"

A beat, then, "That's not important."

"Help her how?" Resisting a sigh. Already resigned.

"A building is on fire in the district. I don't have any details, but people are missing and feared trapped inside. Ivy has been assigned to the story and would like you to talk about what happens during the processing of fire scenes containing dead people."

"Why me?"

"You wrote an article about—here's a shocker—processing fire scenes containing dead people. Ivy found it, knows you're my mother, contacted me."

I had to think a moment. Bingo.

The publication had appeared more than fifteen years earlier in an obscure journal for arson investigators. I was astounded the piece was still available.

"Where did she dig up that bit of genius?"

"Mom. Nothing ever dies on the World Wide Web."

True. But the fact that Doyle had unearthed it told me she was one dogged sleuth.

"Ryan is flying down from Montreal tomorrow. I'm picking him up at five-thirty in the evening, then we're leaving town."

"Ivy can set up a Zoom meeting whenever you want. You pick the time."

"Why does this smell like an ambush?"

"The entire thing will take five minutes."

Except for the whole hair and makeup effort I'd have to make.

"Fine. Eight a.m."

"Ivy will send you an email with a Zoom link. Have I told you that you're awesome?"

"No."

"You're awesome."

Five hours later I was seated at my computer, blush on my cheeks, hair in a reasonably stable ponytail. The face filling the left half of my screen was that of a thirty-something with aquamarine eyes, perfect teeth, flawless skin, ginger hair, and a provocatively asymmetric nose. A combo that might have landed it on the cover of *Vogue*.

To say Ivy Doyle was charismatic would be like saying the Atlantic Ocean was damp. Even digitally, the woman radiated a force that was almost palpable.

So why was it such a big deal to interview me?

"I can't thank you enough for doing this. Perhaps Katy mentioned it, but I'm pitching a show to the network. It's called *ID: Ivy Doyle Digs.* Get it? The title uses my initials."

"Clever."

"Currently, I do *ID* as a podcast. But I don't want to stay a local reporter and podcaster forever. I know this fire isn't the story of the century, but scoring an on-air interview with a celebrity scientist will improve my visibility. Which never hurts in the TV biz."

Celebrity scientist?

Unsure how to respond, I said nothing.

"To not waste your time, I'll do an intro later and paste that part in, explaining that the building has been burning since sometime after midnight, and that recovery will begin as soon as the site is deemed safe. This morning, I'll just outline your qualifications, then go to my questions. You cool with that?"

"Let's do it." A tad uneasy not having seen those questions.

Ivy's shoulders squared. She nodded, then, receiving a signal that the camera was rolling, began in a voice deeper and more modulated than the one I'd just heard.

"With me is Dr. Temperance Brennan, consulting anthropologist to the Mecklenburg County Medical Examiner in Charlotte, North Carolina, and to the Laboratoire de Sciences Judiciaires et de Médecine Légale in Montreal, Canada."

Doyle's French pronunciation, usually mangled by reporters, was perfect.

"One of only a handful of experts ever certified by the American Board of Forensic Anthropology, Dr. Brennan is a specialist in the recovery and analysis of burned human remains. Thank you so much for being here, Doctor."

"My pleasure."

Christ. I sounded like a waiter at the Ritz.

"Dr. Brennan. The fire has been raging since approximately two a.m., and at least four people remain unaccounted for." Slightly breathy. "The building is close to a century in age. Sections of its interior have collapsed. What are scientists up against in cases like this?"

"The search for victims can't begin until the rubble has cooled and the surviving parts of the structure have been declared sound. Once those conditions have been met, search and recovery can begin."

"I imagine the process will be slow and painstaking. What difficulties will searchers encounter?"

"One problem might be floor collapse."

"Please explain that."

"Though stone or brick walls may survive the flames, wooden floors may collapse and accordion down onto each other. Bodies of victims often end up at the lowest level under layers of debris. But not always."

"Investigators are trying to establish the names of the missing. People known to live or be renting rooms in the building. How helpful will that information be?"

"Extremely."

Doyle waited for me to elaborate. When I didn't, "You say recovery will largely be a matter of working through layers." She frowned, an appropriately troubled wrinkling of her brow. "What will searchers find?"

"It's hard to say. Prolonged exposure to intense heat coupled with crushing pressure from the weight of fallen debris are not a good combination."

A beat, then Doyle shifted gears.

"Once a body is brought to your lab, what procedure do you follow?"

"In the jurisdictions in which I work, a pathologist would be in charge. In a specialty situation, he or she would call for anthropological expertise."

"A specialty situation such as a fire death?"

"Yes."

"Because the deceased isn't visually recognizable."

"Yes." Uncomfortable with such a grisly point.

"What would your role be?"

"I would help to establish identifications."

"How?"

This interview was getting more detailed than I liked. Mindful of victims' friends or relatives who might soon watch it, I chose my words carefully.

"I would examine the remains to determine age, sex, ancestry, height, the presence of medical or genetic anomalies—any particularities observable on the bones. I would construct what I call a biological profile. A forensic dentist would observe the teeth and create a dental chart."

"You're assuming these poor people will be burned beyond recognition."

"I'm assuming nothing." Sharper than I intended. Or not.

"What about fingerprints?"

Images of charred corpses bombarded my mind. I saw the scorched flesh. The curled and blackened limbs. The distorted or missing digits.

"One can always hope, but the hands would have to be in printable condition, and even if they were, the prints would have to be in some database to be useful."

"Of course. I'm told that family members will be asked to provide DNA samples. Is it possible to get genetic information from a burned skeleton?"

"It's possible." The subject was far too complex, so I left it at that.

"What are your thoughts when you're doing this kind of work? Are the victims always foremost in your mind?" Bright red lips pressed grimly together.

"Yes. But at the scene or in the lab I remain focused. Completely objective. My goal is to get every victim back to his or her family, whatever may be left of them."

"What can you say to those anxious for word on their loved ones?"

"I know that waiting must be unbearably hard. But proper recovery and identification takes time. It's heartbreaking, but be patient. Those working are doing the best they can."

"Thank you so much, Dr. Brennan."

"My pl— You're welcome."

When we'd disconnected, I sat a moment replaying my comments in my head. Decided it wasn't a great interview, not a bad one, either.

Still, the exchange with Ivy Doyle hadn't altered my view that only woe comes from media exposure.

Within hours that view would be proven correct.

CHAPTER 2

y cell phone rang as I was packing.

The caller's number began with the digits 202. The area code for Washington, DC.

Normally, I ignore unknown numbers. Something told me to make an exception.

I looked at Birdie.

If a cat could shrug, he did.

Tossing a swimsuit into the rollaboard, I tapped the green icon.

"Temperance Brennan."

"Dr. Brennan. I'm so glad I caught you. It's Jada Thacker." The voice was female, and clearly nervous.

"Yes?"

"I don't know if you remember me. We met years ago at an AAFS meeting in Seattle. I'd just graduated med school and was about to begin a residency in pathology."

"Of course." Total blank.

"I asked your opinion on a field course in forensic archaeology that I planned to take."

A vague recollection began to coalesce. A very large young woman with enormous earrings and hair the shiny black of crow's feathers.

And far too much bubbly enthusiasm for that late in the day.

Now that woman sounded pinched and anxious.

"What can I do for you, Dr. Thacker?"

"I just watched the interview you did for WTTG. I got your contact information from Ivy Doyle. The reporter. I hope that's all right."

"Uh. Huh." It wasn't.

"I'll come straight to the point. Based on witness accounts, we believe people perished in this fire. I'm the interim medical examiner for the District of Columbia, so handling those deaths is my responsibility. As you so brilliantly pointed out in your responses to Ms. Doyle, proper processing of a fire scene requires a very specific skill set. A skill set no member of my staff possesses."

Nope. No way.

"My techs are capable of basic recovery, of course. Most have worked fire scenes. But they'll need expert direction and oversight for this one. Guidance from someone with extraordinary knowledge and vast experience."

"Isn't there a board-certified anthropologist in the DC area?" I asked, ignoring that Thacker was laying it on thick.

"Normally I'd rely on Gene Raynor. But Dr. Raynor is in Portugal and unavailable."

"Aren't there others?"

"I want you."

I braced. Anticipating that for the second time in twenty-four hours a forceful young woman was about to try to sell me a line.

"I need your help, Dr. Brennan. I owe it to these victims and to their families to get the job done right."

"I'm so sorry, Dr. Thacker. I have plans that will tie me up for the next few days. But I'd be happy to refer you to—"

"I'm going to share some intel. What I say must remain strictly between us."

Confidential info was the last thing I wanted.

"The authorities suspect that the property was being used as an illegal Airbnb."

"It was unlicensed?"

"Yes. According to witness statements, the second and third floors were subdivided into a warren of rooms, many without windows, none with fire escapes. One long-term renter claims there were at least four people sleeping on the upper levels when the fire broke out."

"Why wasn't the place shut down?"

"I don't know. What I *do* know is that the poor souls inside that building didn't stand a chance."

A new collage of images strobed in my brain, vivid as the day it happened. To me. The old row house in Pointe-Saint-Charles. The acrid smoke. The reeking gasoline-soaked rug. The hungry flames devouring the ancient wood.

Thacker's voice snapped me back to the present.

"—obtained some names. One of those feared dead is a nineteen-year-old Canadian named Skylar Reese Hill. I've heard a recording of Hill's nine-one-one call. The terror in the girl's voice is heart-wrenching."

"Hill is among the missing?"

"Yes. And her husband is demanding answers and not bothering with polite."

I really didn't give a damn about the husband who is suddenly greatly concerned, perhaps because he senses the possibility of money. But I was touched by the death of a nineteen-year-old struggling to stay alive.

Thacker allowed a moment of silence to emphasize the gravity of her next words.

"I'm begging you, Dr. Brennan. Please find it in your heart to help me. To help them."

My gaze dropped to the half-filled suitcase. To the sundresses and sandals stacked beside it. While I'd been thinking about juleps and pecan pie, innocent victims had been perishing in an inferno.

Damnitdamnitdamnit!

"Okay."

"Really? You'll come?"

"Yes." It was so far from *okay* it wasn't even in the same galaxy.

"Thank you so, *so* much." There was that bubbly that I recalled. "How soon can you leave?"

I glanced at the clock. Nine-seventeen. I had to repack, placate and deliver Birdie to my neighbor, then drive to the airport.

"Eleven."

"I'll book a hotel and a flight and call you right back."

"Right back" was almost an hour later. The bubbly was gone, replaced by an elevated level of distress.

"I'm sorry this took so long. My secretary, my assistant, and I have all been on the phone. In addition to the normal Memorial Day frenzy of tourists, DC is hosting WorldPride 2025 and there's some mammoth event this weekend. The district will be insane. The good news is that I managed to finagle a room at the Hyatt Place, which is right across the street from our office.

"The bad news is that there isn't a single seat on any direct flight from Charlotte. I could get you here by seven, but it would involve changing planes and a long layover in Philadelphia."

Mother of God. Could this get any worse?

"I'll drive," I said.

"Are you sure?"

"It's only six hours." In the wrong damn direction.

"I can't tell you how much I appreciate this. Text when you're an hour out and I'll arrange for a meet in my office. The fire investigator will be thrilled to have you."

He wasn't.

I don't mind long road trips. Cross-country travel brings out the pioneer in me. Not that I was migrating west in a covered wagon. Or blazing a trail through uncharted wilderness.

I'd made the trip to DC many times. Still, I enjoyed reading each exit sign as it flew by. Mooresville. Greensboro. Richmond. Fredericksburg.

I played mental games imagining life in those towns. The school plays. The office rivalries. The neighborhood dramas.

The lure of the open highway. Unknown people. Unknown places.

At the height of the craze, my father owned a CB radio. When I could score the family car, I'd put my "ears" on and chat with Thunderman or Big El or K-Bone, believing they had no idea I was only a kid. *Breaker! C'Mon!* My handle was Scooter.

Eventually, my sister, Harry, ratted me out. Mama shut down my trucker pastime, fast and hard.

The day was warm and muggy, with fat dark clouds rolling and shouldering low in the sky. The farther north I went, the more imminent the rain seemed. I hoped the storm would hold off until I'd reached the hotel.

As soon as I'd disconnected with Thacker, I'd phoned Ryan. The call had not gone well. Though he'd tried to mask it, I could read the annoyance in his voice. The frustration. As he correctly pointed out, it was the second time that spring I'd canceled plans with him.

Suck it up, dude. I was disappointed, too.

The hasty transfer of the cat was also unpleasant. Released from his carrier, Birdie had shot under my neighbor's couch and begun howling like his genitals were on fire.

Same sentiment. I wasn't going to a damn spa, Bird.

Now and then an eighteen-wheeler went by too fast, a black or red blur that rocked my Mazda and roused me from my thoughts. I'd brought coffee in one of those insulated Yetis. With each blast, I downed more, and was soon afloat on caffeine.

For a while I listened to an audiobook. When that ended, I went back to the radio, switching stations as I left different NPR broadcast areas.

I am not a slow driver. Ryan tells me I have a lead foot. An overused descriptor but, in my case, accurate.

I took I-85 to I-95 and made good time. Was near Stafford, maybe an hour from the capital, when two things happened.

The storm broke.

Traffic ground to a halt.

Noting the sea of red taillights ahead, I braked.

Waited.

Nothing moved.

I waited some more.

Cursed.

I am also not a patient driver.

Irritated, I shifted into park and leaned back, resigned to the delay.

Rain slammed the windshield and drummed a million tiny bullets against my hood and roof. The wind gusted, swirling the deluge and occasionally yielding glimpses of the world outside my little bubble. During those brief intervals, vehicles emerged and took shape before vanishing back into the gray void.

As with most thunderstorms, this one passed quickly, and traffic began to crawl. In ten-foot bursts. Accelerate. Brake. Accelerate. Brake. I spent the next hour lurching my way forward.

I'll be the first to admit that I have a temper. Always have had. My grandmother attributed this character flaw to my Irish genes. But Gran credited everything, good or bad, to that same Gaelic DNA.

As a kid I wasn't great at keeping my temper in check. It had a high trigger point but once tripped, I'd spew venom on anyone and anything within range.

As an adult I've developed techniques to catch myself in that split second before I detonate and let loose. Sometimes I count. Sometimes I do yogic breathing. Sometimes I run through the lyrics of a song in my head.

The shattered plans for Savannah. The cranky cat. The long drive. The unforgiving traffic. The grim task ahead.

Alone in the car, I didn't even try restraint. Letting the disappointment and frustration blast free, I cursed and wished pestilence on the unseen drivers in the vehicles around me.

The internalized tantrum helped. If not with the clogged artery that was I-395, then at least with my frazzled nerves. When the private outburst had played itself out, I asked my cell phone to dial Thacker's number. She answered on the first ring.

I reported that my navigation app was putting me at forty minutes away. She commiserated about the traffic and said she'd meet me at the hotel.

With its stacked windows and lighted overhang projecting above glass front doors, the Hyatt Place looked like a thousand other high-rise inns in America. One corner of the building was all glass and steel. Flags flew from poles on the roof. Signs identified the brand in enormous vertical and horizontal letters.

It was almost seven when I pulled up to the entrance. A doorman with chocolate skin and smoke-yellowed teeth queried my intent. His name tag said T. Valentine.

I told T. Valentine I was checking in. Accepting my car keys, he offered help with my luggage. I thanked him and said I'd prefer to pull the bag myself.

The lobby was spacious and done in what the designer might have labeled cubist modern. Rectangular sofas and desks. Square footstools. Oblong slashes on the carpet. Lots of gray and yellow.

I looked around. Saw no one I thought could be Jada Thacker.

Why did I find the woman's absence surprising? Nothing else was going as expected.

I crossed to one of the desk clerks, an Asian man so small his chin barely cleared the top of the counter. His tag said H. Cho.

I told H. Cho that a reservation had been made in my name. He beamed and asked for ID.

After a quick glance at my license and my face, H. Cho typed my name into the system. His smile held as he studied the screen. Faltered as his fingers again flew over the keyboard.

"I'm sorry, madam. Could the reservation be under a different name?"

"Perhaps Jada Thacker?"

More typing.

"No."

An eight-hour drive that should have taken six. No holiday with Ryan. No room. No Thacker.

The tripwire in my brain tightened.

I took a deep breath.

It wasn't H. Cho's fault.

I opened my mouth to express my displeasure.

"Dr. Brennan." Breathless.

I turned.

The person rushing toward me was not who I expected.

CHAPTER 3

The woman looked like an ad for Paris Fashion Week. Standing maybe six feet tall and weighing no more than one-fifty, she had high cheekbones and short black hair gelled straight back from her face.

"Dr. Brennan." Fashion Week extended a hand. "I'm Jada Thacker."

We shook, *moi* hoping I was hiding my surprise.

Apparently, I wasn't.

"I know." Thacker smiled broadly. "I've dropped a few pounds since that meeting in Seattle."

"Such a long time ago." Too flummoxed to summon a wittier response.

"My apologies for being late. Something came up as I was leaving the office."

"Of course."

"All set here?"

"Actually, no. The gentleman can't find a reservation for me."

"What seems to be the problem?"

H. Cho, who'd been following our conversation, perked up when the attention shifted to him.

"We're fully booked, ma'am. The lady's name isn't in the system."

"The *doctor* has come to DC to assist with the recovery effort at the Foggy Bottom fire. She's just finished a very long drive and would undoubtedly like to freshen up. Surely, we can resolve this quickly."

H. Cho raised both palms in a "what can I do" gesture.

Thacker turned to me, smile now a bit strained. "Please have a seat while I straighten this out."

I nodded, crossed to one of the yellow sofas, and dropped. Snugging the rollaboard to my knees, I looked around.

The lobby was slowly filling with patrons. Or maybe I hadn't noticed them when I'd arrived.

Across from me, a couple in matching stars-and-stripes sweatshirts studied a tourist brochure and seemed to agree on nothing. A teen slumped boneless in a chair to their right, working patterns on the armrest with one fingertip.

An old geezer in a rainbow blazer and red bow tie entered from the street and crossed to the elevators. When the doors opened a family of five bustled out. The tense hunch of Dad's shoulders suggested he was not a happy fellow.

I was checking my watch, again, when a shadow fell across my wrist. I looked up. Thacker was standing close, proffering a room key.

"We're good for one night."

"One night?"

"Don't worry. We'll sort it. Are you hungry?"

"Yes." The term didn't do justice to the grievance my stomach was registering.

"How about I give you twenty minutes to get settled? I'll order take-out and text the deputy fire chief to meet us at my office."

"Sounds like a plan."

"What would you like to eat?"

"An entire Chinese buffet."

DC's chief medical examiner facility, the OCME, is located in the Consolidated Forensic Laboratory. Sharing the same address at the CFL are the Department of Forensic Sciences and the Metropolitan Police Department. Odd bedfellows. Nerds and cops under one roof.

That roof topped a six-story modern colossus at the intersection of 4th and E Streets in Southwest Washington. Lots of concrete, steel, and glass, with sun-activated solar panels shading one side. Pretty landscaping. And, blessedly, just steps from the hotel.

After swiping her security card, Thacker led me across a lobby whose speckled black-and-white tile gleamed with the commanding appearance of a surgical suite. At eight p.m. on the eve of a holiday weekend the cavernous space was largely deserted.

When I'd signed a register and presented ID, a bored-looking receptionist issued me a pass proclaiming *VISITOR: Escort Required* in bold block letters. Apparently, I wasn't to be trusted unaccompanied.

Thacker and I crossed to the elevators, her three-inch stilettos clicking sharply. Thumbing a button, she explained that her office used a portion of the lobby level for intake but was mostly housed on the fifth and sixth floors.

When the car came, we ascended in silence, both doing that eyes-on-the-floor-indicator-lights thing. A previous occupant must have showered in Brut. The small cell reeked of the stuff.

Exiting on five, we walked a long hallway, Thacker's stilettos muted by the institutional gray-on-gray patchwork carpet. As had been the case downstairs, I saw no one except a receptionist.

Thacker continued her tour, pointing out that the floor above was dedicated to administration, the floor we were on to death investigation. Located on our level were a tox lab and several autopsy rooms. She suggested we skip those areas, since I'd be seeing them soon. I agreed.

The offices we passed were set off by orange walls down low and frosted glass panes rising above. Plaques identified the occupants as pathologists, anthropologists, medico-legal investigators, and forensic identification specialists. A roster as familiar to me as my own hand.

Thacker's digs—not small and not large—were nicer than most government accommodations I'd seen. Directly opposite the door, an L-shaped desk pointed across the room, then turned left along the wall. Matching wood cabinets hung above the wall arm. A computer sat in the desk's center.

Occupying every other horizontal surface was evidence of the endless bookkeeping associated with handling the dead. Stacked printouts I suspected were intake rosters, correspondence, lab test results, and reports. Antemortem medical records sent from clinics and hospitals. CDs holding stored X-rays. Manila case files, some thick, others strikingly thin.

Floor-to-ceiling glass formed the back wall. Beyond the plants lining its double sills and the movable solar panels outside, I could see I-395. Twinkling ribbons of head- and taillights streamed in both directions, one white, one red.

Under the desk's outward-projecting arm was a NASA-level ergonomic seat. Facing it were two chairs, each a complicated arrangement of black Naugahyde and chrome. A grease-stained white bag sat on the desk's blotter.

Thacker had taken my quip literally. The bag looked enormous. The smells of garlic, ginger, and sesame sent my stomach into a full-gainer flip.

While Thacker got plates and utensils, I withdrew a collection of little white cartons, each decorated with a cheerful red pagoda. We were serving ourselves kung pao chicken, Sichuan pork, dumplings, and fried rice when a loudly cleared throat caused us to turn.

A figure stood framed in the doorway. Maybe five-six, the guy had the body of a former gymnast nurturing a fondness for pastry. Narrow face and shoulders. Pale gray eyes the size of dimes. Thinning blond hair combed painfully forward.

A patch on the man's black shirt showed the Capitol with US and DC flags above, fire and medical symbols below. The words *District of Columbia Fire and EMS* wrapped the periphery.

A smoky film on the man's face suggested he'd come straight from work. Its expression said he was not happy about being called away.

"Ah, Sergeant Burgos. I was expecting Captain Hickey."

"He's a tad busy." The voice was high and nasal, the tone sarcastic as hell.

"Of course." Thacker arced a palm toward the food. "Please join us."

"No, thank you."

"Dr. Brennan, I'd like you to meet Luis Burgos. Goes by Lubu if I recall correctly?"

Burgos didn't confirm or deny.

"Sergeant Burgos is the investigator assigned to this terrible fire."

I extended a hand.

Burgos didn't shake it.

Alrighty, then.

"Please, have a seat." Thacker's palm was now aimed at the Naugahyde and chrome.

Burgos yanked the closest chair and sat. Raised his left ankle onto his right knee, body language radiating his eagerness to be gone.

Plate in hand, Thacker circled to her ergonomic perch. Noting that she'd taken only a few spoonfuls of edamame beans to gnaw on, I moved to the seat beside Burgos.

"Dr. Brennan is the forensic anthropologist I told Captain Hickey about. She's come—"

"Where's Gaynor?"

"Portugal."

Burgos flicked the upraised foot several times but said nothing.

"If I'm not mistaken, Engine Company 23 was the first unit to respond to the fire?"

Burgos nodded.

"And you've been there with them right from the start." Thacker's voice oozed compassion and gratitude.

Burgos's foot flicked again.

To me, Thacker said, "Sergeant Burgos is here to brief you on the situation."

Burgos spoke to Thacker, ignored me. "The *situation* is that the bastard's still hot and I've gotta get back there."

"Of course. A short summary will give Dr. Brennan an idea of the conditions she'll encounter."

Burgos sighed. "What do you wanna know?"

Having worked with equally hostile cops, I recognized the signals. The man thought his time too valuable to be wasted on coaching a geek scientist.

"It would help to have a sense of the fire's intensity," I said.

"The call came in as a two-alarm, quickly went to three. Right now, there's six engine companies with four personnel each, three ladder companies with five personnel each, a heavy rescue squad with five, an ambulance with two EMTs, a medic unit with two paramedics, an air unit, and a rehab unit on site. That give you some *sense*?"

"Thank you. That's very thorough. What does the air unit do?" I asked, unfamiliar with the term.

Burgos answered, still without looking at me. "Refill the firefighters' air bottles."

"The rehab unit?"

"Provide a rest platform and rehydration liquids."

"That's a serious crew."

"Look, lady. You gotta understand." Slow, a teacher to a dull student. "It's Foggy Bottom. The building's old and full of all kinds of flammable shit. The fire's been burning since two in the morning. The motherfucker's still got fuel and she don't wanna give it up."

"I *understand* that people may have died in that building. That there may be bodies in the rubble. I'd like to *understand* when I can recover those victims."

"You go in when we say you go in."

"Will that be tonight?" Thacker asked affably.

"Not a chance." Sharp and officious.

On the desktop, beside the blotter, a miniature red rubber corpse lay with a single pen rising from its chest. I knew the medical supply company that had gifted that little gem to Thacker. Had one of my own.

Eyes on the macabre swag, I silently counted to three.

Drew a breath.

"Have you obtained an architectural plan of the building?" I asked.

"People are looking."

I raised my brows in question. Pointless. Burgos still refused to make eye contact.

"Sir?" I prodded.

"Hickey can explain the layout."

"You can't?" Chilly. This guy was an arrogant prick.

"The structure dates to the turn of the century. The *last* century. No codes back then. The place was a disaster waiting to happen."

"It was currently being used as an Airbnb?"

"So I'm told."

I looked at my watch. The fire had been burning for more than eighteen hours. Since no one could have survived such an inferno, there was no urgency to my task. Still, the guy's callousness was grating.

"How many stories?" I asked.

"Three. And a basement. A portion of the sonofabitch has pancaked down to that level."

"Should I expect to go in tonight?"

"No way in hell."

"When?"

"When every friggin' hotspot is cool and Hickey gives the go-ahead."

"I'll be ready at dawn."

"Suit yourself."

Burgos pushed to his feet and strode from the office.

"That was pleasant," I said to Thacker.

"Always is."

"I think the gentleman dislikes me. Any idea why?"

Thacker forked an edamame bean. Pointed it in my direction.

"I believe it has to do with you not having a dick."

Thacker jotted an address on a yellow Post-it and leaned forward to hand it to me.

"I'm sending a recovery team that knows a little about fire scenes. They'll be there early. Join them." A long brown finger pointed my way. "Make Lubu's day."

CHAPTER 4

The US capital was established in 1790 by an act of Congress authorizing a federal district. President Washington chose a hunk of land lying where the Anacostia River meets the Potomac River, a location that offered easy access to the western frontier and was diplomatically sandwiched between the northern and southern states.

Washington's choice of architect was Pierre Charles L'Enfant, a Frenchman who came to America to fight in the Revolutionary War. In 1791, L'Enfant began designing the District of Columbia from scratch—that scratch being plantation acreage, much grudgingly yielded, rolling hills, dense woodland, and soggy marsh. L'Enfant imagined a grand city of wide avenues, public squares, and inspiring buildings, his concept based on European models adapted to the New World notion of egalitarianism.

True to this crazy American ideal, instead of reserving the grandest spot for the leader's palace, L'Enfant placed Congress at the highest elevation, a hill with a commanding view of the Potomac. Central to his scheme was a public walkway, a tree-lined grassy strip running for two miles from Capitol Hill to the river.

Today, Smithsonian museums flank both sides of that strip, now dubbed the National Mall. Natural History. Portraiture. Art. Air and Space. Other creations George and Pierre would never have imagined. War memorials sit among stately monuments to Lincoln, Washington, Jefferson, and others.

Setting forth at seven the next morning, cranky at having to check out of my room, I thought about the best way to navigate. I knew that modern DC is divided into four quadrants called, uncreatively, Northwest, Southwest, Northeast, and Southeast. That numbered streets run north and south, lettered streets east and west. That avenues named for the fifty states cut diagonally through the grid, often meeting at traffic circles or squares.

Smooth sailing, right? Not under normal circumstances. Definitely not with Memorial Day and WorldPride 2025 madness clogging every square inch of town.

My hotel—former hotel—was in the Southwest. The address Thacker had provided was in the Northwest, not far from Washington Circle and smack across Monsieur L'Enfant's grand *oeuvre*. I hoped that the hour was too early for curious tourists, flag-waving pedestrians, gender-affirming rallies, and patriotic parades.

The kind WAZE lady giving traffic advice suggested taking D Street across to Maine Avenue, then Independence Avenue to Rock Creek Parkway. Seemed reasonable, so I did. Encountered only minor delays and enjoyed the parkway's stretch of winding two-lane through the wooded urban canyon.

Exiting onto K Street, I made my way toward Twenty-sixth. Toward an address at the edge of Foggy Bottom, a hodgepodge hood composed of single-family homes dating to the 1800s, blocky midrise condos and apartments, and daunting buildings like the Kennedy Center and the Watergate Hotel. Throw in George Washington University and the area is a real mix.

Well before reaching the fire scene, my ears informed me that I was near. Through the car's fully closed windows I could hear the muted *whup-whup-whup* of chopper blades overhead. The steely *rattle* and *clank* of girders and chains. The *shush* and *thud* of displaced rubble.

A sooty smell slowly infused the car's interior. With every breath I imagined minute but toxic particulates gleefully worming their way into my lungs.

One block out, an MPDC patrol unit—all red, white, and blue—barricaded the street. A cop stood beside it, shoes ruthlessly shined, arms folded across her uniformed chest. Bronze aviators hid the woman's eyes. A black mask covered her mouth and nose.

Ten yards from Officer Shiny Shoes, I spied a gap in the row of vehicles parked along the opposite curb. Quick U-ey. Then, with much sweaty maneuvering, I wedged my Mazda into the roller-skate-sized space with only inches to spare between a red Jeep Wagoneer and a piss-yellow Camry with a window sticker declaring *I Brake for Aliens.*

I sat a moment, cooling down and assessing. Wondering who'd ever paint a car that color.

A lot of the equipment and personnel on Burgos's list were now gone. I counted only two engines and two ladder units, all bright shiny red. All with the Engine Company 23 logo on one side. Heavy construction paraphernalia had replaced the departed fire trucks, and search and recovery were in full swing.

A pair of EMTs leaned against a clunky, cuboid ambulance, one smoking, the other just leaning, both looking tired and bored. I assumed their presence was for the responders, not for the building's inhabitants, now elsewhere or dead.

Reinforcing that assumption was an ME van sitting directly behind the ambulance. Its transport team dozed in the front seat, one with head resting on the wheel, the other with booted feet on the dash.

A pair of techs in protective gear stood outside a second vehicle bearing the OCME shield. Thacker's death recovery team, I assumed. My crew.

I shifted my gaze to the reason we were all there.

Though smoke-blackened and badly damaged, with its easternmost section largely collapsed, the building had held on to enough of its original construction for those present to appreciate that it had once been a beauty. And grander than most of its neighbors.

Located on a corner, separated by a narrow gap from the rest of the row, the three-story brick Victorian had a rounded front topped by a copper-roofed turret. Lots of recesses and ornately trimmed balconies, windows, and doors. Wide steps.

An arrow of sadness pierced my chest. People had ascended those steps to enter that building. And they would never descend.

Chill, Brennan. Do your job.

Nerves hot, blood cool, I alighted and drew my recovery kit from the trunk. Pausing to tie my boots together at the laces, I looped them around my neck and started toward Officer Shiny Shoes. Seeing me, she straightened, spread her high-sheen footwear, and thumb-hooked her utility belt.

I smiled and waved my free hand.

Officer Shiny Shoes did not wave back. Merely followed my progress with unreadable eyes.

Drawing close I could see that the woman's name tag said L. Comer. Knowing cops, I wondered how many ribald jokes that surname had prompted.

"Officer Comer," I said.

Tight nod.

"Temperance Brennan." I set down the case and pulled an ID from my pocket. "I'm here to help with recovery."

Comer pointed the aviators at the small plastic rectangle, my Charlotte-Mecklenburg OCME security pass, then handed it back.

"Go ahead." Chin-cocking the scene behind her.

"I'm to contact Captain Hickey."

"He's here."

"Where?"

Comer shrugged, never disengaging the thumbs. "You'll know him. Guy looks like André the Giant."

That reference seemed oddly dated for a thirty-something cop. Wondering, pointlessly, if Comer was knowledgeable about wrestling history, I circled the cruiser and headed toward the action.

Comer hadn't exaggerated.

At five yards out, I could see that one form loomed larger than life amid the firefighters still present. Though the double-layered turnout suit rendered accuracy difficult, I guessed the man's weight at two ninety, his height at six-eight in stocking feet. Which must have been size sixteen.

I slowed to observe. The team appeared to require no direction from its leader. They spoke little, each doing his or her job confidently and efficiently.

Those jobs now seemed to involve wrapping up. Stowing ladders. Coiling hoses. Rinsing and decontaminating gear.

I expected to be approached and asked for ID. Either no one noticed me, or no one cared I was there.

"Captain Hickey," I called out.

No response.

"Captain Hickey!" Too shrill?

Hickey's head whipped around. I imagined him taking in my boots, jeans, and white tee. My death scene recovery case.

Maybe Burgos or Thacker had briefed him. Maybe he was just curious. A word to the colleague beside him, then Hickey strode in my direction.

Big strides.

As with Comer, Hickey's face was largely concealed, the chinstrap, visor, and earflaps on his helmet hiding his expression. Only one clue. Through the clear plastic eye guard, I noted dark brows angled down and drawn together.

In puzzlement? Disapproval?

I braced for the same hostility Burgos had shown.

While walking, Hickey removed his helmet and tucked it under one arm. The sun was higher now and, despite the smoky haze, my mind logged an itemized first impression.

Sweat- and grime-covered skin, lighter in starburst creases cornering each eye. Irises the green of a Limerick spring. Rusty hair going every direction at once.

"Declan Hickey." An enormous hand shot my way. "I'm guessing you're the anthropologist."

"Temperance Brennan."

We shook. Hickey's grip could have remolded steel.

"Thacker said you were coming." Voice deep as an operatic basso. "Glad to have you on board."

"Burgos told me you're the man of the hour."

The man of the hour? Seriously, Brennan?

Hickey shrugged a modest shoulder. "I was the first arriving chief so I'm in command. Burgos ran things down for you?"

"Sort of."

"Burgos is an ass."

I couldn't disagree.

"What's the current status?" I asked.

"The fire's out. What remains of the structure has been deemed sound."

"How many presumed dead?"

"The building was being used as an illegal Airbnb so who the hell knows. I'm told that reports submitted to the DC short-term rental hotline complained of no fire extinguishers, smoke detectors, alarms, or sprinklers. In other words, the place was a death trap."

"Burgos said you'd interviewed one of the tenants?"

"Yeah. A guy named Billie Norris, an artist who's rented one of the first-floor apartments for fourteen years. Odd duck. Norris thought there were four people in the upstairs rooms. A young woman from Canada, a gay couple, some guy he's sure is a spy."

"Really?"

"That was Norris's take. Probably because the Harry S Truman is so close."

I looked confused.

"The headquarters for the State Department. Like I said, the guy's an odd duck."

"How did Norris know who was in the building?"

"He gets reduced rent for issuing keys."

"Who owns the property?"

"Norris says he's never met the guy, does everything online. Guess title is a question for the cops."

And the lawyers. I didn't say it.

"Am I green-lit to go in?"

"Assuming everyone's wearing proper safety gear."

"I think the ME team is ready. Where do I suit up?"

"Follow me."

"You familiar with DC?" Hickey asked as we walked toward a tent several yards up the sidewalk. He walked. I did more of an antelope caper thing to keep pace.

"I know we're in one of the older parts of the district."

"Foggy Bottom. You gotta love that name, eh?"

I did, actually. Nodded.

"The area's hot now, listed on the national register of historic places.

But Foggy Bottom started life as a blue-collar community of Irish and German immigrants and African Americans. Folks who worked local, you know? At the breweries, the glass plants, the gas and light company."

"You're a native Washingtonian?"

"Born and raised. My grancie's house is right around the corner. The old gal's lived in Foggy Bottom since before I was born. Keeps getting crazy offers from realtors wanting her to sell."

Arriving at the tent, Hickey said, "The fire's no threat now, so all you need is standard PPE and a hard hat. I'll wait by my truck."

I unzipped the door and stepped through the opening. The interior smelled of grass and sun-heated canvas tainted by the faint stink of burning.

Coveralls, helmets, gloves, and goggles filled portable metal shelving at the tent's center. Boots lined the ground beside one wall.

I chose the smallest Tyvek suit in the stack. Was moving toward a curtained-off partition when my mobile rang. Sang.

Digging the phone from my pocket, I clicked on.

Bad news.

Thacker's staff were still trying but had yet to secure a hotel room for me. They were now looking into short-term rentals.

Disconnecting with a not so gracious thank you, I slipped into the coveralls and snapped the fasteners with agitated thumbs. Laced on my boots.

Deep breath.

Grabbing the final items to accessorize my fetching look, I stepped out into the bright morning.

And felt my irritation skyrocket.

Ivy Doyle of the flawless skin, ginger hair, and Ruby Woo lips was talking to Hickey. Down the street, a two-man crew was unloading a camera and boom mic setup from a WTTG van.

On spotting me, Doyle beamed her perfect teeth and gave me a five-finger waggle. A few more words to Hickey, then she hurried my way.

"Dr. Brennan. How awesome to see you here."

I may have nodded.

"Oh, don't worry." Raising a reassuring palm in my direction. "I wouldn't dream of bothering you. I know you're about to begin recovery of these poor lost souls. We're here to get a few ox pops."

When I didn't respond.

"You know. MOSs? Man on the street comments?"

"Uh-huh."

Not exactly comfortable in all the safety gear and wanting to get on with the grim task ahead, I started to move off. Doyle hadn't finished.

"I have a little something for you. No biggie, just a trinket I thought you'd find amusing. If you tell me where you're staying, I'll just leave it at the desk."

"Actually, I don't know where I'm staying." Mildly surprised that a journalist would offer a gift, I assumed the gesture was because of her friendship with Katy.

"I'm sorry?"

"The ME is finding that every room in the district is booked."

"That's totally unacceptable."

Ya think?

Doyle's mouth twisted to one side in fierce concentration. Then her face lit up.

"But this is so simple." Spreading her impeccably manicured hands. "You must stay with me."

"I couldn't possibly do that."

"Why not? I have a huge house and I'm hardly ever there."

"Your offer is very generous. But I wouldn't feel right imposing."

Doyle produced a card and handed it to me, her smile a brimming red bucket of warmth.

"If you change your mind, just give me a jingle."

"Okay," I said.

Hell no, I thought. Colossal hell no.

We both knew I'd never make that call.

We were both wrong.

CHAPTER 5

Even quick, hot flare-ups can cause death from smoke inhalation. People killed in this way often appear unharmed. With higher temperatures or longer burn times, or both, the eyes and tongue swell and the skin blisters. Though disfigured, these DOAs may also remain visually recognizable.

Those are the best-case scenarios. Raise the heat or increase the length of exposure and death by fire is far more brutal.

This blaze had been a ballbuster. I feared we were facing the worst-case alternative.

While I was changing, Hickey had issued a general all-clear signal, so Thacker's team had moved from their vehicle to the base of the front steps. I walked toward them, every neuron in my brain firing.

Imagining the people trapped in that building, I wondered about their last moments. Had the couple clung to each other for solace? Had the Canadian teen cowered alone in her room? Had the foreign national knelt to pray, terrified of dying far from his homeland?

Or had each made a wild dash to escape? Might all four have ended up in the same location? Finding no exit, had they huddled together in a place they hoped was protected?

My thoughts weren't simply morbid speculation. A victim's final actions are pertinent in the search for remains.

If the four had dispersed throughout the building, their bodies could be anywhere in the debris. Finding them would be the challenge. Had they died together, commingling could be an issue.

Commingling occurs when parts of one person break off and mix
with parts of another. Heads detach and reposition. Arms entwine.
Legs overlie torsos. Individuation can be a bitch when separate bodies
have congealed into one amorphous mass of charred muscle and bone.

I also considered the legal implications of the task ahead.

Every fire triggers an investigation. Where was the origin? What
was the spread pattern? What was the cause of ignition? Was the blaze
accidental or intentionally set?

I knew from Sergeant Burgos that fatalities mandated activation of
the Joint Arson Task Force. That the JATF consists of representatives
from the DC Fire and EMS Fire Investigation Unit, the Metropolitan
Police Arson and Explosives Unit, and the Bureau of Alcohol, Tobacco,
Firearms and Explosives. And that a homicide detective might also get
involved.

I also knew that this inquiry would go beyond the routine. Had the
property been operating as an illegal Airbnb, its owners could be subject
to criminal charges. That meant that painstaking evidence collection
and scrupulous maintenance of chain of custody would be essential.

Looking around, I noticed that the crowd had grown. Was thankful
for the police tape barricading both ends of the block.

A fire often triggers a media circus. Throw in deaths, and coverage
can grow frenzied. We've all seen the footage. A bar pyrotechnic display
gone wrong. A high-rise gas explosion. A post–plane crash inferno.
All the pics fit to print. All the human tragedy capable of boosting
viewership

Doyle's coverage had already drawn public attention to the Foggy
Bottom blaze and her rivals were now parking their vehicles by hers.
FOX5. NBC4. WJLA. All local, nothing national.

A good fire also piques the morbid interest of Joe Q. Citizen. Despite
the early hour, the usual nosey gawkers were gathering. A tall skinny
man in a red tracksuit. A woman pushing toddlers in a stroller. A
couple sipping coffee from Starbucks cups. A preteen on a scooter.
The kid and the mom were holding smartphones above their heads
and clicking away.

Nearing the ME team, I raised an arm in greeting. The shorter of
the two gestured back.

"Temperance Brennan."

I proffered a hand to the tech who'd returned my wave, a small man with haphazard dreads and skin the color of week-old tea.

"Jamar Delson." We shook, with Jamar doing some fancy finger thing at the end. "Dr. Thacker said you was coming."

Cocking his chin up and left, he said, "My pale pal here is Ace Bagget. He's a bit slow but listens real good."

Ace rolled his eyes. Which were so velvety brown they made me think of Bambi's mother. Badly scarred skin bore witness to acne that must have made his teen years difficult.

Both men appeared to be in their late twenties. While Jamar topped out at about five-five, I put Ace at six feet minimum.

"Dr. Thacker said you two were crackerjack with burn vics," I said, exaggerating a tad.

"Snap!" Jamar shot a bony finger my way.

Ace said nothing.

"I assume you've worked a few fires?"

"Does a goose shit every ten minutes?"

Assuming the question was rhetorical, and clueless about the answer, I offered no response.

"People lost their lives here," I said. "The authorities, friends, relatives, insurers, lawyers, you name it, will all want to know why. And who. So, a critical first step in this investigation will be victim ID. The more of each corpse we recover, the easier that will be."

"Yes, ma'am." Jamar over-nodded his agreement.

Ace started working a cuticle with his front teeth.

"This fire was a doozy," I said. "I suspect the bodies will be in bad shape."

"Yes, ma'am," Jamar repeated himself.

Ace said nothing. The cuticle was now red and raw.

"Captain Hickey has cleared us to enter the building. I'd like to begin by walking each room in a grid pattern."

"We go in squarin' and starin'," Jamar said.

"Exactly. If you spot remains, stop and alert me."

With that rather nebulous plan in mind, we donned the rest of our PPE, raised our N95 masks to our faces, and climbed to the front entrance, now *sans* door. Here and there, through the shattered cellar and first-floor windows, I saw gossamer wisps of smoke feathering up from the wreckage. And the occasional firefighter still probing it.

Picking our way through ash and chaotically piled rubble, carefully testing the placement of each booted foot, we took a quick tour. Confirmed that the building's interior was as devastated as the damage to its exterior had suggested.

The roof's eastern third had fallen in, taking with it significant portions of the inside walls on that side. As expected, sections of both upper floors had collapsed down onto each other. Much of that wreckage had then ended up in the basement.

On each level, metal fixtures, knobs, appliances, and hinged cabinet doors had warped and distorted. Porcelain sinks and commodes had cracked. Upholstery, carpeting, and drapes had been reduced to charcoal vestiges.

Every item in the house was darkened and covered with soot. The air coming through my mask reeked of the plastics, oils, chemicals, varnish, and paint recently consumed by the flames.

Having evaluated the situation, and sensing that these guys knew their way around a fire scene better than Thacker had let on, I suggested we split up. Jamar volunteered to search what remained of the upper floor. Ace took the second. I headed to the main level.

For more than an hour, the only sounds were the muted thudding of our footfalls, the soft tapping of our probes, the raspy crunching and scraping of displaced debris. Occasionally, one firefighter called out to another.

Then Jamar whistled.

Rising from a squat—a move decidedly unpopular with my ankles and knees—I gingerly worked my way up two flights of stairs. Thankful they were located in the less damaged western portion of the house.

Jamar was standing at the back of a charred shell that had probably been one of the jerry-rigged bedrooms. A singed mattress lay half-off a blackened bedframe. A metal rack leaned at an impossible angle against one wall, its rubber wheels melted, the hangers at its base twisted into grotesque shapes.

Seeing me, Jamar pointed at a slag-coated mound underlying the hangers. I crossed to him.

Typically, the scalp goes first in a fire. The human brain is roughly 75 percent water and fills most of the 1,200 to 1,700 cm of the cranial cavity. Deprived of its insulating helmet of hair and tissue, the skull's outer surface heats up and its contents cook and expand. Pressure builds and eventually the cranium splits.

As the head is destroyed, the facial skin bubbles and crisps. The features melt, eliminating that external façade by which we all recognize each other.

Further south, dehydration and protein denaturation lead to muscle shrinkage throughout the body. Since the bulkier flexors contract more than the extensors, fire victims frequently curl in on themselves, assuming the "boxer" or "pugilistic" pose.

Much of this had happened to the person lying at our feet. Oddly, his or her headgear, though singed, was largely intact.

Ignoring the warning emanating from my knees, I squatted for a closer look. The hat was a baseball cap, with a red, white, and black patch above the bill. A pair of stars on the white stripe suggested the emblem might be a flag.

It was impossible to guess the victim's gender, or the nature of the rest of his or her clothing. All other fabric had been reduced to a crumbly black residue adhering to the scorched flesh.

Unfolding to upright, I said to Jamar, "Good eye."

"Poor bastard." He crossed himself with one gloved hand.

"The body looks fragile. What's your plan?"

"First, I troll through the rubbish above and around him, bagging and tagging every friggin' thing."

"Recording detailed notes and taking pics," I said.

Jamar looked at me as though I'd suggested babies need feeding.

"Then I get Ace up here and we slide a stretcher under the guy's ass. If that don't work, we use plastic sheeting and plywood to get him onto a gurney."

"Yo."

As one, we swiveled.

"Found a stiff." Ace was standing in the hall. "Maybe two."

We descended single-file down one floor into what looked like another small bedroom. Ace's "stiff" was wedged into a back corner, behind the gutted frame of an overturned dresser. Cranial fragments stood out pale against the backdrop of flame-darkened wood.

I counted at least six limbs, each now a charred and desiccated cylinder. The lower torsos and thighs, composed of solid, heavy bones encased in thick muscle masses, had congealed into one shapeless glob.

As with the third-floor victim, the body parts having little or no flesh exhibited the most damage—the fingers and hands, the toes and feet. The few surviving digits had been reduced to clawlike hooks.

Four melted sneakers. Two scorched zippers suggesting more than one pair of jeans. I suspected we'd found the couple.

After discussing strategy, I left retrieval to Jamar and Ace and returned to the main level. Spent another hour searching the rubble. Found zilch. Assured several skeptical firefighters that I was doing just fine.

Since a large portion of the parlor floor had fallen into the basement, I proceeded to that level. The air was danker, the light gloomier, but little else differed.

Except that I scored body number four.

The remains resembled those we'd found on the upper floors. The features were toast, and only a hard blackened mask covered the under-lying facial bones. But this corpse featured one added twist.

As flames heat a torso, the internal organs and intestines expand, and the viscera may burst through the abdominal wall. Here the full sequelae had played out in all its gory splendor.

Not wanting to slow the recoveries taking place above, I opened my kit and began this one on my own. Had taken pics and was shooting video when I heard boots clumping the stairs behind me.

Thinking it was Jamar or Ace, I lowered my camera and turned.

Hickey stood halfway down the treads, a shaft of dirty gray light casting shadows across his features and sparking the neon strips on his turnout suit.

"Hey," I said.

"Hey." The baritone voice boomed loud in the small, enclosed space. "How goes it down here?"

"Good. How goes it up there?"

"Good."

I gestured at the subject of my photography. "All four vics are now accounted for."

"Impressive."

"Thanks."

A moment of awkward silence. Hickey broke it.

"I'm about to release most of my crew. Before I give the word, I'd like to walk the cellar, make sure there's nothing below ground that might still go hot."

"You won't disturb me."

"I'll be quiet as a mouse." Finger pressed to his lips.

I smiled and gave a thumbs-up.

Jesus. Were we flirting?

Returning my gesture, and smile, Hickey stepped onto the cellar floor and set off to his right, here and there kicking at heaped debris or lifting an object with the toe of his boot.

I idly followed his progress.

Until the man suddenly vanished.

CHAPTER 6

A million questions ricocheted in my brain.

Had I imagined it? Was the light playing tricks? Did I glance away at the precise moment Hickey stepped sideways?

No. The man had disappeared.

"Captain Hickey!" My shout muted by my mask.

No answer.

"I need help here!" Upping the volume.

Fearing Hickey could be hurt, I grabbed a penlight from my kit and scrambled to my feet.

"Anybody!" I screamed as I crept toward the spot where I'd last seen the fireman.

No one appeared or shouted back.

I felt the electric current of fear race up my spine.

"Officer down!" Did one say that about a firefighter?

Still nothing.

I called out again.

Zilch.

Where the hell were all the Galahads so recently worried about my safety?

Twenty wary steps brought me to the edge of a gaping hole.

In the first split second, my mind logged the following facts.

The basement was floored by hard-packed clay. That clay had overlain and disguised a hinged wooden door. That door had broken under the pressure of Hickey's weight.

I aimed my light down into the opening.

Hickey lay prone at the base of a weathered staircase, maybe eight feet below me.

I watched for signs of life. Movement. Breathing. Saw no indication of either.

"Hickey!"

Zero response.

My stomach went into free fall.

I was gripping the penlight with my teeth, preparing to descend, when Hickey's left elbow re-angled and his palm pressed the ground. His upper torso arced up and he pivoted to his back. Groaning, he rose to a sitting position and drew his knees to his chest.

Relief flooded through me. Not wanting to blind him, I pointed my beam at his boots and shouted. "Are you okay?"

Hickey glanced up, a puzzled look on his face.

"Shall I call for the medics?"

"No. No. I'm cool."

"You're sure?"

"Just embarrassed." Hickey's chuckle had a brittle edge to it. "What happened?"

"You pulled an Alice and tumbled down a secret passage. Could be they'll charge you for damage to the trap door."

"I'm a firefighter. Property damage is our forte."

"Uh-huh." I was happy the guy hadn't lost his sense of humor. "What do you see?"

"Nothing. It's a black hole down here."

"Probably a subcellar."

"It being below the main cellar."

I ignored the sarcasm.

"Is it big?"

"Hard to tell."

"Are you alone?" Joking.

"I goddam sure hope so."

I watched Hickey get to his very large feet. Lighted a path as he climbed up the treads.

"Shall we explore?" Hickey asked when topside.

"Once I'm done with this guy." Hooking a thumb at the corpse with the popcorned innards.

Hickey nodded. "I'll shed some of my gear and score some headlamps. Let me know when you're ready."

"Roger that." I saluted.

Cringed inwardly, wishing I hadn't.

While I'd finished with the fourth victim, a member of Hickey's team had determined that the subcellar had been negligibly impacted by the fire. Some buckling of the staircase and warping of its banister. Significant smoke damage to the overhead timbers and support beams.

The guy hadn't mentioned the smell.

While I was following Hickey down the steps, paranoically testing each, the stench almost made me gag. Rotten wood. Damp earth. The acrid reek of burning. The occasional glob of fire suppressant foam dripping onto my head did nothing to settle me. Or improve the look of the hair escaping my hard hat.

Nearing the last tread, I peeled my eyes from my boots and glanced up. My headlamp glinted off a pair of bare bulbs dangling by fuzzy dark cords. They were the old-fashioned clear glass kind and, despite the shroud of ash coating the outer surface of each, I could see the delicate filaments inside.

Hickey and I spread out at the bottom, groping the walls to locate a switch. I found one first, beside an opening in the east wall, embedded in an upright of dubious reliability.

I flipped the little lever, expecting nothing. To my surprise, one of the ancient bulbs fired to life. Not exactly the Vegas Luxor Lamp, but the amber glow provided sufficient illumination to allow a sense of our surroundings.

Hickey and I were in a room measuring approximately ten by ten. Low ceiling. Flagstone floor. Earthen walls.

Five barrels stood directly opposite the stairs we'd crept down, arranged in a semi-orderly row. We crossed to them.

Up close I could see that the barrels weren't round, but oddly ovoid. Their wood was weathered, their iron banding rusty as hell. Each had a metal spigot down low and a round hole plugged with a wooden peg on top.

"Looks like oak." Hickey ran a gloved finger through the layer of grime and soot darkening the nearest of the casks. "With brass taps."

"What do you suppose they held? Hold?" I asked.

Hickey hiked both shoulders. Beats me.

The movement sent a shadow dancing across the brass triangle forming the barrel's tap handle.

"Look at the spigot," I said.

"You think it's a spigot?" He leaned close. "It's lettering."

"Can you read it?"

Some serious squinting. Then, "Albany."

"As in, the capital of New York?"

Hickey shrugged again, one shoulder this time.

"That's underwhelming," I said.

"You were hoping for what? Russian crude oil?"

"I don't know. Whiskey? Wine? Maple syrup?"

"Could be anything. The house is old."

"How old?" I asked, growing more intrigued.

Hickey gave another of his trademark shrugs. The guy could have taught a master's class on the nuances of the gesture.

I turned and shone my headlamp through the opening in the east wall.

"Looks like there are rooms beyond this one. Shall we search the rest of this level?"

"Hell, yeah. Let's search the bejeezus out of her."

I led. Hickey covered my six, as he put it.

The place was a labyrinth of tunnels and crannies and chambers, often with one room dead-ending into another. Reminded me of a scene in a Stephen King novel.

As did the fact that I had absolutely no phone signal that deep underground.

There were a few overhead bulbs along the way. Unlike the one by the stairs, none worked.

Not surprising. Still. No light. No means of communication. Not good.

Maybe it was my imagination gone haywire, but the passageway seemed to grow darker and danker the farther we went. Hickey didn't always keep up but lingered now and then to toe or poke at something of interest.

We traversed nine rooms in all. Some showed blackening due to smoke infiltration from above. Three were empty. Four held barrels. Two were furnished with cots, chairs, small tables, and lantern-style oil lamps. The meager furnishings suggested use as a short-term hideaway or safe house.

Beyond the ninth room, the narrow passageway split. By then I was certain we'd completed a bejeezus-grade search. I was cold and hungry, and my headlamp was showing signs of betrayal. Still, I refused to be the one to pull the plug.

I took the left branch, Hickey went right.

Ten reluctant steps. Then my wavering beam fell on an unopened door.

I glanced over my shoulder to call out to Hickey. He was nowhere to be seen.

I strode forward and turned the knob.

The door swung in with an overly theatrical B-grade horror movie squeak.

The darkness beyond was tomb-like, barely penetrated by the faltering beam from my headlamp. My eyes detected no shadowy shape. No silhouette denser than the surrounding blackness. Nothing.

I took a cautious step forward.

The air smelled different from that in the corridor. Mothy, like old wool. Organic, like seaweed baked on a beach. Dry and papery like mummified flesh at the morgue.

Sweetly fetid.

Like putrefying flesh at the morgue.

Swiveling my head slowly, I swept my headlamp around the small space. Saw nothing along the right-hand wall. Nothing in the right back corner. Nothing along the opposite wall.

In the left back corner, the lower edge of my beam reshaped in the shadows where the wall met the floor. I dipped my chin to angle the light downward.

It took a moment for my brain to process the message my eyes were sending its way.

A large burlap sack lay on the flagstones, the kind that might have held potatoes or grain. A rope secured one end, triple looped and loosely tied.

A bulge inside the sack suggested a body. A slender braid snaking from a gap in the coiled rope suggested that body was human. Both the sack and the hair were caked with a mildewy crust darkened by soot.

Had I found a fifth fire victim? A survivor who'd fled to this level to escape the flames?

Seriously, Brennan? And crawled into a bag and tied off the opening?

My headlamp was now cutting on and off and flickering badly. I couldn't tell if the person in the bag was breathing.

Not wishing to frighten him or her, should they be alive, I called out from the doorway.

"Hello?"

The person didn't flinch. Didn't respond.

I tried again.

"Are you okay?"

Nothing.

Pulling surgical gloves from a back pocket, I donned them and took a tentative step forward.

Saw no movement. No signs of life.

Another step.

Another.

Drawing close, I circled the sack, braced a hand on the wall, and squatted. Using one finger, I loosened the knot and dragged the edge of the burlap downward a few inches.

One look told me the person inside was dead. And that it was probably a female. Her eyes were half open, her shriveled and clouded pupils mid-dilated and fixed in the cadaveric position.

I aimed my erratic beam down into the opening I'd created.

My heart threw in a few extra beats.

CHAPTER 7

As Jamar and Ace finished upstairs, each appeared and offered assistance belowdecks. I accepted, but my instincts told me I should handle this fifth victim personally.

Not that the techs hadn't followed protocol with the other bodies. Contrary to Thacker's tepid assessment, they'd performed superbly. But something told me to be extra careful with this lady.

I spent what remained of the day teasing the sack free and digging around and below it. Carefully labeling and packaging everything I found.

Jamar took endless photos and shot hours of video. Ace set up a temporary screen and sifted. Not much of interest turned up. Pebbles. Snail shells. Two rusty nails.

The exception was a small collection of glass shards. The three of us studied each as it appeared in the mesh. On one we could make out the letters *Alk—*. On another, the partial phrase *Green Cou—*. Ace made repeated trips ferrying Tupperware tubs of varying sizes up two sets of stairs to the main level.

By the time I resurfaced, my watch said seven-twenty p.m. I was weary and my back and knees ached from kneeling and bending to disentangle, trowel, and tease items free from the crusty sediment covering them.

I smelled of mold, mildew, and sweat, and desperately needed a shower. My fervent wish was that Thacker had found me a room.

The first person I laid eyes on topside was Ivy Doyle. Who was, as usual, immaculately and stylishly coiffed and attired.

My initial reaction was surprise that the cops had let Doyle into the house. Then irritation. Had the woman *never* splashed coffee onto her blouse? Missed a fragment of lettuce riding a lip? Smeared the perfect crimson lipstick onto a tooth?

I also felt unease. I'd sent the sealed tubs up ahead of my reemergence from the underground. Had Doyle grabbed an opportunity to sneak a peek at the contents? To snap a photo? Would she air the purloined info and pics? *Breaking News! Anthropologist fails to maintain proper chain of custody of human remains!*

Doyle was talking on a cell phone, holding a long, rolled paper in her free hand. She turned as I stepped from the top stair into the kitchen.

Ace and Jamar also tracked my odoriferous entrance.

"We should jet to the morgue with these?" Jamar gestured at the tubs.

"Yes, please. Text to let me know how you log the vic in."

"Yes, ma'am."

"Thanks for your help today."

It took them two trips to haul everything out to the van. When we were finally alone, Doyle's lips reshaped into a smile bright as a Kmart Christmas flier.

"Dr. Brennan. You must be wrecked." Almost breathy. "How long were you down there?"

"Hours."

"A fifth victim. How terribly sad."

I was spared the need to respond when my mobile picked up signal and sang in my pocket.

I dug it out and glanced at the screen.

The phone icon indicated four voice mails.

I opened the app.

Ryan had called at three.

Thacker had called at two, four-thirty, and six.

"Excuse me a moment," I said to Doyle.

She nodded and turned her back to give me privacy.

To listen and take notes?

You're paranoid, Brennan.

I played the last of Thacker's messages, hoping for info on accommodations.

"Jada Thacker here." The woman sounded desperate, so I suspected her news wouldn't be good. *"I've tried and tried, but I'm still unable to find a single district hotel with any availability before Tuesday. At least not in an area I consider safe. An alternative would be to drive out into Virginia or Maryland?"*

A pause. Then,

"I feel horribly guilty, but who knew? I've never encountered this situation before."

Who *knew*? WTF? This was Thacker's turf.

Sounding uber apologetic, and decidedly unenthused, Thacker continued.

"You're more than welcome to stay in the guest bedroom in my condo in Arlington. Just let me know what you'd like to do."

"Sonofabitch!" I thumb-smashed the screen.

Startled by my outburst, Doyle swiveled back to face me, brows tucked into their on-air "sincerely concerned" pose.

"Is something wrong?" she asked.

"Not at all! I'm just the hired help! I can sleep in a friggin' park!" Doyle didn't deserve the temper. But she was in range, so she was taking the blast.

"I don't understand." The ginger brows dipped lower.

I drew a deep, calming breath.

"I'm sorry. It's not your fault. Or your problem."

"What *is* the problem?"

"The ME can't find a hotel for me."

"Has she called—"

"She claims to have tried everywhere." Way too brusque.

"Well, this is so simple." Without hesitation. "You are dear Katy's mother. You must stay at my house."

My face moved into an expression. Weary, I was unsure what it was trying to convey. Hoped it was gratitude. At least not repulsion.

"I can't do that," I said.

"Why not?" Doyle spread her hands, the empty one palm up. "I have an enormous home, and it's only me rattling around in there. I'd love the company."

"It's just—"

"I'm serious. I have a boyfriend who stays over now and then, but that's not a problem."

I drew a reusable water bottle from my kit and took a long swig. Not thirsty but wanting time to consider my options.

There were only two.

I could drive into the boonies searching for some fleabag motel that might have me. I could crash with Thacker.

Or I could sleep in my car.

I guess that made three.

"Could you give me a moment?" I punched auto-dial as I moved toward the door.

Katy answered on the third ring.

"What's the mood, dude?"

"Not real perky." I explained my lack of a bed.

"How could the dimwit let that happen?"

I ignored that.

"Here's my question. Ivy Doyle has offered to put me up. What do you think? For just one night?"

"I think, hell yeah."

"She claims to have extra bedrooms."

Katy nose-blew one of her irony snorts. "Do you know who Ivy is?"

"You said she's a friend from your army days."

"Let me rephrase. Do you know who Ivy's *family* is? Think about it. Doyle? Virginia?"

"I didn't know she was from Virginia."

"You do now."

"Katy, I've spent all afternoon peeling a dead lady off a flagstone floor."

"Ew. Why?"

"Irrelevant. I'm filthy and exhausted and ill-disposed to guessing games."

"The Doyles of Richmond, Virginia, pour millions into various philanthropic foundations established at their direction. The Jordan V. Doyle Foundation for Literacy. The Abigail Harmony Doyle Foundation for Coastal Conservation. The Ivy and Timothy Doyle Foundation for the Abatement of Childhood Hunger. Th—"

As she rattled off names, my memory cells grudgingly admitted to knowledge of the topic. To having heard of the charities on NPR, another of the Doyles' favored beneficiaries.

My higher centers crafted a startling realization.

Ivy Doyle came from money. The very big, very old, very powerful kind. Factoids clicked in.

Back in the day, J. V. Doyle—a great, great, great someone and founder of the lineage—earned his fortune growing tobacco. Acres of the stuff. J.V.'s descendants managed the plantations well, but also diversified and invested in other ventures. Today the Doyle family was involved in multiple enterprises, including companies that owned and operated radio and television stations around the globe.

"You're saying Ivy really does have room for me?"

"Duh. Yeah."

"She won't insist on talking all the time?"

"Ivy reads an audience well."

"Got it."

"Let me know how it goes."

"Will do. Thanks."

I returned to the kitchen. Doyle's attention was again focused on her mobile.

"So. Did I check out?" Question posed with a grin, but also with a hint of something else beneath.

"Busted." I felt my cheeks redden under the grime. "Katy gives you a two-thumbs-up."

Doyle waggled the paper cylinder.

"Guess what I have?"

Christ. Was everyone playing the twenty-questions game?

"Kerouac's on-the-road scroll?"

Doyle ignored my sarcasm. "The architectural plans for this building."

"Seriously?"

"Yep."

"I'm impressed." I was.

"They're photocopies, but the detail is pretty good."

"Where did you find the originals?"

"The Recorder of Deeds is located on Fourth Street Southwest. Are you hungry?"

"Does a dog have three eyelids?"

Eyes crimping slightly, Doyle said, "We can study the layout while we eat. Is there anything you don't like?"

"That maggoty cheese from Sardinia."

Brennan!

The quip earned me another questioning squint. And a stab of guilt for the attitude.

"Would you like to follow me to my place?"

"Thanks, but I can find it. And please excuse my prickliness. It's the fatigue talking."

"I totally understand."

"I really do appreciate your generosity."

"Not a problem."

Doyle gave me her address and I entered it into my phone.

As I peeled off my coveralls, the evening air felt warm and moist on my skin. A gentle breeze lifted clumps of damp hair off my sweat-slicked forehead and neck.

The sky was velvety gray, the overhead leaves, branches, and wires black shapes lifting and falling against it. In the distance, through a confusion of buildings and utility poles, the sun was a fuzzy orange ball hovering low over the horizon.

Free of my PPE, I settled behind the wheel and dialed Ryan. Glad he could neither see nor smell me. He answered quickly.

"Bonsoir, ma chère."

"Hey."

"You sound tired."

"Does a dog have three— Never mind."

"Rough day?"

"It wasn't my favorite."

"Tell the tale."

I described the house in Foggy Bottom, the four fire victims, the fifth body from the subcellar. Thacker. Burgos. Hickey. Doyle.

Ryan listened without interrupting, as was his style. It's one of the things I like about him.

"What's your take on the burlap body?"

"Nice alliteration."

"Thanks. Your take?"

"No idea."

"Sound thinking."

"That way I can't possibly be wrong."

"Be of happy heart, my lovely. A hot sudsy shower and room service await."

"Hah!"

I explained the hotel debacle, Ivy Doyle and her background, and the young woman's gracious offer to host me.

"A sleepover. You can do each other's nails."

My eyes rolled of their own volition.

"I'm curious," Ryan said when I failed to acknowledge his joke. "You say Doyle is Katy's age and seriously ambitious. If her family is wealthy and connected, why isn't she already the next Barbara Walters?"

"I've asked myself the same question."

"And?"

"I don't know."

Following a few tantalizingly unrepeatable suggestions from Ryan, we disconnected.

My navigation app sent me along K Street, eventually onto Mac-Arthur Boulevard, from which I made a right turn onto Chain Bridge Road. Palisades Park stretched to my right, a vast expanse of forest and parkland growing shadowy in the last light of dusk. Well-hidden homes peeked from heavily wooded properties to my left.

Thirty minutes after leaving Foggy Bottom, I pulled onto a winding driveway leading to a very large house. Lots of wood, stone, and glass. In the twilight the roof appeared to glow like copper.

Pulling to a stop in a concrete oval bordered by surgically groomed hedges, I studied the scene.

Certain that the WAZE lady had steered me wrong.

CHAPTER 8

Doyle's residence was so enormous I wondered if the navigation app had mistakenly sent me to one of DC's myriad obscure little museums. The Museum of Architectural Ostentation? The Museum of Outrageous Geometrics? The Museum of Creative Concrete?

That last was pushing the simile. But you get the picture.

The ultra-modern design involved the stacking of square and oblong cubes at startling angles. The massive concrete components were white highlighted by black trim around the windows and doors, and black handrails bordering the walkways and stairs. Horizontal surfaces formed patios and walled beds planted with shrubbery and brightly colored flowers. Hidden spotlights illuminated the structure at every architecturally appropriate point.

I was reaching for my mobile when the colossal front door swung inward. Doyle stepped out onto the porch. I guess you'd call it a porch.

Seeing my car, Doyle gestured "come on" with double arm loops.

Alighting, I dug my overnighter from the trunk, climbed the steps, and joined her under the portico.

"This is quite the place," I said.

"Thanks. I designed it myself."

Of course, you did. I didn't say it.

"There was a sad little dump here when I bought the property. The neighbors were outraged when I had it knocked down to build this. But they got over it. Most of them, anyway."

"Not all?"

"The old fart next door still thinks it's a crime against humanity. Screw him. The lots are narrow, but you can barely see my house from his."

"Must make for cordial over-the-fence chats."

"Like *that* would ever happen." She reached for my rollaboard. "Let me take that."

"I'm good. Lead the way."

"Yes, ma'am."

The smell of cooking enveloped me the moment we crossed the threshold into the chandeliered foyer. Curry? Mango? Coconut?

Ignoring the growls arising from my belly, I followed Doyle down a long hallway toward the back of the house. The plan was open, and I caught glimpses of many of the first-floor rooms.

Like its exterior, the home's interior featured beaucoup black and white. Lots of gleaming stone and tile. Granite? Marble? Limestone? Porcelain?

The furnishings looked like imaginings straight out of the minds of Gehry or van der Rohe. Many of the sofas, chairs, and stools were oddly shaped, making me question the level of comfort they provided. The upholstered pieces were done in animal prints or fine-grained leather. The side and end tables were mostly chrome and acrylic.

The wall art was tastefully indecipherable, with each painting contributing just the right splash of color. The area rugs were precisely calibrated to coordinate with the highlighted pigments on each.

Intricate metal figures and delicate ceramic sculptures topped many of the pieces we passed. I kept a safe distance. Originals or not, I had no desire to send one of Doyle's treasures crashing to its death.

My room was up a short flight of stairs. Opening the door, which was an incredibly beautiful ebony wood, Doyle turned and said, "This one's yours."

"Thanks."

"The only thing that needs explaining is the security system. There's a button in the small recess beside the bed. A panic button. Hit that and a patrol unit is on its way."

I must have shown surprise.

"The buttons are all over the house. You may have noticed one beside the sink in the kitchen?"

I hadn't.

"The police don't call to verify before showing up?" I asked.

"Nope. I chose the option that law enforcement respond ASAP and enter the premises without asking permission. I know the system is a bit over-the-top. It was my contractor's idea. He was a former cop and sexy as hell."

"Got it."

"I've ordered a light supper. Have a shower. Come down when you're ready. No rush."

"I don't want you to go to any—"

"It's absolutely no trouble." Flapping a dismissive hand.

"How'd that turn out?" I asked as she was disappearing into the hall.

"What?"

"The contractor?"

"He married his boyfriend the second week into construction. Let me know if you need anything."

The only thing I felt I might need was a map.

The room was the size of a Vegas casino and took up the entire rear portion of the home on that level. The back wall was glass, the area rugs faux zebra, the bedspread a pattern of intertwined twigs that created a dizzying 3D *trompe l'oeil* effect.

Open cubes sat to either side of a simple black headboard, their interiors emitting a soft electric glow. A complicated steel-and-bronze lamp occupied the top of each.

A long tripod desk paralleled the wall to the right of the door, black like the headboard. The leather and chrome seat snugged below it could have given Thacker's ergonomic throne stiff competition.

The only touch of whimsy was a swoopy, high-backed armchair covered with curly white fur deep enough to house small mammals. Icelandic sheepskin? Tibetan lamb?

That was it for furnishings. Except for the long-haired pelt, everything simple and sleek. Not a ruffle or flounce in sight.

Disappearing closets formed the room's eastern wall. Not wanting to waste time figuring out how to work them, I set my bag on the floor, dug clean undies and a tee and jeans from it, and beelined toward a door opposite.

The bath stayed true to the minimalist vibe. Subtly patterned gray stone floor, probably marble. Two double sinks. Polished nickel fixtures. Profoundly fluffy white towels and mats.

The freestanding glass shower was big enough to accommodate the bathing of thoroughbreds. Shedding my smelly clothes, I stepped in and twisted two of the motherboard's multitude of levers toward what I hoped was a reasonably hot setting.

Lucky choice. Warm drops rained down on my head while a trio of spigots sprayed my neck, chest, and southern parts.

A small niche held enough products to open a beauty supply chain. I shampooed with a peach-pear combo, then lathered my skin with a pineapple-aloe body wash.

Were it not for my vociferously assertive hunger pangs, I might have stayed in that shower all night.

Doyle's "light supper" consisted of green chicken curry over jasmine rice accompanied by a watermelon, mint, and feta salad. Dessert was blueberry cheesecake.

A woman named Lan served. She was round in the middle, with skinny arms and legs that didn't match her torso. Tawny skin. Black hair coiled into a braid on the top of her head. I assumed it was Lan who had also prepared the meal.

We ate at a dining table whose top had started life in a quarry in Carrara. No idea the heritage of the shiny metal legs.

We kept the talk light. I didn't query her plans for broadcast. Doyle didn't ask about the subcellar corpse.

Before serving the cheesecake, Lan inquired about coffee. Doyle and I both requested decaf. Doyle asked that it be brought to the library.

We took the rolled pages that Doyle had showed me as I'd emerged from the Foggy Bottom basement to a room with floor-to-ceiling bookshelves and another large table, this one made of polished burl wood. The coffee arrived shortly, looking out of place in an old-fashioned silver service.

I filled an alarmingly delicate porcelain cup—probably Qing Dynasty—and placed it on an equally alarming saucer. Added cream. Sipped.

Dear God. Could this really be decaf? I wondered about the appropriateness of asking the brand.

Setting our java aside, we unfurled and spread the four photocopies flat. Secured the corners of the pile with random volumes pulled from the shelves.

I felt a flutter of excitement. Why? I had no intention of returning to the Foggy Bottom house. My interest in the layout was pure curiosity. Though it was possible I might learn something about the subcellar lady.

Doyle and I both leaned in.

The topmost page showed the building's exterior, prefire. A few minor elements differed from what I recalled, a handrail on the main staircase, a third-floor window box, but there was no doubt we were looking at the recently devastated Foggy Bottom Victorian.

It was also obvious that the original documents were old and weathered. The hand-sketched lines were fuzzy and indistinct on the photocopied version. Here and there, a tear or crease obliterated a detail.

A scrawled note along the page's lower border provided a date and what appeared to be a name.

"Does that say Hiram L. Pepper?" I asked.

"That's my read. Then July 1911."

"Pepper was the architect?"

"Probably. I'll research the name." Doyle pointed to a series of digits. "That's probably the lot number. I'll research that, too."

Allowing the top sheet to pop free and roll sideways, we viewed the second page in the stack.

"It's the main level." I moved my index finger over the layout. "There's the kitchen with the steps leading down to the basement. The dining room, parlor, hallway, foyer, stairs going up to the second floor."

"And down from it."

"Yes."

"No bathroom."

"That must have been added later."

"I see zero surprises."

"None."

We moved on to the second level. Saw the hallway and bedrooms as they'd been before being chopped up.

Ditto for the third.

No shockers on either.

The last page showed the basement.

A behemoth coal-burning furnace stood center stage in the open area at the foot of the stairs. Several small chambers circled the periphery, perhaps a pantry, a room for coal storage, another for tools.

"Odd," I said.

"What?"

"There's nothing to indicate the presence of a subcellar. The entrance should be there." I pointed to the spot where Hickey had so ungracefully disappeared.

"Also added later?"

"Why?"

"Good question."

"Did you find anything else pertaining to this address?"

"There's nothing on file but the original plans."

We were pondering that when Doyle's mobile rang.

"I should take this," she said after checking her screen.

"Of course."

As she moved toward the hall, I returned my gaze to the plans. Pretended not to do the very thing I'd suspected Doyle of doing earlier. Strained to listen.

Fruitlessly.

What I could hear of Doyle's side of the conversation consisted mostly of monosyllabic questions. When? Where? Often?

After thanking the caller, Doyle reappeared and crossed to the table.

She looked at me. I looked at her. The aquamarine eyes suggested conflict raging behind them. Share with me? Hold back? Order the snakeskin or the red leather pumps?

I waited.

Apparently, the battle resolved in my favor.

"I have a confidential informant who provides me with intel from time to time. That was him phoning." Realizing her mistake: "I use the gender-based term as a generic, not to imply sex."

"Of course," I said, not caring a wit about the identity of Doyle's CI.

"Ironically, this tip had to do with the Foggy Bottom property." Waggling her phone. "Well, not so ironic. I had sent out a bazillion feelers."

Again, I waited.

"It seems the house was used off and on as a meth lab."

"By whom?"

"The caller didn't have . . . that information."

"Or wouldn't share it."

Doyle shrugged one shoulder, conceding agreement.

"How solid is this informant?"

"Rock solid."

I flashed back to the kitchen. Mentally probed the charred and blackened debris.

I couldn't recall seeing any Pyrex, glass, or Corning containers. No mason jars or other glassware fitted with hoses, clamps, or duct tape. None of the usual paraphernalia associated with cooking methamphetamine.

But who knew? The scene had been one of near total devastation. I made a note to question Burgos on what he'd discovered in the course of his arson investigation. An encounter I wasn't eagerly anticipating.

"The fire could have been triggered by a meth lab explosion," Doyle said.

"Happens all the time." I'd watched every season of *Breaking Bad*.

"The four victims are asleep on the upper floors while some creep cooks drugs below them?" Tense. "That's heartless."

"Not to mention criminal."

The image flamed anger in my chest, quick and hot.

"And what about your subcellar victim?" Doyle continued. "Was she involved in the drug operation? Did she die of an overdose? Was she innocent collateral? Did she find out about the meth and threaten to blow the whistle? Who—"

"Speculation is pointless," I said.

"Agreed."

But Doyle had raised some interesting points.

What *about* my belowdecks corpse?

The home had been built in 1911. When had the woman died? How? Why the burlap sack?

How had her body ended up in the subcellar?

The subcellar that was mysteriously absent from the architectural plans.

CHAPTER 9

Thacker held the four fire DOAs for standard postmortems but asked that I remain on call, saying she was certain my expertise would be needed for trauma assessment. Due to my involvement in the recovery of the subcellar vic, she requested that I handle those remains. Said —whined?—that she was short-handed due to staff illnesses, requests for personal time off, a resignation, blah, blah, blah.

Though eager to get back to Charlotte to salvage some sort of getaway with Ryan, I agreed, but added that I wanted to begin without delay. Thacker had no problem with my working on Sunday.

Breakfast was French toast and grilled peaches, served by Lan. Who apparently put in very long days.

DC's Consolidated Forensic Laboratory has four autopsy suites offering a total of seven stations. Though it was Memorial Day weekend, the place was buzzing. *Because* it was Memorial Day weekend. Americans excel at harming themselves and others during holiday breaks. Too much booze? Too much pent-up frustration? Too many contact hours with family? Whatever. Celebratory fiestas send increased numbers rolling through morgue doors.

By eight a.m. I was suited up and prepping in one of the lab's single-table rooms. The equipment was shiny new but standard. Stainless-steel counters, fixtures, and scales. Computer terminal. Whiteboard. Smartboard. Sealed waste receptacles for biohazard materials. Plastic-lined cardboard boxes for regular trash. Overhead fluorescents. Epoxy-coated concrete floor.

Jamar was already there when I arrived. Like Lan, the tech logged some serious hours. In response to my comment about his holiday schedule, he smiled, tipped his head, and purred one word. "Overtime!"

While I created a case file on my laptop—call me paranoid, but I always keep my own copy, both hard and digital—Jamar went to the cooler in search of the subcellar DOA. Case #25-02106.

I was masking and pulling on surgical gloves when Jamar reappeared, dreads bobbing, pushing a rolling gurney through the door. Centered on the stainless-steel was the burlap sack.

Slowly, the room began yielding to the familiar odors of death. Mildewed fabric. Moldy leather. Refrigerated flesh.

After snugging one end of the gurney to the sink, Jamar moved to the computer terminal and worked the keyboard to log us into the system.

Meanwhile, I ran a quick check of my tools. The lab's tools.

Satisfied that all was in order, I turned my attention to #25-02106.

The burlap bag looked more colorful than I recalled. Though faded and stained, I could make out a logo that had once been bright red and green. The words *Swifty Spud* and *Potatoes* arced above and below a cartoonlike potato running in bipedal fashion.

The bag also looked smaller than I remembered.

As did the lumpy object it held.

Had I been mistaken? Were the contents not human?

Another, worse thought.

Was I about to examine the remains of a little girl?

Get on with it, Brennan.

Deep breath.

I began dictating notes, taking measurements, and directing Jamar as he shot stills. Videos weren't necessary, as the entire exam was being recorded by overhead cams.

Having considered options, which were few, Jamar and I decided that cutting the bag would be the least destructive approach. When satisfied with my external observations, I gave the word and Jamar untied the rope, then used scissors to sever the burlap along one side. As he snipped, I tugged, gently teasing the fabric free of the thing inside.

The process was painstakingly slow, but eventually *Swifty*'s booty lay fully exposed.

Mixed feelings.

Relief that I hadn't been wrong.

Sadness that I hadn't been wrong.

The bag held the corpse of a very small woman. Its limited capacity had forced her head down onto her chest and compressed her spine and limbs into a fetal curl. Her unknown time in the basement had cemented her into that posture. Her hours in the cooler had added the extra finishing touch.

Jamar and I tried to lay the woman supine and straighten her arms and legs.

No go.

We both knew that exposure to a higher ambient temperature would help somewhat.

While I recorded observations, Jamar captured the body on film. Pixels?

Then we waited.

Ninety minutes of warming allowed us—with a lot of muscle and maneuvering—to roll the lady onto her back and partially straighten her limbs.

The woman had large eyes, a slightly protruding forehead, and a low nasal bridge. Maybe. Decomp and tissue slippage had distorted her face so much it was hard to be sure. Her lower jaw had dropped in death and locked in the open position. While not a good look to wear for eternity, her gaping mouth allowed me a peek at her teeth.

Though I'd be more precise once I'd viewed her entire anatomy and taken X-rays, I estimated she'd died before her fortieth birthday. And that she'd been quite petite.

The woman was fully dressed, her clothing withered and fragile to the touch. And strangely at odds, at least by today's fashions, with my estimated age range.

Her dress, maybe wool, fell to mid-calf and had small pearl buttons down the front and at the wrists. Her legs were encased in hose held in place by old-style suspender garters. Her feet were shod in chunky-heeled black Mary Janes.

Despite the dress and layer of undergarments, I could see that the remaining soft tissue was shriveled and barely holding the woman's bones together. Strangely, her scalp and braided hair, which was thin and silky, remained attached to her partially mummified head.

Another series of pics then, with Jamar lifting and me tugging, I gingerly stripped the corpse. Not an easy task. That done, I asked Jamar to take #25-02106 off for full body scans.

My mobile rang as I was spreading the dress and hose across drying racks.

The number was an extension at the Charlotte-Mecklenburg Medical Examiner facility. I clicked on.

"Temperance Brennan."

"Dr. Brennan. It's Artie Bluestein here. Your dogshit got rolled uphill to me."

I was lost.

"The—" I heard paper rustle. "Mirek case? I was told you needed a verbal ASAP?"

A moment of confusion. Then synapse.

The mysteriously vanished Norbert Mirek. The munching canines. The bone fragments discovered by Mirek's nephew. I'd sent samples of the scat for trace evidence analysis, curious what else might be in the mix.

"Of course," I said. "Forgive me. I'm not in Charlotte."

"First off, thanks a lot for a couple of real crappy days." Delivered with a note of levity. I hoped.

"You're most welcome."

"Jesus. You could open a roadside zoo with the donors to that mess. Loads of hair and fur. Rat. Opossum. Squirrel. Rabbit. Chipmunk. Probably skunk. And of course, dog. At least one poodle."

"Anything of relevance to my vic?" I knew I should be more patient. But I also knew Artie Bluestein. The man loved to talk and right then I was busy.

"Perhaps." Miffed? Hurt? "Some of the hair was human."

"That's great. Preserved enough to snag a few chromos?"

"Perhaps."

"Can you send samples on to the DNA section?" I asked.

"I can."

"I really appreciate this, Artie. Do you want to give Detective Slidell a call?"

"How about I leave that to you."

When we'd disconnected, I sat a moment, not relishing the idea of the upcoming exchange with Skinny.

And troubled.

Why?

Then it struck me.

Norbert Mirek. The case I'd been pushing to finish so I could enjoy a getaway to Savannah with Ryan. A getaway that never happened. Clicking over to the Mirek file, I pulled up a picture of Uncle Norbert.

Sonofabitch.

Six hours later I was done with what cutting and dissection was possible for #25-02106. I'd finished collecting and packaging specimens for DNA, hair and fiber, toxicology, odontology, and other analyses. I'd successfully plumped two fingers and managed to roll a pair of partial prints.

Based on gross anatomy and careful observation of the full-body X-rays—that Smartboard projected one whiz-bang display—I knew the following.

The deceased was female.

She had died between the ages of twenty-five and thirty-five.

Despite some saddling of the bridge, the woman had an extremely narrow nasal aperture, suggesting she was of European ancestry. The straight and silken brown hair supported this conclusion. Though her skin appeared to be pale, the postmortem conditions to which she'd been subjected rendered this observation of dubious value.

The woman had stood four feet eleven inches and, based on muscle mass and the weight of her desiccated body, had tipped the scales at around eighty pounds. She would have gotten no bigger. Every growth plate in every long bone was fused.

The woman's teeth had all erupted and completed full root development. Except for one rotated canine, her dentition was in reasonably good alignment. She had a single cavity in an upper left first molar. She had undergone no restoration or other dental treatment.

The woman had no scars, moles, congenital or medical anomalies. No evidence of healed fractures, surgeries, or disease. No tattoos or piercings.

The woman's bone density appeared normal for someone her age.

Though decomp made it impossible to say much about the state of her internal organs, overall, #25-02106 presented as a healthy young adult female.

A young adult female with a depressed fracture of her right parietal radiating out into an explosion of linear fractures. A jaw broken in two midway up the right ascending ramus.

What caused the trauma? A transportation accident? A fall? A blast? A blunt instrument blow? Repeated punches to the face?

I couldn't say.

Had the trauma killed her?

I couldn't say.

I could state nothing concerning manner of death. Homicide? Suicide? Accident? So why was the woman's body secured in a bag?

I could state nothing concerning time of death.

For now. I hoped the clothing and potato sack could be used to bracket a possible time range.

At four-ten, I headed to the locker room to shower and change back into civvies. It had been hours since Lan's breakfast. My stomach was again on a rampage.

Except for the security guard and a man approaching the elevator from which I was exiting, the lobby was deserted. I was heading for the doors, thinking about the food trucks I'd seen on the street the previous day, when I noticed the man cut sharply to his left.

To avoid me?

I took a closer look. Narrow shoulders, pudgy body. Thinning hair swirling his scalp like a blond fingerprint.

Snap.

Luis "Lubu" Burgos.

Clearly the fire inspector had no wish to talk to me.

I decided to make his day.

"Sergeant Burgos." Waving and cutting right so our paths would intersect. "It's Tempe Brennan."

Burgos slowed but, unsmiling, stayed the course toward me.

"So nice to bump into you," I said when we were face-to-face.

Burgos made some sort of noise in his throat.

"You're also working on a Sunday on a holiday weekend? I guess we both need to get a life." Accompanied by my most self-deprecating smile.

"I have a report and pics for Doc Thacker." Burgos tapped a large brown envelope tucked under his left arm. "I was nearby, figured I'd just leave this on her desk."

"Conveyed the old-fashioned way." Delivered with another big grin.

"I suppose."

"I've just completed my examination of the body from the subcellar."

Since Burgos was overseeing the arson investigation, I saw no problem sharing, and gave him an abbreviated version of the profile.

"So, your bag lady didn't die in the fire." He sounded grudgingly interested.

"Definitely not. I found no smoke or soot in her trachea or in what remained of her lungs." I left it at that.

"When did she bite it?" The tiny gray eyes narrowing slightly.

"I can't say for sure, but her death wasn't recent." You cold-hearted prick. I didn't voice that assessment. "Any news on the four upstairs victims?"

Burgos guffawed, one cold note. Shook his head, careful not to dislodge his carefully sculpted do.

"I talked to this asshole Billie Norris who kinda acted as a gatekeeper at the dump. A brain trust he ain't. By jostling Norris's memory—the few cells able to break through the haze of blow he was floating in—I got him to cough up some leads."

"Names?"

Burgos nodded. "Doc Thacker's headache now. Could be a bitch getting records. The kid that called nine one one might have been Canadian. There was maybe another foreign national in the mix."

"You're sure it was arson?" I asked.

"Sure as my granny shits every dawn."

"Based on what?" Cool. Hopefully hiding my revulsion for the man.

"Origin and spread. The pattern ain't textbook, but it's good enough for me."

"Where did it start?"

"Kitchen area."

"Did you find evidence of accelerants?"

Burgos sighed a most impatient sigh. "Look, lady. There's things I gotta do."

I debated sharing Doyle's phone tip concerning the meth lab. Decided that wasn't my place.

"Do you think one of the four upstairs vics might have been targeted?"

"Them or any of the scumbagfest in and out of that hole."

Without so much as a nod, Burgos sidestepped me and strode off.

CHAPTER 10

I was on E Street, approaching the Mucha truck, when my mobile sounded.

Seeing the number, I groaned inwardly, but felt compelled to answer. After all, the woman was housing me until Thacker could secure a hotel room.

"Hey, Ivy. What's up?"

"*Les oiseaux dans le ciel.* You?"

"I just finished analyzing the subcellar remains," I said, puzzled by her reference to birds in the sky. To impress me with her command of French?

"Any surprises?" she asked.

"There are always surprises."

Careful, Brennan. The woman is a reporter.

Doyle didn't press.

"I've been digging into the Foggy Bottom property. Did you find anything else down below that you might feel comfortable sharing?"

As a gesture I offered an insignificant detail. I told her about the glass shards.

"Awesome. The place has quite the colorful history. This is going to make a fantab story."

Offering nothing further on her fantab scoop. Fair enough.

"I'll be home by seven," she went on. "Are you interested in dinner?"

"I don't want to—"

"What shall I have Lan make?"

"I'm good with anything."

"Any food allergies?"

Jesus. Was I going on a cruise?

"I don't care for eel."

"No eel it is. See you later."

"Later."

We disconnected.

The menu was staring right at me from the side of the truck. One small starter couldn't hurt.

I went with a pork taco with mango salsa. A horchata to wash it down. What were the chances Lan would cook Mexican?

Lan went full-bore Thai.

Som Tam. Kaeng Lueang. Khao Pad. Khao Niao Mamuang.

Spicy green papaya salad. Yellow curry. Fried rice. Mango sticky rice. She explained each dish as it hit the table.

Despite my earlier snack at the Mucha truck, I did my share. More than my share.

Doyle and I exchanged small talk as we ate.

She asked how I'd come to be a forensic anthropologist. I outlined my post-Northwestern years in academia, my early focus on bioarchaeology, my unforeseen shift into the medico-legal world.

Out of courtesy, I queried her career path. She described the tortuous climb toward her current job at WTTG.

Following the completion of a degree in communications and journalism at Brown, Doyle said she'd taken jobs in Yuma, Arizona; Springfield, Missouri; and Sioux City, Iowa. After almost a decade in smaller cities, she'd been lured by an incredible offer to a station in Columbia, South Carolina. A midsized market.

While in Columbia, she'd been sent to cover the war in Afghanistan and had met Katy. Those reports had led to her shot at the big time: Washington, DC. The position wasn't exactly what she'd envisioned for herself, but the US capital was a huge broadcast area and being there would put her close to breaking national stories.

At first, she'd covered traffic for the local CBS affiliate. After that, she'd worked as a field reporter and occasional fill-in anchor at the regional NBC station. Six long years, then a FOX producer took notice and offered her the position she now held.

As Doyle spoke, giving dates and durations at each location, I did that math thing you do in your head. Realized the woman was older than I'd estimated. Older than she looked.

Doyle's dream was an anchor desk with a major network. And a nationally syndicated true crime series. For now, she was reading the news at four, seven, and eleven p.m., doing her podcast, and hoping to be discovered again.

Ivy Doyle was a poster child for the bright and attractive young women currently in demand by TV news departments. And definitely ambitious. Why, I wondered, had her career not progressed more quickly?

Eventually, inevitably, the conversation shifted to the Foggy Bottom fire.

When Doyle asked about the subcellar vic, I laid out the basics, essentially the same spiel I'd given Burgos.

"Impressive that you managed to lift prints."

"I only got two partials. And that took some doing."

"Thacker will have them run through IAFIS?"

Doyle used the acronym for the FBI's Integrated Automated Fingerprint Identification System, a massive database used for the storage and analysis of fingerprint records. A latent print examiner once told me that the IAFIS software was so sophisticated it could search more than a billion prints in a single second.

"She will," I said.

"Do you really think she could get a hit?"

"If the lady's in the system."

"What might get her in there?"

I shrugged. "Criminal record. Job application. Military service." The last seemed unlikely, given the woman's diminutive size.

"How early are the oldest records in the database?"

"I'm not sure. But cops started using prints back in the 1800s."

Doyle thought about that, then asked,

"COD?" Cause of death?

"Undetermined."

"Suspicious?"

"I doubt the woman stuffed herself into that sack."

Cringe face. Then,

"PMI?" Doyle was certainly up on her forensic lingo. This one was an acronym for postmortem interval. I assumed her familiarity was due to her frequent coverage of crime stories.

"Hard to be exact. But given the state of the woman's body and clothing, and the conditions in the subcellar, I'd say a minimum of five years."

"Could it be much longer than that?"

"Absolutely. Why do you ask?"

Doyle waited a beat too long before answering. A revealing tell. Though willing to take, the reporter in her was hesitant to give.

"No reason." Doyle flashed me the smile that melted the hearts of millions.

No reason, my ass.

"I found more info on the building." Doyle shifted gears. "Want to hear it?"

"Sure."

Doyle rose and crossed to the Louis Vuitton purse she'd dropped onto the sideboard. I'd had a knockoff once, purchased from a street vendor in New York. The strap broke within a year. Hers was the real deal. As was the notebook she withdrew, pen clipped to its blue leather cover. Small white symbols identified both as Montblanc.

Lan reappeared as Doyle was returning to the table.

"Would you like coffee here or in the study, ma'am?"

We chose the study. Lan dipped her head ever so slightly and disappeared.

Minutes later we were settled in two Herman Miller Eames lounge chairs, our feet on the plush white leather ottomans. The Montblanc journal lay on Doyle's upraised knees.

"The property has had surprisingly few owners over the years." Splaying the pages open with the press of one palm.

"Unusual for such an old building."

Lan tiptoed in and placed a steaming mug beside each of us. We took a moment to sip.

"Would you like something stronger?" Doyle asked.

You bet your ass, I thought.

"No thanks," I said.

"We know that the house that burned down was designed by Hiram L. Pepper," Doyle continued. "I confirmed that it was built in 1911."

"The date on the plans."

"The first title holder was a man named Ansel Dankworth. Dankworth owned a paper box factory on the northern edge of Georgetown."

"Paper boxes must have been profitable."

Doyle's eyes rolled to meet mine. "Until the factory went up in flames in 1924. Six women died because the fire doors were locked to prevent employees from sneaking in late or slipping out to smoke. The media made a circus of Dankworth's unsafe working conditions. He sold his Foggy Bottom home the following year."

I'd seen photos of turn-of-the-century workshops and sweathouses. Felt sadness imagining the terror experienced by those trapped workers.

Doyle's gaze dropped back to her notes.

It was almost ten. I'd slept poorly the previous night, awakened at dawn. Put in a long and difficult day at the morgue. Ingested at least ten pounds of Thai food. Despite the coffee, my brain was signaling its intent to clock out. Still, I tried to pay attention.

"The next owner was Caleb Sheridan. Sheridan owned three hardware stores. Lost them all when the market crashed in '29. Declared bankruptcy and sold the Foggy Bottom property in 1930."

Focused on her notes, Doyle didn't notice that I was fading.

"The third owner was a woman named Unique Swallow. Documents described Swallow as a spinster, her occupation as 'business owner.'"

Doyle looked up and flashed an apologetic look. "I could find nothing in the archives specifying the nature of Unique's enterprise."

I nodded, thinking of the more colorful possibilities. Had Miss Swallow supplied services of a personal nature?

"Not sure what happened to Unique, but in 1942 the house sold to an entity called W-C Commerce. W-C still owns the property today."

"Is it a partnership or a sole proprietorship?"

"I don't know. But I intend to find out."

"How?" Stifling a yawn.

"I have my sources." Coy.

Though I was fighting the good fight, the exhaustion must have shown on my face.

Doyle closed the Montblanc with a definitive snap.

"Off with you now." She stood. "I'll have more tomorrow."

"I really am intrigued."

"Get some shut-eye."

"Are you on-air tomorrow?"

Doyle nodded. "The news rests for no man. Or woman. As a matter of fact, it's time I go to the station now."

I'd just crawled under the covers when the dreaded, though not unexpected, phone call came.

CHAPTER 11

Before she spoke, I knew Thacker's ask.

"Tempe, I hope I didn't wake you."

"Not at all."

"I won't keep you up."

That was for damn sure.

"I have potential IDs for the Foggy Bottom DOAs. My investigators have requested dental records and alerted family members of the need for DNA samples. Hopefully, the dentals will arrive within the next twenty-four hours."

"I understand there may be foreign nationals in the mix."

"Yes." A note of surprise that I knew that? "Autopsies will begin first thing Tuesday morning. I hope you can attend. Visual IDs will not be possible."

Crap!

"Of course."

Thus died my last lingering hope of recouping a sliver of the holiday weekend to spend with Ryan.

With a sigh nearly as dramatic as Burgos's, I disconnected and hit speed dial.

Ryan picked up with his usual cheery salutation.

"*Ma chérie.* What a lovely surprise. I figured you'd be asleep by now."

"I'm in bed and about to turn off the light."

"What are you wearing? Is it that lacey—"

"I'm in a UNCC tee and plaid boxers."

"*Très* sexy."

The guy never changed. I loved that about him.

"Thanks."

"Will you model your chic ensemble for me tomorrow?"

"Ryan, somethi—"

"I've cleared my schedule for the entire week. How about I take the dawn flight to DC tomorrow, then we set off for Savannah together? Road trip! You can be Thelma, I'll be Louise."

"They were both women."

"I'll work on my costuming."

"They died at the end of the movie."

Ryan ignored that.

"Lordy chile, I hear the song of Dixie calling me home."

"That's the worst southern accent I've ever heard."

"I surely do thank you, ma'am." Thick as syrup on grits.

"Stop," I said.

"*Oui, Madame.*"

I closed my eyes and drew a deep breath, hating that I was about to disappoint him again.

"I've got bad news."

Five hundred miles to the north, I sensed Ryan stiffen.

"Thacker has asked me to attend the postmortems for the Foggy Bottom fire victims."

"Why does she need you?"

"There's no possibility of visual IDs. And trauma analysis could be complicated."

"Why you?"

"She's heard I'm a superstar?"

Ryan didn't laugh at my joke.

"When?"

"The autopsies will begin Tuesday morning."

"Four of them." Flat.

"Yes."

"You've agreed?"

"I have."

Ryan is affable by nature, his ignition for annoyance or offense less sensitive than mine. That said, I could sense that I'd triggered it.

"You're telling me not to come," he said.

"I'm sorry."

Ryan's breathing shifted and started going hard through his nose. I pictured his lips compressing, the skin around them turning white.

For at least ten seconds, there was no other sound on the line. Just that breathing.

I broke the tense silence.

"It's not what I want. I feel terrible."

"You always do." The words sluiced like cold shards through the miles between us.

"I—"

"This happens all the time, Tempe. We make plans, you back out. Your commitments to me mean nothing. *Rien.*"

"That's not fair."

"Isn't it?"

We were both forcing our voices calm. But I sensed an entire soap opera's worth of anger and resentment pouring from Ryan.

Felt similar emotions sprouting in me.

"You would have me refuse Thacker?" I asked, the effort to keep my voice down actually hurting my throat. "Have me turn my back on the innocent people who lost their lives in that fire?"

"Here's the thing, Tempe. I'm tired of performing somersaults to fit into your schedule. Tired of always putting my needs second to yours. Maybe this is for the best. Maybe we need some time apart."

Three beeps.

Dead air.

I sat, mobile pressed to my sternum, emotions roiling in my brain. Anger. Hurt. Confusion.

Mostly confusion.

Why such flash-fire rage? It wasn't like Ryan. Was he correct? *Was* I always putting myself before him? Was I taking him for granted?

Or was Ryan being unreasonable? I felt a responsibility to the Foggy Bottom victims. Was his reaction to my commitment inappropriate?

Contrary to my earlier expectation, sleep was a long time coming.

When it came, it did so hard and deep.

It was almost nine when I awoke from a dream I couldn't remember. Uncertain of my location, I sleepily surveyed my surroundings. Cavernous room. Space rocket lamp. Wooded view of half the East Coast.

Right.

Lan insisted on making an omelet for me. Doyle was gone, so I ate her marvelous eggs alone at the shiny marble table.

My mind kept replaying the previous night's quarrel. I debated whether to call Ryan to apologize.

A gaggle of kindhearted neurons urged me to pick up the phone. A less-forgiving cluster said absolutely no.

In the hours since the argument, I'd decided that Ryan's response had been childlike and selfish. I was certain I'd never ask him to put my desires ahead of his professional obligations.

Given that, I decided to go with the nos. Let the guy cool down for a while.

After breakfast, I took coffee to my room and booted my laptop.

I began by checking my inboxes.

Seven emails from political candidates, all asking for money. Three from TV stations informing me of upcoming shows. Two from Chewy alerting me to products for cats. One from an online retailer from whom I'd purchased makeup two years earlier. One from an outfit trying to sell me solar panels.

The only personal message had come from my mother. Daisy was considering signing up for a cruise along the western coast of Africa. Wanted my thoughts.

Deleting all but Mama's communique, which I would address later, I began my research by googling the phrase "historic burlap sack." This produced a half dozen links for buyers and sellers of antique bags. Apparently, there was a small but enthusiastic community of collectors. Who knew?

I clicked over to the website of the NYP Corp., a company that described itself as a provider of burlap and other agricultural supplies and textiles. NYP's home page offered contact information for locations in New Jersey, Pennsylvania, Tennessee, Missouri, Ohio, and my own fair state.

I prowled around on the NYP website a while, clicking from page to page. Learned many useful facts, including the following.

Jute is an annual plant of the genus *Corchorus*.

Jute is grown entirely for its fiber.

Burlap is made from jute.

For centuries, people in India used jute to make rope, paper, and handwoven fabrics.

Early on, English traders saw jute's potential as a substitute for hemp and flax.

The East India Company exported its first hundred-ton shipment of jute in 1793.

While interesting, none of this info was relevant to the question I wanted answered.

Ninety minutes after starting, I sat back, frustrated.

Returning to the NYP home page, I drank tepid coffee while staring at the shifting images topping the screen. Tree root baskets. Deer corn bags. Ground covers. Seed sacks.

What were the chances anyone at NYP would be at the office on Memorial Day?

Zero to none sounded like a reasonable estimate.

What the hell.

Figuring shared roots might make the person answering my call more receptive, I phoned the plant in Lumberton, North Carolina.

Four rings. A voice answered as I was about to disconnect.

"NYP Corp. Colt's my name. Burlap's my game." Drawl thicker than sludge in a sewage pipe.

I was so stunned I didn't respond immediately.

"Y'all there?"

"Sorry, Mr. Colt. I didn't expect to find anyone working on a holiday."

"That's not how I view it, ma'am."

"Excuse me?" At a loss what Colt meant.

"For me, burlap is a labor of love."

"I see." I didn't. "I'm interested in a particular item. Wondered if you might—"

"Is that a Carolina twang I'm hearing?"

"Yes, sir. I live in Charlotte."

"Privileged to make your acquaintance. Go Panthers!"

"Yahoo. I'm calling because I have some questions about the manufacture of burlap."

"What do you know about our little op?" Colt asked.

"Not much."

"Well, then."

Cellophane crinkled, then a pop-top *whushed.* I feared I was about to learn far more than I needed. I was right.

"NYP has been a wholesaler of burlap products since 1936. Nursery and horticulture needs. Agricultural and industrial packaging. We do it all."

"I read that on your website."

Colt made a throaty noise meant to convey contempt, I think.

"Upholstery supplies, emergency sandbags, landscaping materials, ground covers, bales and rolls—"

"I'm wondering if someone could provide details about one particular sack. I'm especially interested in pinpointing the period during which it was produced." I left out that the sack in question had held a corpse.

"And you would be?"

"Dr. Temperance Brennan."

"Are you a collector?"

"Mm."

"Can you describe y'all's sack?"

"It's big and has the words *Swifty Spud* written above a cartoonlike potato, the word *Potatoes* written below."

"Are the lettering and the picture in color?"

"Both are red and green."

"What's the potato doing?"

"Running." Weird question.

Colt gave a noncommittal grunt. Then,

"Where was the sack found?"

"In a basement in Washington, DC. The image is faded but readable. I—"

"Shush. I'm thinking."

I waited.

"What's the bag's capacity?"

"It measures approximately forty-eight by seventy-two inches." Big enough to hold a body.

Colt *tsked*, displeased with or skeptical of my answer.

"Can you text me a photo?" he asked.

"Of course. To this number?"

"To my personal cell." Colt slowly and carefully dictated the digits for his mobile.

"I'll do it right now, sir."

Seconds later I heard the text land with a soft bong on his end.

A beat, then a sharp intake of breath.

"This gage thingy. Is it accurate?"

"Very." Out of habit, I'd included an ABFO ruler in the shot for scale.

"Oh, my stars," Colt said.

"What?"

"This is an ultra-large sack. And a real beauty. What did you say your name was?"

"Brennan. Do you recognize the logo?"

"No. Well, maybe. I'll have to do some digging to establish when and where this burly gal was made. This is truly exhilarating."

"How long might that take?"

Colt ignored my question. Or missed it in his excitement over the burly gal.

"This is a marvelous specimen. May I phone you back on this number?"

"Yes."

"Thank you so, so much for sharing your find with me." Gushy.

"I appreciate your willingness to help."

Colt lowered his voice to a conspiratorial whisper. "I will be totally discreet."

"Thank you."

"No. Thank *you*."

By the time we disconnected I was sure Colt was planning to send me flowers and candy.

Instead, by day's end I'd get a far less pleasant surprise.

CHAPTER 12

My eyes drifted to the top right corner of my screen.
12:15 p.m.
Monday, May 26.
Memorial Day.
I wasn't within miles of Savannah.
Or Charlotte.
Or Ryan.
I'd made almost no progress identifying the tiny subcellar woman.
Restless, I swiveled, grabbed the remote, and turned on the TV. I could always count on my pals at CNN to be there for me.

Wildfires were raging in California. Six died in a plane crash off Cape Cod. Two white cops were relieved of duty for mistreating a Black prisoner in Baltimore. Fifteen were injured in a boat explosion at Lake of the Ozarks.

I've no idea why I'm such a news addict. Newscasts are like factory-produced clocks, each broadcast composed of interchangeable parts. On any given day, swap in different names, different places, different details, the main storylines remain predictable. With seasonal variations.

Today's twist was that the whole country was decked out in red, white, and blue. CNN showed clips of preparations underway for celebrations in New York, Atlanta, Minneapolis, and Chicago.

Alas, I was not participating in the patriotic display. Instead, I was stuck killing time before being able to autopsy four charred corpses.

Christ on a cracker, Brennan. Quit the pity party.

Motivated by my well-deserved self-admonishment, I googled the times and locations of the district's major festivities.

The National Memorial Day parade would begin on 7th Street, turn north onto Constitution Avenue, proceed west and end at 17th Street. The high-stepping and confetti tossing would start at two p.m., street closures at noon.

I phoned Uber.

Forty minutes later Diego arrived in a gray Honda Accord bearing Virginia license BRX-4237.

Virginia Is For Lovers, declared the plate's slogan.

But not for me.

I walked through the doors of the E Street lab at six-forty-five Tuesday morning. Was delighted to see Jamar on the far side of the lobby.

We traded quick waves, Jamar again doing something intricate with his hand, then headed to our respective locker rooms to change.

Thacker was already in the large autopsy suite. To my surprise, she announced she'd be cutting the Ys herself.

Body bags lay on three of the four tables. Two had contours of reasonable size. The third looked like it might hold a full adult hippo.

Thacker and I exchanged a few words about the weekend.

Yes, I'd gone to the parade. Yes, I'd seen the fireworks. Yes, the weather had been hot.

"And you?" I asked her, mostly out of courtesy.

"I avoid all public gatherings. Too many nasty microbes waiting to pounce."

With that, Thacker turned to Jamar.

"Roll the credits."

Jamar worked the keyboard and four names appeared on the Smart-board. He read the list aloud, adding a few pertinent details for each individual.

"Case number 25-02102, Skylar Reese Hill, female, age nineteen, white, foreign national, Canada."

"Was Hill the young woman who made the nine-one-one call?" I asked.

"Assuming this DOA is Hill, yes."

My cheeks reddened at Thacker's not-so-subtle reprimand.

"Where was that body found?" the ME asked her tech.

Jamar clacked more keys. "Basement level, east end, buried in rubble from the collapse of the upper floors."

The victim I'd recovered.

"Next." Thacker was all business now.

"Case number 25-02103, Danny Green, male, age twenty-nine, white, no accompanying intel.

"Case number 25-02104, Johnnie Lamar Star, male, age thirty-four, Black, US citizen, last known address Philadelphia. Star and Green were in the west bedroom on the second floor." Looking up, Jamar added: "I did that pair. The two beside the bed, all tangled up together."

No one restated the obvious concerning unproven assumptions.

Jamar continued.

"Case number 25-02105, Jawaad el-Aman, male, age twenty-one, foreign national, Syria. Body recovered from the third floor, west bedroom."

"We'll have to be extra careful with him," Thacker said. "The kid was an ambassador's son."

"What was an ambassador's son doing in a rented room in a cheap Airbnb?" I asked.

"I don't know. But I don't want the State Department getting its nuts in a knot."

"Assuming the DOA is el-Aman." I matched Thacker's admonishment word for word.

"Assuming that." Raising her mask to her face, Thacker added, "Let's start with el-Aman." Turning to me. "The body presumed to be el-Aman."

Her eyes suggested a grin behind the blue polypropylene covering her mouth.

Crossing to the closest autopsy table, Jamar clicked on and adjusted the pull-down surgical lamp. The bright LED lit the black body bag like a spot on a darkened film set.

Thacker nodded.

The zipper rent the silence with a loud *whrrrp.*

The remains were as I recalled.

The man had died wearing a baseball cap. A quick google revealed the emblem on it was a Syrian flag.

The facial features were gone, the skull cracked, its contents reduced to a shriveled dark mass. The torso was blackened, the forearms history, the limbs curled into the pugilistic pose.

Jamar shot pics. Thacker and I tweezed debris off the charred flesh, setting each item aside for future analysis. A zipper and studs from jeans. A belt buckle in the shape of a star. Fragmented teeth. Amorphous globs that had probably been dental restorations. A melted and warped metal comb.

Then, with much maneuvering, the three of us managed to roll the corpse to its back.

I stood aside while Thacker dictated what comments were possible. She noted the remnants of a penis and scrotum, the genitalia protected from the flames by the well-muscled lower torso and thighs. The eyes, stomach, and other organs were too damaged to yield any info. Inking prints was impossible.

Using a scalpel, Thacker verified the presence of smoke in the victim's mouth, lungs, and trachea. The kid had been breathing at the time of the fire.

When Thacker finished, Jamar wheeled the body off for radiography.

After a quick coffee break, Thacker and I viewed the projected images together. As she recorded facts about soft tissue, I focused on the skeleton.

Based on the state of epiphyseal union in the clavicles and long bones, I estimated that the victim had died in his late teens to early twenties. Using measurements taken directly on the handy-dandy Smartboard, I calculated that he'd stood sixty-eight to seventy inches tall.

Neither of us spotted anything suggestive of factors other than death by fire.

The bio-profile was consistent with that of Jawaad el-Aman. As was the cap bearing the flag of his homeland.

Beyond that, all we could do was collect samples for DNA testing.

Another short pause for lunch, then we moved on to the hippo bag. To the commingled bodies found on the second floor, presumably Danny Green and Johnnie Lamar Star.

As with the vic presumed to be el-Awan, the body parts having little or no flesh exhibited the most damage—the fingers and hands, the toes and feet. The few surviving digits had been reduced to blackened twigs.

While at the scene, I'd counted six limbs, each a scorched and shriveled spindle. That tally held true. The lower torsos and thighs, composed of solid, heavy bones encased in thick muscle masses, had congealed into one shapeless glob.

Neither man's head had survived intact. Cranial and dental fragments coated the macabre black mass like sprinkles on a cake. Others had been collected and sealed in a small Tupperware tub. From the accompanying debris we retrieved parts of four melted sneakers, two scorched zippers, and fourteen more teeth.

By eight-forty-five Thacker and I had completed our analyses of #25-02103 and #25-02104, using the same protocol we'd followed for #25-02105. Brennan bones. Thacker organs and soft tissue. Jamar, brawn.

The bio-profiles were consistent with Green and Star.

Neither corpse yielded prints.

Thacker was pleased and asked if I'd be there for Hill the following morning.

Presumed Hill.

I agreed and left.

Exhausted.

Never wanting to see charred or seared meat again.

Hoping to avoid social interaction of any kind, I grabbed a spicy turkey club at Rich Coffee on MacArthur Boulevard—Thacker's recommendation—then headed to Doyle's house, thumbed the code into the keypad, and slipped in as quietly as I could.

Luck was with me. I encountered no one. Presumably, Doyle was at work and Lan had punched out for the day.

After showering in the hundred-acre glass cubicle, I ate my sandwich while entering notes onto my laptop.

When finished, I again considered calling Ryan. Peeks at my voice mail, email, and text messages throughout the day had shown that he hadn't tried to contact me.

My phone said 10:40.

Screw it. Someone had to be the adult.

I dialed. Got voice mail. Disconnected, leaving no message.

I killed the light and collapsed into my mound of goose down pillows.

Was asleep in seconds.

I awoke to cloud-shrouded moonlight filtering through glass. To shadows dancing a shape-changing ballet on the walls, the ceiling, the quilt.

No shutters. No Birdie.

I wasn't in my own bed.

A moment of cerebral groping, then recollection.

Doyle. DC. The Foggy Bottom fire.

Rain was falling outside the window wall framing the headboard. Tree branches lifted and dropped, occasionally scraping the pane with a gentle *tic tic tic.*

Had the muted staccato awakened me?

I held my breath, listening.

Heard nothing inside but the murmur of air flowing through vents.

Though I welcomed the blissful cooling provided by Doyle's central AC, the intermittent blowing dried the lining of my nose and mouth.

I reached for my drink.

Three hundred and eighty million tons of plastic are produced each year, as much as half that for single-use purposes. Refusing to contribute to that atrocity against the planet, I never buy or drink bottled water.

Damn.

Lan had taken my Yeti to the kitchen for washing. In my exhaustion, I'd forgotten to retrieve and fill it.

Throwing back the covers, I got out of bed and padded across the zebra carpet.

Halfway to the door, a sound stopped me in my tracks.

Scritch.

Fabric scraping a wall?

I froze, every sense straining for further input.

My ears took in nothing but the echo of empty space.

What are you, Brennan? Four years old?

I was reaching for the knob when something went *clump* on the far side of the door.

A footfall?

Whose?

At night, the hall outside my room was lit by motion-activated foot-level spots. I glanced at the crack where the door met the carpet. Noted soft illumination.

Two dark shapes silhouetted in the dim glow.

Feet?

Spread wide in an aggressive stance?

My heart tossed in a few extra beats.

What to do?

Scream?

Lock myself in the bathroom?

Throw open the door?

Swallowing through my dryness, I tiptoed to my suitcase and withdrew a small key-chain baton. Received as a gift from my baby sister following a YMCA course on self-protection, it had been tucked into a compartment and forgotten. Until now.

Thank you, Harry.

Death-gripping the tiny steel bar, I recrossed to the door.

Ready to come face-to-face with anyone from a hophead junkie to Charlie Manson.

CHAPTER 13

A man stood there, a huge one, right hand raised, fingers curled into a fist.

Prepared to knock?

To attack?

The man's face was in shadow, only his lower legs pulled from the gloom by the discretely placed spots.

I saw boots. Cargo pants.

The man leaned toward me.

I may have screamed.

I may have threatened with my ridiculously small weapon.

The man dropped his arm and stepped back.

"Who are you?" I demanded.

Two palms rose, directed toward me. "Easy."

Somewhere below, a door slammed.

"What do you want!?" My throat was parched, and fear wasn't helping my diction.

I heard footsteps. Muffled, like an eraser tapping a chalkboard.

My eyes never left the man. Beyond his massive shoulders I saw a head appear on the stairs at the far end of the hall. A ginger head.

The head bounced up tread by tread and became Ivy Doyle.

"Ben!"

The man whipped around.

"Sorry, babe. You can't work up here tonight. I have a guest bunking in this room."

Doyle must have flicked a switch. Suddenly the hall was bathed in light.

Ben looked like every cell in his body was prickling. I'm sure I looked the same.

"My bad," Doyle gushed, intent on defusing the awkward situation. "Wires crossed? SNAFU? What does one call a failure to give notice?"

I hadn't an inkling of her meaning. Ben's expression, now readable, suggested he hadn't, either.

Doyle hurried toward us, manicured fingers clutching her robe at the throat, slippers softly kissing the hardwoods.

"Tempe . . ." sweeping a hand from me to Ben, ". . . this is my fiancé, Ben Zanetti. Ben . . ." reverse sweep, ". . . this is Tempe Brennan. Dr. Brennan is staying here while she consults to the medical examiner."

Ben and I exchanged nods. His hair was black and curly and leading-man thick, his eyes an unusual amber flecked with bronze. I swear the guy stood six feet six. Almost as big as Captain Hickey. Seemed our nation's capital preferred its men large.

"Tempe's daughter, Katy, is one of my very best friends," Doyle said to Zanetti.

I suspected that was an overstatement but didn't let on.

"Nice to meet you," I managed to get out.

"Ben's the hottest realtor in DC." Doyle smiled coyly at him. "He does paperwork up here when staying at the house." Her grin switched to mildly rueful as she reached for Mr. Real Estate's hand. "Which isn't nearly often enough."

"I'll work on that, darlin'." Ben pulled her in and draped her shoulders with a tree-trunk arm.

"I'm so sorry to inconvenience you," I said, suddenly aware of my inelegant boxers and tank. "I'll be out of here tomorrow."

"Absolutely not," Doyle said. "You are welcome here for as long as you need."

As things turned out, my stay was far longer than anticipated.

I awoke to another soggy dawn unfolding in shades of gray. Pewter sky. Slate trees. Ash walkways and drive.

I lay a moment, experiencing a twitchiness I couldn't explain.

Out of habit, I reached for my phone.

Checked my voice mail.

Found nothing from Ryan.

Fine. Two could play that game.

What are you, Brennan? A high schooler scorned?

Still, I declined to dial his number again.

After dressing in jeans and a tee, I ran a quick brush through my hair and over my teeth. Different strokes, different brushes.

Given the hour, I figured I'd slip out unnoticed.

Not so.

Today, Lan offered oatmeal sprinkled with granola and raisins. No Quaker instant for this gal. The woman really knew her way around a stove.

I saw no sign of Doyle. Or Ben. Big Ben as I'd come to think of him overnight. I assumed both were still sleeping.

As I pushed from the table, my body-image neurons sent an unwelcome warning. Keep eating like this and you'll need all new pants. Or serious alterations.

Grabbing purse and keys, I headed for my car.

The morning couldn't make up its mind what it wanted to do. Carry on with the rain? Yield to the sun?

On one thing it was certain. The day would be hot.

It was a quick drive back to Southwest Washington. After finding a parking spot—trickier than I would have thought at 6:50 a.m.—I set out for the Consolidated Forensic Lab.

While walking, I passed the usual urban players. Early-bird office workers talking into their phones. Students in running gear sweating off hangovers. The homeless. The addicts. Most looked post-sunrise bleary, uncurious about what the next twenty-four hours would bring.

Outside the glass doors, two young dudes argued loudly in Polish. Maybe Czech. As I stepped around them, neither missed a beat in pressing his point.

Twenty minutes after my arrival, Jamar, Thacker, and I were attired in scrubs, ready for the analysis of #25-02102—presumably Skylar Reese

Hill, the victim I'd recovered from the basement rubble in the Foggy Bottom house.

I was surprised to see a man in one corner of the autopsy room, mask covering his nose and mouth, paper gown carelessly thrown on over his suit. Long face, long neck, Adam's apple the size of a kiwi, prickly gray hair in the act of retreating from his forehead. Not the homeliest guy I'd ever seen, but a contender.

Thacker looked grim. The man looked stoic. Jamar looked his usual chipper self.

Thacker introduced the visitor as Detective Merle Deery.

Deery dipped his chin but said nothing. The wide-footed stance and tense cant of the long neck screamed "cop."

A male tenor crooned from a powerful purse-sized speaker on one of the stainless-steel counters. Verdi. Maybe *La Traviata*. Opera was a requirement for Thacker when cutting Ys.

Without further ado, we got down to business.

Except for postmortem trauma caused by impact and crushing, the remains on the table resembled those found on the upper floors. The features were gone and only a mask of blackened flesh covered the underlying facial bones. The limbs were truncated. The viscera had exploded through the abdominal wall.

Thacker had requested an antemortem photo of Hill. Deery had brought one. Thacker and I leaned our heads together to view it.

The picture showed a young woman with long blond braids sitting on a bench on a sunny day. Wind teased her bangs and lifted the collar of her mint green shirt. Her smile, wide as the Mississippi, spoke of confidence in a future rolling on forever.

A future denied her.

I felt my usual melancholy on seeing a frozen moment in a life cruelly ended.

And resignation.

The shot was useless. There wasn't a chance of a visual ID.

As with the other corpses, I knew the bones would tell most of the story.

I was right.

The pelvis and skull verified that the victim was female.

Surviving cranial and facial details hinted that she'd been of European ancestry.

Long bone measurements said she'd stood sixty-three to sixty-five inches tall.

The incomplete union of several growth plates suggested she'd died between the ages of eighteen and twenty-five years.

A bio-profile that fit that of Skylar Reese Hill.

The victim's right humerus threw in one bonus nugget. On X-ray I spotted a slight deformity just above the elbow, an indication of a healed fracture.

A check of Hill's medical records, also supplied by Deery, confirmed that she'd broken that arm the previous year.

Throughout the procedure, Deery never uttered a word. He left as Thacker was dictating her final observations and I was scribbling my last few notes. I'd just finished when my mobile sounded.

The digits on the screen identified a line at the Charlotte-Mecklenburg crime lab.

Snapping off one of my gloves, I thumbed the icon.

"Dr. Brennan."

"—stein. Have more inf—your sam—"

"Artie?"

"—es. I got the res—"

"I'm sorry. You're breaking up. Give me a moment."

"—leave for a meeting short—ought you'd—to know."

Phone pressed to my ear, I hurried out into the corridor. Still, the reception was lousy.

As I passed through the sliding doors, three beeps told me the call had been dropped.

Damn.

Once in the office temporarily assigned to me, I hit redial, hoping Bluestein was still available.

"Was that Pavarotti?" he asked.

"Yes."

"I didn't know you like opera."

"Who doesn't." Rhetorical.

"I have season tickets to Opera Carolina. We should catch a performance sometime. My wife hates it."

"Mm. You have more info on the Mirek sample?"

"Asian female."

That took me off guard.

"What?"

"The hair in the fecal matter came from an Asian female."

"You're sure?"

Bluestein didn't bother to respond.

"Thanks, Artie."

"You're welcome. Shall I email the report?"

"Please."

I stood a moment, totally baffled. Was repocketing the phone when it sounded another incoming call.

Ivy Doyle.

"Can't talk." Sounding rushed. "I'll be home for a bit before my eleven o'clock. Wondered if I should bring takeout. Wednesday is Lan's night off."

Thank God. The woman did get time to herself.

"Please don't bother—"

"It's no bother. I've been AWOL and it will be nice to catch up. Do you like Greek?"

"Love it."

"See ya!"

I expected gyros on pita with fries.

As usual, Doyle had gone all out.

Feta-brined roasted chicken. Braised lamb shanks. Lemon broth poached asparagus. Goat cheese smashed potatoes. And, of course, baklava.

We exchanged updates as we ate.

Doyle had zip. Was still researching W-C Commerce. I suspected Big Ben was the distraction causing her lack of progress.

The night was warm and Potomac-basin sultry, so we took our pastries to a deck at the back of the house. Using her mobile, Doyle put Sinatra on the audio system. It was pleasant watching day yield to night as Frank crooned and June bugs body-slammed the screening around us. For a while we said nothing.

Old Blue Eyes was singing about strangers in the night when we began discussing the arson examiner, Lubu Burgos. Neither of us had much confidence in the guy. Burgos was convinced the Foggy Bottom fire had been deliberately set. Had it? We both sensed his investigation had been cursory. Were we right? Or was our judgment clouded by our impression that the man was a jerk.

The Foggy Bottom building was more than a hundred years old, a tinderbox of dry timbers, untreated plywood, ancient appliances, and outdated wiring. Might the fire have been accidental?

We considered multiple possibilities.

Was the blaze triggered by a spark from a socket? A gas leak? A faulty circuit? An overloaded breaker? An ash from a carelessly discarded cigarette or joint?

Burgos consistently refused to explain how he'd ruled each of these out. Had shared only that the place was definitely being used as an illegal Airbnb.

Though loath to reveal her source, Doyle viewed the meth tip as valid. That led to a new pathway of speculation.

Might the building have been torched by a rival drug dealer? Might the lab have exploded due to sloppy cooking protocol? Faulty equipment?

I shared the fact that the four upstairs vics had been IDed, pending verification by DNA. Jawaad el-Aman. Johnnie Lamar Star. Danny Green. Skylar Reese Hill.

Then the conversation ambled off into other twisty hypotheses.

Was el-Aman targeted because he was Syrian? Because of his accent? His hat? His Middle Eastern appearance? Because of his father's state department connections?

According to background intel provided by Billie Norris, Star and Green were gay. Had the couple been in someone's crosshairs because of their lifestyle? Had some homophobic nutjob been incensed by DC's hosting of WorldPride 2025 and chosen two random victims to vent his rage? Had the fire been a solo act of terrorism? Had it been set by a group?

Did some aggrieved psycho want Skylar Reese Hill dead? Had she offended someone? Seemed unlikely, the kid was Canadian. And only nineteen. Still.

And for each speculative theory the same unanswered questions.

Who?

Why?

We'd been at it far too long when Zanetti's large form framed up in the doorway.

We both turned toward him.

Crossing the deck, Zanetti proffered an object to Doyle, another to me.

"Sweets for two sweet ladies."

The word "cornball" popped into my forebrain. I shoved it back down, and, smiling, accepted the cornball offering. A chocolate lollipop in the shape of a rose.

Doyle and I thanked him for the candy.

"Did you close the deal?" she asked.

"Tomorrow is another day," he said.

I assumed that meant no.

As did Doyle. "Sorry, babe."

Zanetti shrugged, bright Hollywood smile never faltering.

Doyle was pushing to her feet when her mobile sounded.

Raising an apologetic "just a moment finger" she answered.

"Ivy Doyle."

As the caller spoke, a shadow slipped across the perfectly *maquillaged* face.

"No way. You're solid on this?"

Zanetti and I exchanged puzzled glances.

"Hold on," Doyle said to the person on the other end of the line. "Dr. Brennan needs to hear this. I'm putting you on speaker."

I listened.

Felt the expression on Doyle's face take over mine.

CHAPTER 14

Doyle's informant was calling with a tip about another fire. In Foggy Bottom.

"Is it still burning?"

"Oh yeah. But not quite as hot as before."

"Where?" Doyle gestured that I should take down the info.

The caller, clearly a smoker, probably male, reeled off an address. I entered it into the Notes app on my phone.

"How close is that to the previous fire?"

"I could maybe spit. 'cept I'd—"

"Is it another illegal Airbnb?"

"Negatory. Single-family rental, outa my range by a zillion—"

"Is anyone inside?"

"Word is the happy couple is doing the season in Vienna."

"Do you have their names?"

"Phil and Devira Aaronson. The assholes left their parakeet behind." Before Doyle could query how her CI knew that, he added, "The whole goddam brigade had barely landed when a kid showed up claiming to be the house sitter."

"Who is he?" Jiggling a finger at me.

"Chippy Bennett. With two *n*'s, two *t*'s. Who the hell goes by—"

"Did Bennett call it in?"

"Yeah. The little capitalist lives two doors down. Spotted smoke."

"Engine Company 23 responded?"

"Yeah. Guy running the scene's the size of a SpaceX."

"Hickey?"

"Rocket Man wasn't in the mood to chat."

"So they've got the flames contained?"

"Yup. Show's pretty much over. I'm about to haul ass. You want I should send pics?"

"Yes."

"I snapped a few, but they'll cost extra."

"No problem."

"Coming atcha. And whoever's listening there in the wings, you never hearda me."

I assumed that comment was for my benefit.

"You picked up the alert on your scanner?" Doyle asked.

"Affirmative. By the by, he made it."

"Sorry?" Doyle tilted a questioning palm. Pointless. The caller couldn't see her.

"The bird. They got him out."

Two minutes after disconnecting, a trio of photos landed on Doyle's phone.

The three of us drew close to view them. Zanetti smelled of something probably costing a thousand bucks an ounce and produced in only one village in France.

The first image was time stamped 19:40:03 EDT. Centered in it was a two-story white townhome with a bay window on the left and a red door on the right. An extension ladder leaned high up against the front-facing wall. Brick steps led from the sidewalk to a walkway bisecting a tiny front yard. Hoses crisscrossed the trampled grass like eels on a riverbank.

The structure's lower level looked largely intact. Not so the upper. Orange flames licked from shattered windows. Dense smoke billowed out around them.

The second shot, a view up the block, showed contiguous row houses, some frame, some brick, each painted a kitschy rainbow shade. Window boxes, shutters, doors, and trim were done in harmonizing HOA-approved tones.

The third pic was taken with the lens pointed a full one-eighty away from the fire. It captured a narrow, cobbled street hectic with equipment and personnel. Gawkers. Patrol units. Yellow police tape.

"This address isn't far from 26th and K," Doyle said.

"Geographically speaking." I referred to the vibe I was getting from the photos, one of Persian rugs, Waterford goblets, and Italian espresso makers. Not seedy lodgings leased out at rock-bottom rates.

Doyle caught my meaning and nodded.

"Thank God no fried foreigners this go-around," Zanetti said.

I cocked a brow at Doyle. She hitched one shoulder, acknowledging that she had, indeed, shared details of last week's blaze with her boyfriend.

"So what?" Her tone was mildly defensive. "It was breaking news anyway."

I said nothing.

"The proximity of the two fires is probably coincidence," Zanetti said. "Much of Foggy Bottom is old. I'm sure houses go up all the time."

"Your CI said this is a rental." I indicated Doyle's screen. "Did he say who owns the property?"

"He didn't know. But I intend to find out."

"And she definitely will." Using one finger, Zanetti looped an errant curl behind Doyle's left ear. "This gal's a tiger."

I couldn't disagree.

"Can you forward those pics on to me?" I asked, not sure my reason for wanting them.

"Sure."

"I'll probably hit the road tomorrow," I said.

"Aw." Sad faces. "Ben and I will be sorry to see you go."

Seriously? Zanetti and I had hardly met.

On that note, we headed to our respective rooms.

Sleep came easily.

Understanding the drama it brought along did not.

I'm standing on a beach watching the ocean swell and recede. A low-hanging moon spreads a narrow cone of light across the roiling water.

A sound distracts me and I turn, straining to understand the source.

My eyes take in nothing but darkness.

My ears hear only the angry sea.

The sound crystallizes into footsteps, heavy and gritty.

A figure appears in the far distance, a black cutout denser than the night from which it emerges. He or she walks toward me. Unhurried, steady. Darkness obscures his or her features.

I hold my breath.

Then Ryan is there, his expression saying he's piqued.

What's happened to you? he asks.

I don't understand.

You aren't with me.

I'm working a case.

Ryan's feet spread and brace. Behind him, the sand crumbles.

There. Go there. He points at something over my shoulder, his finger unnaturally long.

I swivel. See a house silhouetted in eerie moonlight.

I've no wish to approach it, but feel compelled to follow Ryan's directive.

Drawing near, I note that the structure is old and weathered, its wooden exterior the color of dirt from a grave. Its carved front door is painted bright red.

I turn the knob and push the door inward.

Air rushes out, damp and rotten. Angry at being contained against its will?

Then I'm inside, wandering from one gloom-shrouded room to another. The place is unique, I think. Like a brothel, only less tasteful. Red velvet. Tarnished brass. An overload of tassels and fringe.

As I cross a wide threshold into a large empty chamber, a figure crawls the triple panes of a big bay window.

I open my mouth to scream.

Realize I am seeing my own reflection.

Without warning, I'm descending steep stairs, a tiny woman beside me. Her feet get tangled in her long skirt.

Help me, she pleads.

I don't know how.

It's in the bag, she says.

Then I'm on a two-lane blacktop.

Rain is falling hard.

A storm drain runs alongside the road, clogged and overflowing. I watch puddles merge to form a shallow lake on the pavement, its surface pock-marked by the deluge of drops.

When I glance up the whole street is submerged.

A shaft of light appears on the horizon, then separates into two beams.

A car. Approaching fast.

Spray plumes up from the vehicle's wheels, sending an object drifting out of the culvert.

A woman, floating, eyes wide open, the ripples around her tinted blood red.

I backpedal to get away from the corpse.

My feet are caught.

I pinwheel.

Throw my arms out, desperate to regain my balance. To grasp whatever I can.

My eyes flew open.

My pulse was racing. My tee and hairline were soaked with sweat.

I lay still a moment, fingers death-gripping the quilt.

Mind struggling for clarity.

Only a dream, one sleep-drugged cluster of neurons reassured.

You're fine, their snappy-happy colleagues added.

My language center was far less subtle.

WTF?

No sector of my brain was enthused about a return to dreamland.

The last time I checked my phone said 4:21 a.m.

Again, I awoke to a gloomy sky and the soft patter of rain.

Did the sun ever show itself in DC?

I realized I'd been roused by my latest grating ringtone.

My phone's screen now reported an astonishing 9:42 a.m. And that the caller was Katy.

"Hi, sweetie."

"Hi, Mom. Uh . . . brace yourself. You won't like what I have to say."

"Hit me." Heart knotting in my chest.

"When I checked the Annex as you'd asked, I found that your ice-maker had malfunctioned and flooded your kitchen and parlor."

"Sonofabitch! I can be there—"

"Do *not* come home. I've called a plumber, a floor guy, and the insurance company. The water's off and there are big-ass fans going full boogey in there. They plan to refinish the hardwoods as soon as the moisture level drops enough."

"Thank you so much. But shouldn't I—"

"Stay where you are. The place won't be livable for at least a week. Maybe longer."

"Birdie?"

"Your neighbor is happy to keep him. Should that change, I'll pick him up."

"Oh my God. I owe you big-time."

"And I will collect. Count on it."

I debated. Decided, what the hell. Following my conversation with Ivy over Lan's Thai dinner, I'd been curious about something. And an online check had yielded an odd discrepancy. Katy could probably explain it.

"While I have you on the phone, may I ask you something?" I said.

"Sure."

"It's about Ivy Doyle."

"What about her?"

"You made a comment the night you asked me to talk to her about the Foggy Bottom fire. You said that Ivy really needed the interview."

"So?"

"What did you mean by that?"

"Nothing."

Careful, Brennan.

"Ivy has an extraordinarily charismatic on-air presence," I said. "She's ambitious. Her family must have serious grease in the telecommunication business. I'm curious why her career seems—"

"Seems what?" Familiar with my daughter's every nuance, I detected an unexpected defensiveness in her tone.

"Why she hasn't achieved the national prominence she desires."

"What is it you're not saying, Mom?"

Tread gently.

"Ivy told me she'd been lured from Sioux City by an offer from a station in Columbia. But her résumé shows a two-year gap between her departure from Iowa and her arrival in South Carolina."

"You looked her up?" Not quite, but close to indignant.

"I wanted to find fodder for conversation. You know I'm lousy at small talk." Partially true. What I'd really sought was info on the life-saving incident in Afghanistan that Katy had referenced. No way I'd admit to that.

A pause as Katy worked around my explanation. Then,

"Fine. But this stays between us."

"Of course," I said.

"Ivy didn't leave Sioux City under good terms. She was fired."

"Why?"

"Let's just say she embellished a few details on a story. The station agreed to keep it quiet, but you know how those things go. It took her two years to land another job. But that was a long time ago. She'd never cheat the facts again."

"Thanks for sharing. Ivy's secret is safe with me."

Despite the late hour and the bad news about my town house, I didn't fire out of bed.

Now what?

I'd completed every task Thacker had requested. Owed her nothing further except for reports.

I lay back against the pillows, reassembling shards of the previous night's kaleidoscope.

My dreams don't require a careful parsing of id, ego, and superego. No need for a Freudian consult. Typically, my subconscious takes recent experiences from my waking hours and weaves them into reimagined presentations, some straightforward, others more cryptic.

The source of Ryan's unhappiness was obvious.

The creepy house was based on the Foggy Bottom property that had burned.

The brothel décor was inspired by Unique Swallow, the place's one-time owner.

The tiny lady wearing the entangling skirt was undoubtedly the nameless subcellar vic.

The corpse in the culvert was anyone's guess.

But why that theme? Why that cast of characters?

Had my id recognized something that I hadn't? Was it suggesting the tiny lady could be Unique Swallow? I'd wondered about that. Swallow had sold the property to W-C in 1942. I had no idea what had happened to her after that.

If I'd known the answers then, things might have been different.

CHAPTER 15

Doyle returned as I was finishing my French toast with whipped cream and berries.

No kidding. If I kept gorging like this, I'd need new pants.

"I understand you'll be staying with me a bit longer," my host said brightly as she shifted a long-handled satchel from one shoulder to the other.

"You've talked to Katy?"

She nodded.

"I can probably find a hotel—"

"Don't be silly. I'm happy you're here." A long moment passed. Then, "And I'm happy you know about the debacle in Sioux City."

"We all make mistakes," I said.

"It was an unbelievably stupid and unethical thing to do. Got me canned and sent my self-confidence into the toilet for years."

"You were young," I said. "I'm sure you learned a valuable lesson."

"You can take that to the bank. Thanks for not judging me."

"I've seen your broadcasts, Ivy. You're a good reporter."

"That means the world coming from you." An introspective moment, maybe thinking about the world, then her face lit up with a sudden idea. "Want to help me with Chuck?"

"Chuck?"

"I've agreed to take care of a friend's chinchilla while she's away visiting her father. He's been diagnosed with the big C. The father, not the chinch."

"Of course," I said.

"Apparently, chinchillas need food, water, and a dust bath daily."

"What's a dust bath?"

"No idea."

"How does one bathe a chinchilla?"

"No idea."

"When does Chuck arrive?"

"Later today. I'm afraid the little guy will have to stay in his cage most of the time he's here. Ben is allergic to every mammal that ever evolved." Eyes rolling. "That's why I have no pets."

Lan topped off my coffee and looked a question at Doyle.

"Why not. I've only had six gallons." Then, as Lan poured, "I've learned something you won't believe."

"Donuts are high in nutritional value."

"I wish."

Doyle and I—yep, you guessed it—relocated to the study. Not my preference. I wanted to return to my room and hop back onto the internet to verify my theory about Uncle Norbert Mirek. Her eagerness made refusal impossible.

Doyle and I had barely settled into our cushy Eames loungers when she yanked a yellow legal pad from the satchel and placed it on her knees, one of which was pistoning up and down.

I noted that the pad's top page was filled with scribbling. That the satchel's remaining contents looked quite hefty. Clearly, my hostess was now serious about fact-checking.

"W-C Commerce," Doyle began without preamble.

"The owner of the illegal Airbnb that burned," I said.

"Bingo!" Way too pumped.

"And possible meth lab."

"Probably not."

That surprised me. I let her continue.

"I'm still working to verify what the initials stand for. If anything."

Doyle's coffee arrived. I waited while she thanked Lan, then drank, thinking to myself that caffeine was the last thing she needed.

"Do you know the purpose of a holding company?" Doyle asked.

"Vaguely."

"I'm not a lawyer, so I'll summarize to the best of my understanding." Quick skim of her copious notes. "A holding company is a financial entity that owns and controls other assets."

"Things like real estate, stocks, firms," I guessed.

"Yes. Typically, a holding company conducts no business operations of its own. It produces no goods or services, but has controlling interests in other companies, which are called subsidiaries."

"I get it."

My expression must have said otherwise. Doyle elaborated.

"A parent corporation can control the policies of its subsidiaries, maybe oversee management decisions, but it won't run the day-to-day activities. The structure is used by businesses of all sizes and in all industries."

"Why? I mean, what's the advantage?" Not sure where the conversation was heading.

"The parent company is protected from losses accrued by its subsidiaries."

"So, if a subsidiary goes bankrupt, creditors can't go after the holding company."

"Exactly," Doyle said. "I think there can also be tax benefits."

"Is there a disadvantage?"

"For investors and creditors, yes. It may be difficult for them to know the actual financial health of the holding company."

"Let me guess. Unethical directors could hide losses by moving debt among the various entities."

I dredged that from a barely absorbed conversation with Ryan about a client who'd suspected just such a scenario.

"Damn. You're good at this."

"Hardly." Not false humility. Finance interests me about as much as the taxonomy of molds.

"Don't sell yourself short, girl."

Girl?

I thought a moment.

"Can a holding company also be a way to protect the identities of the subsidiary businesses?"

"Absolutely."

"What does this have to do with the Foggy Bottom fire?"

"Right." Doyle again checked her notes. "W-C Commerce dates to 1941, a year before Unique Swallow sold the Foggy Bottom house to it. W-C was established as a *personal* holding company wh—"

"A personal holding company?"

"Meaning that fifty percent of the ownership stake is controlled by five or fewer individuals . . ." squinting at the scribbles ". . . and that at least sixty percent of its income derives from passive sources."

"Passive sources?"

I was beginning to sound like a parrot.

"Income from sources like financial investments, stocks, mutual funds—"

"Rental properties?"

"Yes."

"How many entities make up W-C?"

"Three or four."

"Not exactly Berkshire Hathaway."

"No."

"What does this have to do with the fire?" I asked with some giddy-up in my voice. I feared a brain bleed if this discussion continued much longer.

"Right. Have you ever heard of the Foggy Bottom Gang?"

Again, I shook my head no.

"This stays between us for now, right? I mean, the information is out there for anyone clever enough to find it. I did. But why wave a red flag?"

"Sure," I agreed. For now.

"Emmitt, Charles, and Leo Warring. The Foggy Bottom Gang. I spent hours this morning digging into these guys, mostly in the *Washington Post* archives." Doyle jabbed a thumb at the satchel by her chair. "Found close to three hundred articles mentioning them."

"Why?"

"Back in the day, they ruled Washington's booze and gambling world."

I was lost.

"Bootlegging and the numbers racket." If a human can be said to chirp, Doyle did it.

"And the Warrings are relevant because?"

"First, a bit of history." Flapping a hand to indicate I should settle back.

I did. Reluctantly.

"DC wasn't always the slick, cosmopolitan burg it is today," Doyle began. "Until the sixties, it was pretty much a sleepy, southern town. No Kennedy Center, no Watergate, no metro system. That all changed with the expansion of the federal government in the late sixties and seventies.

"But let me backtrack a little. Before DC was established, Georgetown was a separate municipality. It remained so until incorporated by the district in 1871. Foggy Bottom, which borders Georgetown on the Potomac, was the district's industrial center. Do you know how the area got its name?"

"River fog and industrial smoke."

"Exactly. There was a large gasworks at 26th and G which, according to all accounts, put out a truly noxious stink. A lumber mill, two breweries, a glass factory. The area was totally blue collar."

I'd learned some of this during my brief time with Hickey. Didn't let on.

After running an agitated finger through her notes, cherry-picking facts, Doyle resumed her, what? Tutorial?

"Just after the turn of the century, a man named Bruce T. Warring opened a barrel business on the Georgetown waterfront at K Street. The bucks rolled in, so a few years later he moved his growing family to a large home in Foggy Bottom. Ten kids, an older sister named Esther, blah, blah, blah . . ." One finger slid down the page. "The last three were boys, Leo born in 1903, Emmitt in 1905, Charles in 1907. The youngest Warring brothers were in their teens when the Volstead Act became the law of the land."

"Bye-bye, booze."

"Yep. Prohibition began in 1917 in DC, a bit earlier than in the rest of the country."

"God bless the WCTU." A sarcastic reference to the Woman's Christian Temperance Union.

"Your namesake peeps."

"Not at all." Though I was sober of necessity, a genomic drunk as Katy often teased, I had no issue with others enjoying their martinis or Pinots.

The searching finger hopped down the page.

"Anyway, Bruce's daughter, Esther, and her husband, Bill Cady, were quick to see the opportunities offered by a demand for illegal alcohol. Their residence, a row house at 2512 K Street, served as their base of operation."

Doyle's eyes rolled up to mine. "That's just west of Washington Circle and the present-day George Washington University Hospital."

"Got it."

Lan, having quietly reentered the room, stood awaiting instruction, coffee pot at the ready.

"No, thanks," I said, shielding my cup with one hand.

"I'm good," Doyle said.

Dipping her head ever so slightly, Lan withdrew.

"The Warrings?" I prodded, hoping to get back on track. Whatever the track was.

"Right."

Pause to pick more cherries.

"By the mid-1920s, Leo, Emmitt, and Charlie were in their twenties. For reasons not totally clear to me, around that time the trio began to take over Cady's bootlegging businesses in Georgetown and Foggy Bottom."

Doyle looked up again. "Interesting aside. Emmitt stood only five feet four and probably had scoliosis. Because he was so small the family called him Pudge. Still, he was unquestionably the brains of the outfit."

"Never underestimate the little guy."

"Here's where the story gets good." Gazing back on her notes, Doyle raised a "pay attention" finger. "With the help of family members, Cady modified his home by creating underground compartments for his illicit stash of inventory. One article in there"—the thumb again shot toward the satchel—"describes, and I quote, 'a catacomb where more than five hundred one-gallon containers of alcohol were hidden.' Other stories report secret passageways, panels, circuitous routes, blah, blah, blah."

Doyle's eyes again sought mine, burning with the fire of a hunter closing in on its prey.

"How did you think to look into the Warrings?" I asked.

"Those glass fragments you collected from the soil in the subcellar."

I'd forgotten all about them.

"It took help from a geek buddy, but we figured out that *Alk* was probably part of *Alky* and the other phrase was probably *Green Country*. We did a Google search using those as key words along with 'Foggy Bottom,' 'hidden passageways,' and the address of the fire scene."

"What *were* those shards?" I asked, reluctantly intrigued.

"Emmitt Warring was a huge player in the bootlegging world. At the height of his operation, he managed a distribution network out of ten warehouses in DC, selling over five thousand gallons of alcohol weekly. In bottles labeled *Alky, Green Country,* and *High Noon*."

"I'm impressed." I was.

"Thank you, ma'am."

I thought about everything Doyle had said.

"The Cady home was on K Street, right?" I asked.

"Yes."

"That's some distance from the house that burned down."

"Good point. But stay with me."

I resumed my listening face.

"Throughout the Warring brothers' reign, from the twenties into the fifties, Foggy Bottom had several alley communities, basically courts with single entrance and exit points. A big chunk of their bootlegging operation took place in and around one called Snows Court, a close-knit community that dated back to the Civil War."

"Where was it?"

"Snows Court was bounded by 24th and 25th Streets east and west, and K and I Streets north and south."

I started to ask a question. Doyle cut me off.

"*Is* bounded, I should say. The court still exists, though today it's one of the priciest areas in Foggy Bottom, all swanky town houses, boutiques, and coffee shops."

I conjured a mental map of the district.

"That whole area is close to the fire scene."

"It is. And listen to this. Emmitt Warring and Bill Cady invested their illegal earnings in dozens of properties." The finger jumped a few lines. "Esther Cady owned a home at 39th and Mass Ave. Emmitt Warring owned one at 39th and Macomb."

The ferocious eyes rose again, wide and excited.

"Are you ready for this?"

"Hit me," I said.

Before Doyle could do that, my mobile rang.

CHAPTER 16

The ginger brows floated to the ginger hairline. In a moment of boredom, I'd switched my ringtone to Jelly Roll singing "Need a Favor."

"Sorry," I said, recognizing the number. "This has to do with the subcellar vic."

"Take it," she said.

"Brennan," I answered.

"Waylon Colt here." Then, in case I didn't recall his name, "At NYP Corp."

"Thanks for getting back to me, Mr. Colt."

Doyle made a "who-the-hell" face at me.

"Do you mind if I put you on speaker, Mr. Colt?"

"I sure as sugar don't."

"Thank you, sir."

"Your bag's a good un'," Colt said. "But it took some digging to track her down."

Which was my cue to say how much I appreciated his help.

"I really appreciate your help, sir."

I mouthed "burlap bag" to Doyle. She shook her head, not understanding.

"Yes, ma'am. Your Swifty Spud's a dandy. Can't say as I minded looking her up."

"I'm glad you found the *burlap bag* of interest."

I enunciated clearly for Doyle's sake. She raised a thumb to show she got my meaning.

"I'll cut right to the chase, seeing as that's what you said you was after. That bag was made by KAT, Inc. of Patterson, New Jersey. She was produced as a limited run for only five years."

I waited for Colt to expand. He didn't.

"And those five years were?" I prompted.

Colt made a chuttery noise that might have been a chuckle.

"Your bag is a war baby. Born between 1940 and 1945."

"That's very helpful, Mr. Colt. Thank you so much."

"You're most welcome, ma'am. You ever want to sell that lovely lady, you give me a ring."

"Will do."

"Blessed day," and Colt disconnected.

Doyle and I looked at each other.

"Doesn't help much, does it?" she asked.

"I know the subcellar vic died after 1940. At a time when the house belonged either to Unique Swallow or to W-C Commerce."

"Now you're getting somewhere."

Teasing. But the dig struck a nerve.

"You could just let it go." Doyle reached for her mug. Grimaced at the contents and set it back down.

"You're right. I could." Hearing the lack of conviction in my own voice. "The Foggy Bottom vics aren't my problem."

"True. Thacker will deal with the four DOAs from the fire. If it was arson, as Burgos claims, those deaths are homicides. Deery will investigate that."

Doyle glanced at her watch.

"Yikes! Gotta go!"

Shooting to her feet, she added,

"Thacker constantly struggles with budgetary issues. Will she really give a rat's ass about a woman dead maybe eighty years?"

I had no answer to that.

"DC's homicide rate has increased by more than twenty-five percent over the last few years. Deery's caseload is undoubtedly mammoth. Will he?"

I had to agree. It was unlikely resources would be spent on such an old case.

"I know you want to head home. But think about hanging long enough to check out these articles." Doyle indicated the satchel holding her three hundred printouts. "Or you're welcome to make your own copies. I'm not doing that again."

After Doyle left, I sat a moment, thinking about her question. Questions.

Would Thacker care about the lady in the sack? Would Deery?

Was her death even a murder?

Why *not* let it go?

An hour later, I wasn't loading my rollaboard into my car. I wasn't motoring south imagining the Virginia of days gone by.

I was in an autopsy room at the Consolidated Forensic Lab, standing over a body bag containing the nameless subcellar vic. Her shriveled flesh looked almost colorless under the harsh fluorescents, her bones the pallid gray of molted snakeskin.

The burlap sack lay folded to the left of the corpse. The long, skinny braid was coiled inside a plastic container, dark and murky like a creature seen through frosted glass.

I stared at the cranial and mandibular trauma, searching for any detail I might have missed, one bleak scenario after another looping through my brain. A crash? An accident? An argument? A push?

Why the makeshift burlap shroud?

I imagined a man looming over the tiny woman. Raising an object, maybe a fist, in anger. The bone-shattering blows. The woman falling to her knees. The killer maneuvering her lifeless body into the sack. Dragging the sack downstairs to the basement, then to the subcellar, her battered head thumping against each riser.

I wondered what the woman's life had been like. The clothing in which she'd died suggested one different from that of Unique Swallow or her ladies of the night.

Was she married to a kind man with a friendly small-town face? To a tool who overdrank and mistreated her?

Did she have kids? Want kids?

Did she have a harassing ex? A beau who sent her roses after every date?

The woman had been roughly Katy's age when she'd died, her life barely begun when it was violently taken from her. What direction might it have gone had she been allowed to live it?

Stop! This is getting you nowhere.

I zipped the body bag, then informed the tech—surprisingly, Jamar was not on duty—that I was finished. After stripping off my gloves, I stepped from the gurney and left, heading toward the administrative side of the floor.

The receptionist tried to stop me, firmly but politely. Thacker's office door was open, and I could see her slick-haired head bent over her desk.

Smiling, firmly but politely, I blew past the gatekeeper.

Thacker looked up at the sound of my footsteps.

"Tempe. What a surprise." Tone implying time would tell if that surprise was a pleasant one. "What can I do for you?"

"I'm wondering if you've had any feedback on the prints I lifted from case number 25-02106."

Thacker looked blank.

"The DOA from the Foggy Bottom subcellar."

"Of course. I was about to call you."

Of course.

"I'm sorry to report there were no hits."

"Where did you have them run?"

"Everywhere."

I opened my mouth to query specifics, decided against it.

"Though disappointing, it's not surprising," Thacker said. "A petite gal like that? Unlikely she had a criminal record or served in the military."

"Bonnie Parker stood only four feet eleven," I countered, referencing the legendary bank robber. Where the hell did I pull that gem from?

"Uh-huh. Have you established PMI?"

I told Thacker what I'd learned from Waylon Colt.

"So the woman could have died any time in the last eight decades?" Thacker kept her face and voice carefully neutral.

I described the head trauma, matching the ME's neutral with my own.

Thacker leaned back in her overly complex chair, fingers steepled below her chin. When I'd finished, she said nothing.

"Does DC have a statute of limitations on murder?" I asked.

"No."

"I want to follow up on this."

"On what? People get knocked down or fall down all the time."

"Isn't identifying the victim the first step in any homicide investigation?" Realizing my mistake, "In any death investigation?"

"No dentals, no prints. Extremely vague time of death." Face blank. "What are you proposing?"

I was able to read Thacker now. Knew that behind the blank look her mind was already searching for a path toward additional free expertise.

"What do you know about forensic genetic genealogy?" I asked.

"It's pricey as hell."

"And?"

"The cops in Colorado used it to nail the Golden State Killer."

"In California, actually."

"Isn't Golden a town in Colorado?" Thacker asked.

"Yes, but the killer preyed on victims across California." I was growing impatient. "Do you know how genetic genealogy works?"

"I do. But something tells me I'm about to learn more."

"Condensed version. An investigator collects a biological sample—blood, semen, hair, skin. That sample contains DNA that can be read through genetic sequencing."

"*Might* contain DNA."

I acknowledge Thacker's point with the lift of one hand. "Are you familiar with how that sequencing is done?"

"I am," Thacker said. "And I know that once a genetic profile is created, that sequence is added to a public database of DNA sequences on a website like GEDmatch."

"A database containing genetic profiles uploaded by consumers who've purchased DNA tests."

Thacker had decided to keep playing along. "Yes, kits sold by companies like 23andMe or Ancestry. Why do people *do* that?"

Though probably a rhetorical question, I answered anyway.

"Maybe they're curious about possible genetic predisposition to disease. Maybe they want to find relatives in Zimbabwe. Their motives aren't the point. As you know, cops and coroners do it because they're interested in whether an unknown body or perp, an unsub, is related to other people in the database."

"Sure. Potential relatives are determined by the number of shared genetic variants. But how often does a user actually find a close relative?"

"Rarely," I conceded. "Unless the user comes from a family whose members are all bonkers about genealogy. Usually what they find are third cousins or further out. That's where traditional genealogy comes into play."

Thacker nodded. "Tracking down records like birth, death, and marriage certificates, census data, obituaries, social media, etcetera. That data is then combined with the DNA data to build a family tree of individuals who might be related to the 'unsub,' as you term him or her. Then investigators use conventional methods like physical descriptions, eyewitness statements, timelines, to narrow the field. I don't live in a cave, Tempe."

"I never thought you did."

"You'd like me to try to ID your subcellar vic using forensic genetic genealogy?"

"Yes."

"No can do."

"Why not?"

"Let's loop back to my opening line."

It took me a moment.

"It's expensive?" I said.

"Far too expensive, given my budget. Do you know how many bodies I have in my coolers right now?"

"I don't."

"So many that I can't justify burning funds on a case having such a low probability of success."

"I'll pay for it." Before thinking it through, the words left my mouth. Why not? I'd made the same offer a few years earlier in a Montreal case.

Thacker looked at me with the long-suffering patience of a painted Madonna.

"You'll pay for it?"

"I won't bill for any of the work I've done for you. Everything will be pro bono, reports and all."

Thacker's eyes roved my face, razor sharp, before flicking away. A grin teased one corner of her lips.

"Would you sweeten the deal by agreeing to review a file or two?"

Really? The woman was haggling over price?

"No problem," I said.

We eyed each other a long moment across the wide desk. Then,

"May I ask one question?"

"Sure," I said. Sure that I wouldn't like it.

"Why?"

"Why what?"

"Why such an emotional commitment to this case?"

I hadn't a good answer.

CHAPTER 17

Resigned to the realization that I wasn't going home for a while, I requested file designations for the cases Thacker wanted reviewed. Then, grumpy, I trudged to my office.

First off, I looked up the number of a colleague in Reston, Virginia. Dialed.

"Dr. Lizzie Griesser, please."

"Dr. Griesser is in court today. May I take a message?"

Inwardly cursing, I left my name and contact info, then disconnected.

Using my iPhone, I checked my email. Found news alerts, solicitations from political groups offering to triple-match my donation, pics of animals saved by foundations in need of my money, a notice of an upcoming sale on Spanx.

I deleted all but the Spanx ad. A temporary solution to Lan's culinary overload?

The messages in my voice mail were equally dispiriting.

No texts.

Feeling deficient over my lack of popularity, spurned by my lover, disappointed at not talking with Griesser, and irked at myself for the idiot agreement I'd made with Thacker, I logged on to the OCME system computer.

Both of Thacker's files involved DOAs shelved in coolers for more than a month. I skimmed the summaries.

Cynthia Bierny. White. Age seventy-four. Burned to death in the laundry room of her Southeast Washington home.

I read a note inserted into the file two days after its creation.

DOA was a smoker. Fire sparked by a carelessly handled cigarette? Or did someone torch granny?

The comment struck me as callous. Thacker? Or one of her pathologists?

The second case was that of Harriet Stroby, a twenty-three-year-old American University student decapitated by an excursion train on a route used by the Western Maryland Scenic Railroad. Stroby's file also had a comment inserted by an unnamed reader.

DOA was a poetry major. Self-arranged on the tracks? Died elsewhere and placed there?

Neither case struck me as one needing a forensic anthropology consult. What was Thacker's game?

Pushing from my desk, I hurried toward the chief ME's office. Halfway there, the murmur of voices stopped me in my tracks.

I turned to retrace my steps back up the corridor.

One of the voices rose in pitch, overly loud and buzzing with self-importance. Male. Familiar.

The man's mood was already a snarl of self-pity and resentment, but indignation now elbowed itself into the mix.

I froze.

Listened.

The wanker was sharing intel with the ME but not with me? And goddam Thacker. Why hadn't she included me in the briefing?

Shoulders and spine ridiculously rigid, I reversed and proceeded the last few yards.

"—considering the possibility that it could have been a hit on one of the four."

Burgos, who was holding a mug that said *Have a Nice Day*, stopped midsentence when I came through the door. His expression changed. Then changed again. Surprise. Uncertainty. Irritation. All in one blink of the pale little eyes.

"Tempe." Thacker regarded me with a long, quizzical stare. "You're back."

"I am."

Thacker's lips drew into a smile whose longevity looked dicey at best.

"Sergeant Burgos and I were discussing the Foggy Bottom fire victims. Perhaps you'd like to join us?"

"I think that would be appropriate." Chilly.

I took the chair beside Burgos.

Swiveling back to face Thacker, the arson investigator smacked the mug on the table between us with a hard-edged clunk.

Thacker said to me, "The sergeant is summarizing intel from the Metropolitan Police Department detective assigned to his team." To Burgos, "Please continue."

"As I was saying, if one of them *was* targeted, according to Deery—"

"Merle Deery is the MPD detective you met in the autopsy room," Thacker interjected for my benefit.

"—according to Deery we got us a shit ton of motive. The vic from the basement—"

"Skylar Reese Hill."

Burgos ignored me.

"—hotfooted it south to get away from a guy named Alvon Finrock. The happy couple was married less than a year, but the lady decided she wanted out. Finrock didn't see it that way."

"Finrock has been calling me nonstop for a week," Thacker said. "The man is rude and abrasive."

"That's being kind," Burgos sniffed. Not a pleasant sound.

"Does Finrock have a jacket?" I asked.

"Petty stuff. A couple DUIs, one drunk and disorderly, one juvie B and E." Burgos's eyes remained on Thacker.

"Where was Finrock at the time of the fire?" she asked.

"Deery says he claims he was on his *chesterfield*—that's a couch—in Mississauga binging all twelve seasons of *Bones*. Neither the Mississauga PD nor border patrol is busting ass getting back to him."

A short pause for Thacker to comment, maybe me. Neither of us did.

"Danny Green and Johnnie Star were, how shall I put it, close." Burgos made an obnoxious limp-wrist movement with one hand. "Both are skeevier than slop in a sty. Green worked the Smithsonian metro station offering bargain blow jobs for fifty bucks a pop, supplemented that income stream hawking oxy and K."

Burgos used the street names for oxycodone and ketamine.

"Star was your man if X or speed was your jam."

Ecstasy and meth.

"Deery has two hypotheses. A is that one of them maybe pissed off a competitor by expanding onto the other skeeve's patch.

"B is that some self-appointed vigilante decided to make the world a better place for himself and his red-blooded American brothers. Deery says department moles intercepted a lot of chatter leading up to Memorial Day and this WorldPride 2025 shit, especially a group calls itself Male Order. Catchy, eh?"

"Sounds like a real free-thinking bunch," I said.

"Who are they?" Thacker asked.

"White supremacists. Misogynists. Skinheads. Neo-Nazis. You name it. They're scumbags who hate anyone don't look and think like them. And here's a tantalizing side note. Certain more virulent Male Order members have a history of torching buildings."

"These assholes were in DC this past week?" My words dripped with disgust. "Maybe they got worked up seeing all the rainbow flags?"

"Male Order was one of a dozen hate groups staging anti-gay protests in the district recently," Thacker said.

Burgos took *a nice day* swig before speaking again.

"Here's another lead Deery's chasing. Danny Green was from Birmingham, Alabama. His father, also Danny Green, is a forklift operator there and a candidate for United Neanderthals International. Danny the elder has three assault charges, one aggravated. All old, all dropped, unclear why.

"Danny senior don't like that his boy's gay, and he don't like that his boy's dating Black. Blames the former on the latter. Could be he got tanked and decided to take Star out."

Thacker arched a brow. "Along with his own kid?"

Burgos shrugged one scrawny shoulder. "Maybe Daddy's plan wasn't as brilliant as he thought."

Through the window behind Thacker, I tracked a small plane flying low over the city. A banner dragged from its tail, advertising an event whose name and details were lost on my less than twenty-twenty vision.

"Go on," she said.

"Finally, there's the Syrian slant."

"Jawaad el-Aman," Thacker said. "I understand the kid's father is the Syrian ambassador to the US."

"El-Aman's old man isn't ambassador to shit."

Thacker's gaze hit mine, shock meeting shock.

Burgos pulled the ubiquitous investigator's spiral from a hip pocket. I'd been wondering at its absence. After licking a thumb, then turning a few pages, he selected salient points, much as Doyle had done.

"Deery dug this crap up. Not sure it matters. The diplomatic mission of the Syrian Arab Republic to the United States was suspended in 2014." Pause. "The US subsequently recognized the diplomatic mission of the National Coalition for Syrian Revolutionary and Opposition Forces." Longer pause. "The final ambassador was a guy named Imad Moustapha."

Burgos looked up, expression suggesting he wasn't open to queries. "Arab Spring, al-Assad's crackdown, the Syrian civil war. You know all that. If not, read about it on your own time."

"How are relations between Syria and the US today?" I asked—to no one in particular.

"Nonexistent," Thacker said.

"Does the Syrian embassy still exist?" Again, to whomever.

Thacker nodded. "It's on Wyoming Avenue, in the Kalorama neighborhood, along with several other embassies. The building is noteworthy because former President William Howard Taft lived in it for almost a decade. He died there in 1930." Sheepish grin. "DC's historic architecture is my passion."

"*My* passion," said Burgos, "is that we wrap this up before I have another birthday sitting here?"

What a dick.

"Here's the more pertinent stuff. El-Aman's father is a millionaire businessman and pal of none other than President al-Assad. El-Aman owns properties in DC and Virginia, but his purpose for being in the

States right now is unknown. According to Deery, the guy has more bucks than God and more enemies than a tax auditor."

"If el-Aman's father is wealthy, what was the kid doing in that Foggy Bottom dump?" I asked.

"Unclear. Jawaad had a condo in Georgetown, paid for by Daddy."

"What has el-Aman senior been involved with that might have angered someone enough to want to kill his son?" Thacker sounded skeptical.

"The Arab-Israeli conflict, the Golan Heights annexation, the Iraq war, the occupation of Lebanon, state-sponsorship of terrorism, you name it. Deery found dozens of money trails arrowing straight to Jawaad's old man."

That night it was beef Wellington with minted peas and mashed potatoes. Custard for dessert.

Zanetti dined with us.

Besides the heart-stopping good looks, the man had the warmth of an old parish priest, and the manners of a royal at court. An extremely winning trifecta.

Another endearing quality. From what I observed, Zanetti was totally smitten with his fiancée. Whenever Doyle spoke, he regarded her with the eyes of a cocker spaniel fixed on a treat.

Naming no names, Zanetti entertained us with anecdotes involving clients. His descriptions of their quirks and foibles rivaled standup at its best.

Mostly for Zanetti's sake, I shared what I'd learned regarding how long the subcellar vic had been dead. That I'd narrowed the range to the last eighty years.

"Hot damn!" Doyle said, twirling her fork in the air.

Zanetti shot her a look of *faux* disapproval.

I couldn't disagree with Doyle. My achievement so far was pretty lame.

Doyle had spent the time between her eleven and four o'clock broadcasts researching the second Foggy Bottom property that had burned. As with the first, it had changed hands several times over the years.

"Might turn into a story, might not," Doyle said in conclusion.

"It's a long shot." Zanetti sounded skeptical.

"Better than no shot at all."

"Watergate was a long shot," I said.

"I've heard of that," Zanetti said, deadpan.

Doyle said she planned to stay on it.

As we were finishing the custard, Doyle asked when I planned to head back to North Carolina. I explained that my departure was delayed because of ME files I'd been duped into reviewing.

Zanetti proposed a toast to celebrate my prolonged stay. I clinked the rim of my tumbler to the rims of their crystal goblets. Mine held Lacroix grapefruit sparkling water, theirs a lovely Willamette Valley pinot noir.

We were returning our glassware to the tabletop when Zanetti's phone rang. After glancing at the screen, his face went contrite.

"Babe." Uber apologetic. "I really should answer this."

"Of course," Doyle said.

Holding the phone to his chest, Zanetti rose, circled to his fiancée, and kissed the top of her head.

"Back in five," he said.

Doyle and I chatted for a while. Katy. The weather. A new wrinkle cream she was trying. I admit, I noted the brand.

Doyle described a pair of blue satin Manolo Blahniks she'd ordered from Bergdorf Goodman. I wasn't sure, but figured she meant shoes.

I considered mentioning the Spanx ad. Decided against it.

Doyle reported that she and Chuck were forming a meaningful relationship. I asked how Zanetti was dealing with the chinchilla. Answer: Claritin.

A short silence, not awkward, just there. Then,

"What are these files you're reviewing?"

I explained the deal I'd struck with Thacker.

"You really are committed to that subcellar vic," she said.

I shrugged.

Doyle leaned back and pulled off the elastic binding her hair into a pony at the nape of her neck.

"Discover anything astonishing?"

I debated what to share and what to hold back.

"This is strictly between us, right? No 'breaking news'?" Hooking finger quotes around the hackneyed phrase.

"Jesus, Tempe. Of course not."

"One case is that of an old lady who died suspiciously. Are you aware of how kitty litter and gasoline can be used to start a fire?"

She shook her head and the ginger curls danced wildly. Joyful at last to be free?

"It's an old Boy Scout trick."

"Part of being prepared?"

"I'll summarize. An elderly woman was found in the charred remains of an annex behind her house, a room where she did laundry. At first her death was thought to be accidental. She was a smoker, the cat pan was there, the washer and dryer, the gasoline container. Turned out the fifteen-year-old grandson killed her."

"How?"

"After bludgeoning the old lady to death, the little creep dragged her body into the laundry room. Then he went outside and disconnected a supply line running from a propane tank into the dryer. Next, he disconnected the dryer end of that line."

"Inside the house."

"Yes. Then, he soaked the cat pan with gasoline and tossed in a match. When the litter was burning, he went back outside, reconnected the gas line, and opened the valve. The fire exploded and burned the annex to the ground."

"Holy moly. How did the investigators unravel that one?"

"I'm not an expert. But it had to do with the lack of stripping and the presence of oxidation on the gas line's threads at its point of connection to the dryer."

"She was dead before her body was burned?" Doyle asked glumly.

"That's the questi—"

We both turned on hearing a sharp clatter in the hall.

Zanetti was scooping his mobile from the floor.

"That, ladies, is not recommended procedure for the care and feeding of phones."

He held the device to his ear.

Smiled the toothpaste-of-champions' smile.

"And she keeps on ticking."

CHAPTER 18

I was trying to pull a corpse from a bag. It wouldn't budge. The harder I tugged, the deeper the lifeless limbs entangled themselves in the burlap.

I awoke with my heart busting dance moves in my chest. Sensing the dream had been long and convoluted but recalling no details.

Great. The subcellar vic was now haunting my sleep.

I checked my voice mail. Nothing from Griesser.

My grandmother had a saying. In for a penny, in for a pound. Or something like that. Gran's adages were easily lost in the brogue. But the old saw seemed apt.

I'd come this far with the subcellar vic. Why abandon her now?

I called Pierre LaManche, my boss at the LSJML in Montreal. He had nothing that needed my attention.

I called Nguyen, the chief ME in Charlotte. A teacher had found a human cranium in a storage closet at a high school in Cornelius and dropped it at the MCME. Nguyen was 90 percent certain the skull was an old biological supply house specimen and said there was no reason for me to rush home to see it.

I called my neighbor about Birdie. She was delighted with her feline visitor.

I owed Slidell an update on the Norbert case. Decided to hold off until I'd clarified the presence of female Asian hair in the poop.

To avoid one of Skinny's blustery harangues?

Ryan still hadn't texted, emailed, or phoned.

My hostess was still encouraging me to stay.

Stay and do what?

Easy one.

Do right by the tiny lady in the burlap bag.

Fine.

In for a pound.

I began with a review of what I knew for certain. Which wasn't much.

The subcellar vic had sustained trauma to her face and head. The fractures showed no signs of healing, so she hadn't survived the incident that caused them. A vehicular accident? A fall? An assault?

Unless her body was kept elsewhere and later placed in the sack, the woman's death occurred after 1940, the earliest year in which her burlap shroud was produced.

Why do that? Why not give her a proper burial? Or dump her some-where?

The woman's corpse had been left in one of a warren of rooms below the basement of the first Foggy Bottom property that burned.

Had she lived there? Worked there? Died there?

Been murdered there?

In 1942, title to that property transferred from Unique Swallow to a holding company called W-C Commerce.

In their heyday, Leo, Charles, and Emmitt Warring were a trio of bootleggers and racketeers known as the Foggy Bottom Gang.

Emmitt Warring and his brother-in-law Bill Cady invested their substantial earnings in multiple properties throughout DC.

Bill Cady created a maze of tunnels and hidey-holes below at least one of his Foggy Bottom homes, presumably to hide his inventory.

A maze like the one in which the subcellar victim was found.

Might the initials in W-C Commerce stand for Warring-Cady? Might the Foggy Bottom home once have belonged to Emmitt or Bill?

I sat up and ran my hands over my face, trying to think. Massaged my temples with deep fingertip circles.

I'd taken what partial prints I could, but they'd yielded no hits.

I'd collected samples for potential DNA testing. Until I talked to Griesser that would have to wait.

My thoughts ranged to the satchel Doyle had mentioned. To its three hundred stories on the Foggy Bottom Gang.

In for a truckload of pounds, I thought.

After coffee and a homemade cinnamon bun, I went to the study, snatched the satchel by its straps, and headed for my room, curious as to the origin of the odd penny-pound expression.

Sitting cross-legged on the floor, I sorted the photocopies by publication, placing them in piles around me. Most of the stories had appeared in the *Washington Post*. But not all. The *Washington Herald* was represented. The *Washington Times*. The *Evening Star*. The *Washingtonian Magazine*. The *Chicago Tribune*.

Next, I organized each stack chronologically.

The earliest article dated to 1921. Its headline was a grabber: POLICE RAIDERS FIND UNDERGROUND STORES OF ALLEGED BOOTLEGGER. A 1933 story screamed: NALLEY KILLING BLAMED ON WAR OVER GAMBLING. In 1936, it was: JURY CONVICTS WARRING MOB OF SHOOTING.

It was like binging episodes of *The Sopranos* or *Boardwalk Empire*.

I got sucked in early and hard. Lost all track of time. Sensation in both legs.

I learned that the Warring brothers weren't the first to jump aboard the illegal gambling and booze train in our nation's capital.

In fact, they had plenty of fellow peddlers.

Which made the Prohibition era in the DC-Maryland-Virginia area a very wild ride—the saddest aspect of that ride being the death of innocents.

Example. A series of 1934 reports covered the bungled murder attempt of Edward G. "Mickey" McDonald, a wannabe freelancer in the numbers racket. Assassins mistakenly shot Allen D. Wilson, a newspaper carrier from Silver Spring, Maryland. Allen, guilty of nothing but being in the wrong place at the wrong time, left behind three children: Patricia, age eight, Allen, age four, and Richard, age one.

Another heartbreaking incident involved Doris Gardner, the on-again-off-again girlfriend of Warring henchman Amon "Alarm"

Clock. Gardner was present in 1944 when Clock got into a throw down with a rival bootlegger. Guns were drawn and Gardner was killed. She was thirty-two, the mother of two young girls.

I was moving forward in time when Jelly Roll sang from the bedside table.

Finally! Lizzie Griesser!

I unwound my ankles to stand but my feet, dead asleep, vetoed the move. I pinwheel-lurched across the room like a drunk stumbling from a bar.

Grabbing the phone, I flung myself onto the bed.

"Brennan."

"Are you all right?" It was Doyle on the line.

"I'm good," I said, hopefully hiding my disappointment.

"You sound like you just ran a marathon." I could hear voices in the background, some human, some robotic. I figured she was phoning from her office at the TV station.

"If so, I'd be dead."

"Ben just called and offered to take me to Nara-Ya for dinner. He wondered if you'd like to join us."

"I don't want to—"

"Will you stop it. I've been dying to go there. Meet us at seven. It's in District Square. If you Uber, Ben says he's happy to drive you home."

"Okay."

"What are you doing?"

"Taking a crash course in bootlegging."

There was a moment of indistinct background chatter as she worked through that.

"I'm reading the articles you photocopied. On the Warring brothers."

"Great minds." She truncated the quote. "Keep at it. I think I've made a major discovery along those lines."

"Yeah?"

"Not now. I'll tell all at dinner."

She disconnected.

I noticed the time. One-forty.

Unbelievably, I was hungry again.

Hoping to slip in and out unseen, I crept downstairs to the kitchen. Not a chance.

Lan appeared and offered to make me a sandwich.

Knowing it was futile to refuse, I accepted.

Ten minutes later I was back on the floor of my room, a turkey and Havarti on rye artfully plated on a tray beside me. Green chips, probably something healthy like spinach. Fresh fruit salad. Napkin folded to look like a dove.

I munched as I continued working through the stacks.

Though the bulk of the Warring coverage ran from the thirties into the fifties, Doyle had photocopied several more recent articles. By the late eighties, DC concerns seemed to have shifted away from home-grown gangsters to organized crime.

A 1987 *Post* Sunday edition featured a spread headlined: OUR GANG— WITH THE MAFIA MUSCLING IN, WE SOON MAY LONG FOR THE GOOD OLD BAD DAYS. The tone was close to that of fond remembrance. A good chunk of the treatment was devoted to Emmitt.

The text traced the brothers' rise to prominence during Prohibition, their entry into the numbers business, and their headline-making trials for murder and tax evasion. It referenced Emmitt Warring's appearance before a Senate District Subcommittee, describing his testimony as largely taking the fifth.

Several of the pieces were accompanied by photos of the Warrings and their associates, men with flash and cash, all jaunty fedoras and cocky smiles. Men who'd made their fortunes in booze, numbers, bookie joints, craps tables, and dope. Men who'd partied till dawn at after-hours clubs, paid off cops, fought turf wars, scandalized Congress.

Men who'd killed people.

Had one of them beaten a small woman to death, stuffed her into a burlap sack, and hidden her in an underground chamber?

I'd learned something about the possible early owners of the Foggy Bottom house. Sadly, nothing about the life or death of the corpse in its subcellar.

I glanced at the stacks of unread articles.

At my watch.

Six-thirty.

No wonder a headache was knocking at my frontal bone. I'd been squinting at photocopies all day.

Crapballs!

I had to be elsewhere in half an hour.

An Uber arrived quickly. Still, I got to my destination twenty minutes late.

Nara-Ya was one of many eateries to have sprouted like mushrooms after a rain in the trendy Wharf District in Southwest Washington.

Ornately decorated glass doors opened onto a lobby leading into a tunnel covered on all sides with geometrically patterned and very sparkly foil paper. Backlit flowers hanging from the ceiling and neon-eyed faces lining the walls made for a dizzying effect.

The restaurant itself, a short elevator ride up, was all glass on one side, providing a spectacular view of the marina and Potomac River. The floor was gleaming red tile.

Doyle and Zanetti were seated at a window table. As the maître-d' brought me to them, Zanetti did that half-rising thing men do when women approach.

"I am so sorry—"

"Tempe." Zanetti's smile had enough wattage to attract moths. "I'm delighted you could join us."

Zanetti indicated the chair held open for me. The one with the best view of the water and boats.

I sat. The waiter presented me with a menu the size of a spinnaker.

Nara-Ya described itself as innovative Japanese. Whoever named their cocktails certainly was. *Exit the Dojo. Shogun and Unicorn. Origami on a First Date.*

Doyle's choice of beverage was very large and very pink. Zanetti had a Sapporo Premium. I went with Perrier and lime.

"She won't be needing this." Zanetti gestured to the waiter that he should reclaim my menu. "We've already made our selections."

Normally, such presumption would irk me. This time it didn't. As food started to appear, it seemed Zanetti had ordered every item listed.

Sashimi. Nigiri. Rolls, some of which were called Ballers. And a generous portion of caviar.

As we dipped and devoured, I shared some of what I'd read about the Foggy Bottom Gang. Zanetti talked of a client who turned out to be a scam artist, visiting property after property with no intention of buying.

While eating my green tea ice cream—additional calories I seriously did not need—I felt a bit wistful at how well-suited my dinner partners seemed for each other. And guilty over my antisocial attitude of late. The pair really were good company.

Doyle bunched and set her napkin on the table. From which it was immediately whisked away.

"I hate to be a buzzkill," she said. "But I think I've found intel that will blow the roof off the Foggy Bottom fire investigation."

She wasn't wrong.

However.

Within twenty-four hours another event would blow that roof even higher.

CHAPTER 19

"W-C Commerce also owns the townhome currently rented by Phil and Devira Aaronson?" I couldn't keep the shock from my voice.

"Yep."

"The one with the parakeet?" Stupid question. But my mind was struggling to toggle this new information.

"What?"

"The other house fire?"

Doyle nodded. "W-C holds title to only three or four entities. Two of those are the pair of Foggy Bottom properties that just burned."

"That can't be coincidence," said Zanetti, stating the obvious.

"Duh," Doyle said.

"Have you shared this finding with Burgos?" I asked.

"Who's Burgos?" Zanetti asked.

"Burgos is a dick," Doyle said.

"Major league. But he's the dick leading the team investigating the first fire." An investigation involving four fatalities, I didn't add.

Doyle said nothing.

"Who's assigned to the Aaronson fire?" Zanetti asked.

"Burgos," Doyle said.

"Bloody hell," I said.

"Bloody hell," Doyle agreed.

"You have to loop the guy in," Zanetti said.

"Burgos has an ego the size of a container ship."

"Still, you have to tell him."

"I will."

"There's an MPD homicide cop on Burgos's team," I said. "Merle Deery."

"Dreary Deery," Doyle said.

"You know him?"

"Oh, yeah." Doyle gave a little shake of her head. "I'm not sure the man knows how to speak."

"He is the silent type."

"You've met him?"

"Deery attended the Hill autopsy. Never uttered a peep the whole time."

"That's Deery. He's with the VCB. The Violent Crimes Bureau. His name comes up in a lot of the stories I cover."

"Maybe we could do a side run around Burgos. Use Deery as our point of contact."

"Not a bad idea."

Doyle checked the screen of her mobile. "Anyone think either Burgos or Deery is out there chasing leads at ten on a Friday night?"

Zanetti and I gave almost identical shrugs.

"Besides. It's time I get to the studio."

"You work too hard, babe." Zanetti reached over and ran a gentle thumb down Doyle's cheek.

"Wait up for me?" Coquettish smile.

"You bet."

So, tacitly, we decided that phoning either Burgos or Deery could wait until morning.

A big mistake.

True to his promise, Zanetti gave me a lift from the restaurant. He drove a red Land Rover. Said he needed it for hauling would-be buyers from house to house.

"I'm a rock star with the soccer moms."

"Not to mention the glamping set."

Zanetti swiveled to face me, brows raised in question.

"Campers wanting all the luxuries when venturing out into the wild."

"I could use Big Red to pull my forty-foot RV with AC, flat-screen, De'Longhi, and wet bar? Hot diggity!"

We laughed, rode several minutes without talking. Then Zanetti asked,

"Did Ivy say she's friends with your daughter?"

"Yep."

Oncoming headlights showed brows halfway to the nary-a-deserter hairline. "No way you're old enough to have a daughter that age."

"Ivy may have a few years on Katy," I ventured, successfully quashing an eye roll he wouldn't see anyway.

Another mile of silence. This time I stepped up.

"Are you and Ivy planning a big wedding?"

"Like carny in Rio."

"Have you set a date?"

"For me the sooner the better. Ivy's the one dragging her feet. But, as you may have noticed, until the lady makes up her mind, there's no pushing her."

Thankfully, Jelly Roll interrupted at that awkward point.

I dug my mobile from my purse and checked caller ID.

Lizzie Griesser.

"Sorry," I said. "This is important."

"Of course."

"Lizzie. Thanks for calling back so soon."

"My pleasure. What can I do for you?"

I described the case I wanted to send her. The subcellar environment. The burlap bag. The mummy-skeleton corpse.

"Think there's any possibility of doing a genetic genealogy workup?" I asked when finished.

"PMI?"

"I think she may have died after 1940."

"May have?"

"Yes."

Following a long stretch of dead air, Lizzie asked, "You've cut specimens?"

"One dental, one bone."

"Sounds like low odds."

"But worth a shot?"

"All the good ones are."

"I'll overnight the samples by FedEx. Same address?"

"Yes, ma'am."

"Do you need payment up front?"

"I can bill your ME."

"Do that. I've had to sell her my soul to fund this testing."

"Gotta admire your dedication, girl."

We were on Chain Bridge Road when Zanetti posed his next question. "What did you make of Ivy's W-C Commerce news?"

"I think it shifts focus away from the victims and onto the landlords."

"Meaning the property owners were the targets?"

"That could be, though it seems a stretch that arsonists aiming at owners wouldn't take more care to not set fire to tenants. Still, two houses owned by the same holding company in the same neighborhood catching fire or being torched within days of each other hardly seems random. Tell me if this sounds crazy. I'm thinking the W-C in the name stands for Warring-Cady."

"And that said targets are somehow associated with the Foggy Bottom Gang? Maybe members of the Warring or Cady family? Doesn't sound crazy at all, except for the tenants winding up as casualties. That part looks pretty inept."

"It would be awesome if Ivy could verify ownership."

"Trust me, she's all over this, and she's amazing. She told me that W-C Commerce has no website or social media presence, so most of her internet searches have gone nowhere. But she's checking free databases and subscription databases and looking for official records, court records, that sort of thing. And she belongs to an outfit called the Global Investigative Journalism Network."

"You're confident she'll come up with names?"

"That or she'll find someone who can."

The moon was new, the wooded land beyond my window a shapeless dark void.

The house was quiet as a crypt.

I was still awake at midnight, skimming more of Doyle's photocopied articles. When a voice spoke from the doorway, I nearly jumped out of my skin.

"Sorry. Didn't mean to startle you."

"No, no. I'm good." Willing my heart back into my chest.

"I saw your light and thought you might still be awake."

"Mm."

"After the last broadcast I need time to wind down."

"I think Ben's gone to bed."

"Too early for me. I can never fall asleep much before three."

Not awaiting an invitation, Doyle crossed the room and dropped into the excessively shaggy chair. "Ben and I spoke briefly. He said you and I are tracking along the same lines."

"Given that both homes belong to the same holding company?"

"OMG. I never sent you the Aaronson scene photos, did I?"

"No biggie." I'd forgotten all about them.

She reached into her bag and withdrew her mobile. A few thumb strokes, then the images landed on my phone. I created an album and saved them to it.

"Finding anything of interest in that muddle?" Stretching out her legs, a very long stretch, Doyle cocked her chin at my piles.

"This and that."

"Any hot new hypotheses?"

I shared my speculation about W-C.

"You're thinking someone might dislike Warring or Cady enough to burn down houses?"

"Such a grudge would require some very long-standing resentment and some carefully selected targets."

"True." She recrossed her ankles. "What about an issue with the *current* owners of W-C Commerce?"

"Whoever they are."

"Whoever they are."

Doyle finally left at one-fifteen, off in search of a nightcap.

I did a quick *toilette*, then crawled into bed.

Before turning off the lights, I skimmed the images Doyle had just sent. No reason. An exercise to help me "wind down" as she'd put it.

The pics were as I remembered.

The first was a close-up of the two-story townhome with its bay window and bright red door. Smoke and flames upstairs. Ladder. Brick steps and walkway. Hoses crisscrossing a trampled lawn.

The second was a wider-angle view. Rainbow row houses lining a narrow, cobbled street.

The third was taken with the lens facing away from the fire. Same block, better sense of the chaos. Fire equipment and personnel. Gawkers. Patrol units. Yellow police tape.

Switching my phone to silent mode, I turned off the light.

Suddenly I was wide awake.

For one unnerving moment, I had no idea where I was.

Then recognition.

Chez Doyle.

I felt sweaty and anxious.

Why?

An overload of soy and raw fish?

No. The agitation was due to another barely remembered nighttime drama.

Why was my subconscious nagging me now?

Lying in the dark, I struggled to reassemble the ephemeral fragments.

It seemed my id was processing its most recent intake. As usual.

In the first scrap of dream, I was inside the Aaronson town house. Walking alone from room to room.

In the next, I was out on the street.

I passed two identical boys with two identical dogs.

"Don't do it," the first boy said.

"Don't do what?" I asked.

"There's a car parked behind you, another in front."

"I'll find the key."

"You're trapped."

New scrap. I was alone again, moving from vehicle to vehicle, nose to the windows, hands to either side of my face.

Sonofabitch!

I went bolt upright.

The clock said two-forty-seven.

Heart hammering, I grabbed my phone. Opened the album containing the Aaronson scene pics. Expanded the second image with my thumb and finger.

Yes!

I fired off a text to Doyle.

I've got something.

She answered immediately.

What?

Come up to my room.

Give me ten.

Enough time for me to hop on the net.

She arrived in slippers and a long satin robe.

"Look at this," I said, holding out my phone.

She took the device and studied the image.

"So?"

"Look again."

She did.

The aquamarine eyes rolled up to mine.

CHAPTER 20

"What do you see?" My voice was calm but backed by a fizz of adrenaline.

"The ugliest Camry ever. So what?"

"I parked behind that car when I visited the first Foggy Bottom fire." Jabbing an excited finger. "There it is at the Aaronson scene."

"How can you be certain it's the same Camry?"

"Piss-yellow paint job. Window sticker saying *I Brake for Aliens*. What are the chances?"

"Might it belong to a reporter?" she asked.

I hadn't thought of that.

Doyle's brows dipped as she studied the image.

"The rear bumper is in shadow. I can't read the plate."

"Zoom in."

Doyle expanded the image as I had done.

"There's some sort of decal on the left rear window. Maybe a parking sticker?"

"That's exactly what it is. A Montgomery County DOT residential perking permit."

"It's badly faded." More zooming. "I think the date is 2019."

"Still, it might be of use in tracking the vehicle's owner."

"Fuckin' A." Doyle leaned forward and raised a hand.

I smacked her upraised palm with mine.

———

I awoke to sun—Hallelujah!—and temperatures already in the eighties. Humidity looking to score a personal best.

Walking from my car to 4th and E, I breathed the usual summer-in-the-city smells—wet cement, rotting garbage, diesel, coffee. Now and then a whiff of pizza or fresh bakery.

Odors reminiscent of Montreal.

Still no word from Ryan.

I refused to think about that.

My shirt was clammy by the time I entered the Consolidated Forensic Lab lobby. The blast of arctic air sent goosebumps prickling my arms.

It was Saturday, so I had to work unassisted. I'd already collected samples from the subcellar vic. It took little time to prepare them for shipment to Lizzie Griesser.

Only half my mind was on the task at hand. Assuming neither Burgos nor Deery would take the parking permit lead seriously, I was anxious to do some cyber sleuthing on my own. Starting with the Montgomery County DOT website.

Thoughts focused on my plan of attack, I took no heed of my surroundings. Hurrying down the corridor, I flew through the doorway into my office.

And slammed into a figure exiting from it. Equally startled, we both backpedaled quickly.

"My fault," I said, squatting to retrieve the packet that had flown from my grasp. "I wasn't paying attention."

The figure said nothing.

Stretching to reach my papers, I caught a glimpse of feet.

Badly scuffed Oxfords suggested the wearer was male. Shoe size suggested considerable height.

Packet in hand, I straightened.

Faded blue eyes gazed down at me, dour and unsmiling. A fat dark crescent underhung each.

"Detective Deery," I said. *Why the hell are you in my office?* I thought.

Deery nodded.

"Can I help you with something?"

"Doc Thacker asked that I keep you looped in on the Foggy Bottom fire investigation."

"That would be good," I said, curious about Thacker's motive. The woman seemed to run hot and cold on me, sometimes holding back, sometimes going the extra mile to include me.

"Didn't really expect to find you here on a Saturday."

I said nothing.

"I observed you during the Hill post."

I expected a positive comment. Good job. Well done. Very professional. None came.

"Shall we sit?" I invited, less than warmly.

Not awaiting a response, I circled my desk, placed the packet on the blotter, and sat.

Deery dropped into a chair facing me, knees splayed, ankles crossed. He wore neon yellow socks, brown pants, a melon shirt, and a green-and-gold tie badly in need of cleaning.

I noted that Deery wasn't as tall as his footwear had suggested, maybe five-ten. Like the famed dodo bird, he had feet disproportionately large for his height.

I waited for him to begin.

"I'll cut to the chase. I've got an arson resulting in four deaths. Four homicides. Thinking one of the dead might have been targeted, I researched each."

"Skylar Reese Hill, Danny Green, Johnnie Lamar Star, Jawaad el-Aman."

I listed the names to let Deery know I was already solidly inside Thacker's loop. He ignored me.

"Star and Green are out."

"They were drug dealers."

"Which made them easy to track."

"I take it you have reliable sources on the street?"

"If someone ordered a hit on Green or Star, word would have spread like wildfire."

Given that Deery seemed devoid of humor, I assumed the pun was unintended.

"I brought in the feds for el-Aman," he continued.

"The State Department?"

"Among other resources. El-Aman's father is wealthy and political and has pull with powerful people in Syria. I ran him and every KA through the system." Deery used the acronym for *known associate.* "Floated queries with the Syrian police and Interpol. The man has some unsavory friends and scores of enemies."

"You interviewed him?"

Deery looked at me like I'd asked if fish need water.

"El-Aman stated that he was devastated by his son's death, that he believed the fire was accidental, that he'd pursue prosecution of those responsible for unsafe conditions leading to an accidental fire. Otherwise, on advice of counsel, he said zip."

"Why was he in DC?"

"He said he'd come here to attend a meeting with financial advisors at Bank of America. The bank says no such meeting was scheduled."

"Was el-Aman cooperative?"

"Of course not."

"Might he—"

"I'm working it." Clipped. "Then there's Hill's husband."

"Alvon Finrock."

"Finrock claims he was in Canada when his wife died."

"Mississauga."

"Border patrol says otherwise. Finrock entered the US by car, crossing at Niagara Falls two days before the fire. His MasterCard was used at gas stations in New York, Pennsylvania, and Maryland. The last fill-up was at a Sunoco on Virginia Avenue in Northwest DC. On the morning of the fire."

Holy jumping Jesus.

"Finrock has a jacket," I said. "DUI, drunk and disorderly, a juvie B and E."

If Deery was impressed by my knowledge, he didn't let on. Or maybe he did. Hard to tell with his face.

"Emails and texts sent to Hill indicate Finrock was controlling and abusive. One thread contains threats of violence should Hill not return and commit to their marriage."

"Where is he now?" I asked.

"Still in the States, but in the wind. I've issued a BOLO." Deery used the police acronym for *Be on the Lookout*. "We'll get him."

I told Deery about the Camry at both fire sites.

"Did you get a plate?"

"No." I explained the parking decal.

No reaction.

Sudden thought.

"The house was being used as an illegal Airbnb," I said. "What about the man who handed out the keys? Billie Norris?"

"He's clear."

"Burgos thought Norris was sketchy."

"This is not my first murder investigation, Ms. Brennan."

A tense silence crammed the small office. Choosing my words carefully, I said,

"Are you aware that both properties that burned belong to the same holding company?"

"I am."

That surprised me. I doubted Ivy had found an opportunity to share the intel so quickly. Way to go, Deery.

"Does that seem like coincidence to you?" I asked.

Deery said nothing.

"Do you know the story behind W-C Commerce? That it's a holding company founded back in the forties? Perhaps by Emmitt Warring and Bill Cady, members of the Foggy Bottom Gang?"

The faded denim eyes gave away nothing.

"Have you learned the names of W-C's current owners?"

"The suits are blocking my attempts to obtain warrants."

"Whose suits?"

"I'm not at liberty to say."

We looked at each other across the blotter and the packet.

"Is it possible one of W-C's current partners is being targeted?"

"My colleagues and I feel that's highly unlikely."

"Based on what?"

Deery ignored my question. "The doer was someone associated with Hill or el-Aman."

"Motive?"

"To send a warning, to frighten, to intimidate." Deery pressed down on both knees to push to his overly large feet. "Either way, the bastard killed four people and I intend to net him. Pardon my French."

With that he was gone.

CHAPTER 21

My purse strap was going over my shoulder when the desk phone shrilled, startling me.

I figured the system had been rolled to auto for the weekend. And that the caller was probably Deery, having forgotten some detail and hoping I was still here.

"Brennan," I answered.

"Is this the bone doctor?" The voice was female, and so low I thought the conversation might need subtitles.

"Who's calling?"

"I saw you on TV with Ivy Doyle."

Dear God. How often would that interview come back to bite me in the ass?

"I trust Ivy Doyle. She's an honorable person. I sense you are, too."

"Your name please?"

"No. Not this way."

"You phoned me, ma'am."

"Yes. I did. Wait." The connection muffled, as though the caller were pressing the handset or mobile to her chest. Then,

"You're the expert examining the people who burned to death in Foggy Bottom?" Even more whispery, lips close to the mouthpiece.

"How can I help you?"

The woman's next words sent electricity sizzling through me.

"I know who set those fires."

"What?"

"The two buildings. I know who destroyed them."

"Who?" Too strident. Stupid.

I heard a sharp intake of breath followed by the thud of complete silence.

"I'm sorry," I said, more gently. "I can tell this is hard for you."

The woman uttered a spindly little sound that might have meant yes.

"Would you prefer we meet in person?"

"That would be better."

"Tell me when and where."

"Three this afternoon." Slight hitch in her breathing. "The Einstein Memorial."

"I'll be there." I'd never heard of it and hadn't a clue to its location.

"You cannot tell anyone."

"What about Ivy?"

"Absolutely no one. Promise?"

"You have my word."

"If I suspect you've broken that promise, I won't come."

Dead air.

I sat, immobile, pulse humming.

Asking myself repeatedly.

Was I insane?

Quick stops at a FedEx outlet, then a bagel shop, and I was back at Doyle's house by eleven.

In a rare moment of objectivity, I considered the range of emotions I was experiencing. I was irritated by what struck me as Deery's tunnel vision, agitated by thoughts of my upcoming encounter with the mysterious caller, and curious about the spot allocated to the legendary genius.

After spreading a generous layer of cream cheese on a cinnamon raisin, I booted my laptop and googled "Einstein Memorial."

I learned that Albert's is a private monument located on the grounds of the National Academy of Sciences, about a block north of the extravaganza erected for Honest Abe. That it was dedicated in 1979 to honor Einstein's one-hundredth birthday. That twenty-seven hundred metal floor studs represent the planets, sun, moon, stars, and other celestial objects as positioned by Naval Observatory astronomers on dedication day. That if you stand in the center and talk directly to Einstein, your words will bounce back as if spoken in an echo chamber.

Next, I googled the key words "Montgomery County DOT" and "parking permit." Followed the same link I'd used in my wee hours search.

Temporarily leaving a vehicle in Maryland was as complicated as it was in Montreal. I acquired the following useless information.

Permits had been issued for forty years.

The program was intended for residents of neighborhoods impacted by certain public facilities, land uses, and adjacent commercial districts.

Outside of central business areas, only single-family homes were eligible to participate.

Great. The permit had been issued to someone living beside a uranium mine, a paper plant, or a boutique shopping strip lacking a lot.

Or to the occupant of a single-unit dwelling.

That last could be moderately useful.

Though language made it clear that online interaction was preferred, I managed to find a single discretely placed phone number.

Call a government agency on a Saturday morning?

Right.

It had worked with Waylon Colt on Memorial Day.

Harboring little hope of success, I dialed.

A recording told me that the office was closed and would reopen at seven a.m. Monday.

"Argh!" I actually said it out loud.

Frustrated, I skimmed the site's home page. Found a number for the director's office in a blue band at the bottom of the screen.

What the hell.

In for a penny.

"Archie Baxter."

"Mr. Baxter." Caught off guard, I babbled. "You're the director."

"The office is closed for the weekend." The voice sounded as if it came from a country where people sheared a lot of sheep. "Please try again on Monday," said the Maybe-from-Down-Under man.

"I'm sorry to bother you, Mr. Baxter. I'm sure you're terribly busy. Probably using the weekend to catch up on paperwork. I do that myself."

Baxter said nothing. I heard familiar music in the background.

"Oh, my God. Are you a fan of The Oak Ridge Boys?"

"I am." A minuscule thaw in Baxter's tone?

"The 'Y'all Come Back Saloon' is my absolute favorite." Faux gushy.

"'American Made.'"

It took me a second. "Yes! Great acoustic."

"Who's calling, please?"

"Dr. Temperance Brennan. I'm visiting DC from North Carolina."

"That explains it."

I had no idea what that meant. "Might I ask you a few questions about parking stickers?"

"That's an odd request."

"I'm wondering if it's possible to trace the holder of an old decal."

"How old?"

"Twenty nineteen."

"It's undoubtedly expired."

"Undoubtedly."

"Why?"

Not expecting my call to be answered, I hadn't prepared a spiel.

I was hesitant to share information on the fire victims. And I feared Baxter might claim confidentiality issues if I mentioned the police or ME.

My mind went into hyperdrive.

"It's a silly story, really." Silly-me chuckle. "Not to bore you with details, I'll just say that a lady helped me out of a jam involving my car and my cat. I want—"

"You have a cat?"

"Yes."

"What's his name?"

"Birdie. Anyway, I want to give the lady a thank-you gift. I failed to get her name or license plate, but I have a picture that shows a parking decal on her back window."

"I suppose there's no harm in looking up an old, elapsed sticker. Email me what you've got."

Baxter provided an address at the Montgomery County DOT and I sent him the image.

"Hold on."

A handset clattered.

The Boys sang about Elvira. Bobbie Sue.

I checked my mailbox. Replied to a few messages.

Thumb-nailed a dark intruder from between my upper left molars. Hunk of raisin?

Considered rehab plans for my nails.

An eternity, then Baxter was back.

"Took some creativity but I got it. The sticker was for residential parking in a neighborhood in Silver Spring, Maryland. Issued in 2019 to one Willie T. Pope."

He read off an address. I wrote it down.

"Did you happen to note the vehicle type?"

"Why do you need that?"

"I want to be certain it's my good Samaritan's car."

Uber patient, Baxter complied.

Totally pumped, I thanked him, disconnected, and punched an autodial number.

CHAPTER 22

D oyle picked up right away.

"Where are you?" she asked.

"In my room."

"What's happening?"

I considered telling her about my upcoming rendezvous with the female caller. Decided against it. Meeting someone of my gender in the late afternoon on the grounds of the National Academy of Sciences seemed perfectly safe. And the woman had been adamant. And I had promised. Besides. The whole thing was starting to feel a bit too *Spy vs. Spy* to me.

"I have a name and address for the owner of the piss-yellow Camry," I said.

"No shit. Have you contacted Deery?"

"I just met with him. You're right. The guy's a barrel of laughs."

"You should tell him."

"I will."

"Burgos, too. Give Sergeant Sunshine my love."

With that, Doyle was gone.

I dialed the mobile number the arson investigator had reluctantly shared. He answered on the second ring.

"Sergeant Burgos."

"It's Tempe Brennan. Sorry to bother you on a weekend." I was saying that a lot.

Burgos said nothing.

"I have information relevant to the two Foggy Bottom fires."

More nothing.

Once more avoiding mention of my upcoming meeting, I explained the yellow Camry, the decal, Archie Baxter's records search.

"I suggest you brief Deery."

"I'll phone him next."

For what seemed like a full ten seconds, I listened to the fuzzy hum of cell phone silence. Finally,

"Do you not have a job, Ms. Brennan?"

"I do."

"Then why are you trying to do ours?"

"Do you have any leads?" I snapped.

"Many."

"Leads that actually lead somewhere? Deery seems to be suffering from a severe case of tunnel vision." I knew that was imprudent as soon as I said it.

Burgos disconnected.

I dialed Deery.

Got voice mail.

Fingers tense with irritation, I texted Doyle.

You up for a road trip?

Like a flag on a pole.

An hour later Doyle and I were parked on a quiet elbow of a street not far from the central business district of Silver Spring. Yards were small but well-tended. Here and there, a bicycle lay abandoned on a sidewalk or lawn.

Trash cans dotted both curbs. Utility wires drooped overhead.

Tiny red-brick bungalows lined both sides of the block, all looking like the spawn of one lackluster developer. Shutters and trim were either white or green, probably painted within the last decade. Except for the occasional potted plant or lawn ornament, that was it for whimsy.

The home that Doyle and I were eyeballing had construction debris piled along its right side. Weeds growing amid the rubble suggested aged repairs or renovations. Perhaps a project abandoned midstream.

An ancient car sat in the driveway. Gray, with tires smoother than the skin on a grape.

"That clunker looks like it rolled off the line before I was born," I said.

"Ford Mustang," Doyle said. "Probably a '92. Cool set of wheels."

"But not a piss-yellow Camry."

"Definitely not."

"Shall we see if Mr. Pope is receiving visitors?"

"Lead on."

As with every other home on the block, three steps led up to a small concrete stoop. As with every other home on the block, an outer screen door shielded an inner one made of metal.

We climbed. Doyle thumbed the bell.

The chimes could have announced Mass at St. Peters.

Nothing happened when they'd finished ding-donging.

Doyle was reaching out for another go when we heard the snap of a deadbolt. A second. A third.

The metal door swung inward.

Willie T. Pope might have stood five feet tall in her prime. Though the dowager's hump added a few inches, the most she could claim now was four and a half.

Pope wore a pink floral kimono that pooled on the floor at her feet. Black lace gloves on hands gripping a walker wrapped in green and white satin ribbon. A curly red wig that didn't sit right on her head.

"Ms. Pope?" Hiding my surprise.

"Who's asking?"

"I'm Tempe." Indicating Doyle. "This is Ivy."

"You two sisters?"

"No, ma'am."

"You missioning for the Mormons?" Pope's eyes never stopped shifting between Ivy and me, birdlike, inquisitive. The clearest blue I've ever seen.

"No, ma'am."

"What do you want?"

"We're curious about a car once registered to this address."

"I'm eighty-nine. You think I still drive?"

I hoped not.

"How long have you lived here?" Friendly as a Walmart greeter.

"Forty-two years. By myself since Mite passed. Come to think of it, she'd burn my ass for telling you that."

"Your secrets are safe with us." I resisted the urge to wink.

"Weren't no secret. Mite was queen bitch when it came to security."

"Did Mite drive a yellow Camry?" Doyle asked.

"Mite drove a big-ass Ducati. Damn bike scared the crap out of me."

"Who owns the car in your drive?" Doyle was not one for small talk.

"My nephew's kid. Says he's going to restore the thing, but his parents don't want an old beater spoiling their view of the pansies. What the hell? No skin off my nose if he tinkers with it here."

"Do you know anyone who owns or used to own a yellow Camry?"

"My, my, Miss Ivy. You've really got your tits bouncing over that car."

"Do you?" Doyle's patience was fast evaporating.

"Question asked and answered."

Sliding me a side-eye, Doyle tipped her head toward my Mazda.

"Thank you so much," I said. "Have a lovely weekend."

We were halfway down the walk when Pope called out to our backs.

"Those wheels were mine, you know what I'd dub 'em?"

"What's that?" I asked.

"The Camry Canary."

Shuffling backward without turning, Pope slammed the door.

"Tough old bat," Doyle said as we were buckling our seat belts.

"I liked her."

"Not a chance she's our Foggy Bottom arsonist."

"No. But Deery should still check her out. See what evil lurks in the Pope family tree."

Grinning, Doyle pushed damp curls from her face. "Well, this was a total waste of time."

Was it?

What had my subconscious been trying to tell me?

————

The National Academy of Sciences is centrally located, at 2101 Constitution Avenue NW. I arrived at two-forty-five and hung back by the row of cars into which I'd embedded my Mazda. Before making my presence known, I wanted to assess the woman I'd agreed to meet. Should she appear sketchy, or armed, I'd split.

Einstein's wasn't the biggest memorial in the district. Nor had it been the easiest to find. I'd finally spotted it in an elm and holly grove in the southwest corner of the Academy grounds.

A bronze statue, maybe twelve feet tall and undoubtedly weighing mega tons, depicted the great man casually seated on a three-step stone bench. His left hand grasped a sheet inscribed with what I guessed were mathematical equations.

I couldn't be certain from so far off, but what else would they be? It was Einstein.

The sculpture was burly and craggy and wonderful. Dappled with shadows cast by overhead branches, the effect was truly beautiful. I felt Albert would be pleased.

At the moment only squirrels were present, rooting and rummaging for whatever appealed to their rodent minds. Not sure how Albert would have felt about that.

Three o'clock came and went. No one appeared.

Every few minutes I checked the time.

Three-ten.

Three-fifteen.

Might the woman be doing exactly as I was? Hanging back to see if I was crazy or packing?

Sighting down the barrel of a Mauser M18?

By three-twenty, I felt like I'd downed two triple espressos. Nerves jangling, I threw caution to the wind and strode to the monument.

No gunshot shattered the afternoon quiet.

No figure materialized in the warm summer sunlight.

Only the squirrels reacted, scattering quickly, at least one screeching its irritation.

Time passed.

My eyes roved my surroundings. My pulse did overtime.

I glanced at the star map spread across the monument's base. At the paper clutched in the statue's hand. I could read the inscription now. It summarized three of Einstein's most important scientific contributions: the photoelectric effect, the theory of general relativity, and the equivalence of energy and matter.

Right. I knew that.

A man crossed the grounds, tall and gangly, with wiry hair the color of dead grass in winter. I watched him move from the street to the building, unlock and enter through a side door.

No woman appeared.

I read the three quotations on the bench under Einstein's bum. One struck me as germane to the question both Thacker and Doyle had posed.

The right to search for truth implies also a duty; one must not conceal any part of what one has recognized to be true.

That was the answer. The reason for my commitment to the sub-cellar lady.

I saw it as my duty to find her truth.

That's not *your* whole truth, my subconscious interjected with brutal honesty.

Suppressed for years, the memory roared into my forebrain. I was lying bound, gagged, and blindfolded in a sack on a bank of the Tuckasegee River, the captive of a demented group calling itself The Hellfire Club. For a moment, the long-ago feelings engulfed me anew. The rage, the helplessness, the terror of dying in that bag.

I'd survived my ordeal. I was uncertain what had happened to the tiny subcellar woman. But I knew that she hadn't survived hers.

At four o'clock, I positioned myself at the monument's center, looked directly at Einstein, and said, "Screw this."

My words echoed back as promised.

I headed for my car.

CHAPTER 23

Doyle suggested we share an early meal together. I was starving again. And had no viable plan for feeding myself.

We decided on Mexican. I offered to drive.

We were halfway to Maïz64 at Logan Circle when Doyle's mobile rang.

"Doyle."

A voice buzzed for a long time on the other end of the line. Probably male. Definitely excited.

Doyle listened, a zillion expressions colliding on her face.

"You got names?"

More buzzing.

"Good work. Get me more."

After disconnecting she pressed the phone to her chest.

Inhaled deeply.

"Freakingfuckonafreakingduckfuck!?"

"Bad news?"

Doyle regarded me with flapjack eyes.

"What?" I prompted.

"My CI caught a call on his scanner about a drive-by this morning. A fifty-six-year-old Caucasian male gunned down outside a home on a residential street."

"Dead?"

"As a bug on a windscreen."

"Where?"

"Chevy Chase."

"That's in Maryland?"

"Yes and no. Chevy Chase is also the name of a neighborhood in Northwest DC, just below the Maryland state line. That's where the shooting happened."

"Did your informant get a name?"

"He's working on it. But he did have info on the location." Teasing the suspense.

Not in the mood for drama, I circled a wrist, urging her to spit it out.

"The property is owned by one Lloyd Warring."

That took a moment to compute.

"You're thinking the vic could be related to the Foggy Bottom Gang Warrings? The probable founders of W-C Commerce?"

Doyle's brows, shoulders, and palms rose as one.

"And that this hit could be linked to the Foggy Bottom fires?"

"Seems an odd coincidence."

"We're seeing a lot of those lately."

"Indeed."

"Warring is a fairly common surname," I said.

"Not *that* common."

"What else did your informant say?"

"That Warring has pull and his 'people'"—hooking air quotes—"are pressing to keep the attack out of the news."

"Who'll handle the investigation?"

"MPD. Maybe the Cathedral Heights station on Idaho Avenue. Which would be awesome."

"I'm thick. Explain the importance of that."

"I have an inside source there."

Of course, you do, I thought. I wondered, was this murder really linked to the fires? Or was the journalist in Doyle looking for a story where none existed?

For a long moment, Doyle sat staring up the street. Maybe at the dead insects splattered across the passenger-side glass.

"What's the last thing to go through a bug's mind when hitting a windshield?" she asked, the corners of her lips crimped into a mischievous smile.

"No idea."

"Its asshole."

My eyes rolled with zero input from me.

"Dinner's off?" I guessed.

"Do you mind? I really want to dive into this story."

"Not at all."

I shifted into gear and gunned the accelerator.

After dropping Doyle at home, I looped back to a Walgreens we'd passed along the way.

Ten minutes later my little cart held products I hadn't anticipated needing on a brief trip north. My preferred brands of toothpaste, deodorant, and moisturizer. A pack of ankle socks. A cordless mini flat iron. A pink-and-purple emery board. A few random impulse items, most involving creativity with hair.

Jesus, Brennan. Are you hoping for an invite to the prom?

The self-checkouts were on the fritz and only one register was open. Six customers were queued up to pay, two looking peeved, the others with eyes fixed on their mobiles.

Frustrated on multiple levels, hating weekends and icemaker-caused floods and house fires and drive-bys, I took my place at the back of the line.

While awaiting my turn, I phoned Katy, hoping, illogically, that the Annex was inhabitable.

Nope.

Inwardly cursing, I inched forward, one cart length at a time.

The cashier was a bosomy blonde with dark roots and makeup too garish for the unkind drugstore lighting. Her name tag said Charlaine.

Charlaine greeted each customer with an expression of delighted surprise and a barrage of folksy banter. Which did nothing to speed the process.

Stars were born and died. The earth rotated.

Finally, I was second in line. Bored, I grabbed a half dozen Snickers and Kit-Kat bars from a rack positioned to lure shoppers into doing just that. Within earshot now, I half registered the conversion between Charlaine and an old coot in leather suspenders and baggy tweed pants.

The pair were discussing the inconvenience of home renovation projects. The nuisance of having workers underfoot. The bother of having to register for this permit and that.

One complaint snapped me to attention.

Suddenly, I was on fire to get to my laptop.

Back in my room, eating a Whopper and fries, I booted my Mac and returned to the Montgomery County DOT site.

Quickly verified what I'd overheard.

I was about to phone Doyle when she appeared at my open door, looking like her heart was pumping pure adrenaline.

"Lloyd Emmitt Warring."

"Back up," I said.

"Went by Lew."

"Who did?"

"The man gunned down this morning." Doyle paused to collect all the patience she could take in. "His name is Lloyd Emmitt Warring. Was."

When the significance of her statement penetrated my brain space, "Warring may be a common surname, but Emmitt is not a common first name."

"Damn straight," Doyle said.

"Which gives legs to the theory that one of the Warrings is being targeted."

"Big muscular ones."

"Two W-C properties are torched. Then a family member is shot." Recapping for myself, not Doyle.

"Assuming Lew Warring is related to the Foggy Bottom brothers."

"Assuming that."

"Why?" she asked.

"Why else? Someone holds a grudge against Emmitt. Maybe against the family."

"We both agreed that would be one long-standing grudge."

"The Hatfields and McCoys plugged holes in each other for almost three decades." Even as I said it, I knew the comparison was a stretch. "Of course, that happened in West Virginia and Kentucky in the eighteen hundreds."

"Fine," Doyle said. "Maybe the perp is someone's kid. Grandkid."

"Whose?"

"The Warring brothers ran with a rough crowd. They must have made enemies."

"Everything I've read says that's true."

"You plowed through those articles I photocopied. Float some candidates."

I reached for my notes.

"Okay. Here's a possibility. In 1934, Allen Wilson was shot dead by gunmen hired to kill some Warring-associated gangster whose name I forget. Wilson was an innocent newspaper carrier caught in the crossfire. He left behind three young kids."

"Their names?"

"I didn't write that down."

"That's good. Another?"

"Doris Gardner was the girlfriend of a Warring accomplice named Amon 'Alarm' Clock. Gardner was killed when Clock got into a fight with some rival bootlegger. She was the mother of two young girls."

"Go on."

"I don't like to speculate."

"Do it anyway."

I dug deep.

"For years, Rags Warring—"

"Charles."

"Yes. For years he was in a relationship with Mary Healy, a woman who worked at the National Archives. Because of Warring's unsavory reputation, Healy was given an ultimatum: find another boyfriend or find another job. She dropped Warring cold."

"So, what's the grudge?"

"I don't know. Maybe Rags retaliated in some way? This is senseless. I hate conjecture."

"Fine. But you do grasp my point? At least tell me you grasp my point."

"The cops should be looking into the Warrings."

"Thank you," she said, appeased.

"Deery says he did that and found nothing linking the name Warring to the fires."

"Uh-huh." Doyle's tone was beyond dubious.

I segued to *my* news.

"I may have another angle on the parking decal."

"Willie T. Pope was a bust."

"Maybe not. Did you notice the rubble piled beside Pope's house?"

Doyle nodded.

"Residents of Montgomery County need temporary permits for contractors doing long-term construction or repairs at their homes."

"You're thinking Pope obtained the decal for a worker's vehicle?"

"A worker's piss-yellow Camry."

Doyle's mouth reshaped into a balance between optimism and doubt.

"It's an interesting possibility," she said.

"Yes," I agreed.

"How about you chase down the decal while I contact my guy at the Cathedral Heights station."

I checked the time. Seven-twenty.

"Did we get a phone number for Pope?"

"If she has a landline, that shouldn't be hard. And someone should brief Deery and Burgos."

Before I could suggest she make those calls, Doyle had disappeared.

"Pope residence."

"It's Tempe Brennan, Ms. Pope. My friend Ivy and I visited you earlier today?"

"How did you get my number?"

"It's listed."

"Well don't that beat all."

"It's standard unless you specifically ask to opt out."

"Phone hardly rings except for my nephew. He's the one insists I need the thing. Thinks I'm going to fall on my keester and crack my skull."

"I'm sure—"

"Tell me this. How would I dial if I'm lying flat on my ass?"

"Ms. Pope, I'm wondering if you've had repairs or renovations done on your property in the recent past."

"You do ask the damndest questions."

"I noticed construction debris in your yard. And, well, your home looks so lovely, I was curious who did the work."

"Yeah? You think so?"

"I do."

"Was a pain in the patooty but it needed doing. Had water seeping down my bedroom wall."

"Do you recall the name of the company?"

"What am I, a walking encyclopedia? Hold on."

I heard the clunk of a handset hitting a hard surface. The receding double tap of Pope's feet and walker. I pictured the old woman. The terrible wig. The kimono. The black gloves.

My hindbrain cleared its throat. *Ahem!*

What?

Try as I might, I hadn't a clue what my subconscious was telling me.

An eternity later Pope was back.

"You must live under a lucky star, buttercup. The contractor, or whatever he was, left a business card. I kept it in case there were problems. I'm careful like that."

"A good quality."

There was a pause during which I heard a tsunami of wheezing. I could picture Pope squinting to make out the lettering on the card.

"'Safe and Sound Home Repairs and Renovations.' The print is so small it may as well be on an aspirin bottle."

There followed another lengthy round of wheezing.

I pondered buttercups. Patooties. My favorite brand of aspirin.

"I think it says 'licensed general contractor, insured and bonded.' Yeah. That's it. I vaguely remember the guy. Did a nice job but never smelled too good."

"Do you recall his name?"

"Not sure I ever knew it."

"Do you see contact information?"

"There's a phone number." She read off the digits. "No address, but the area code is out in Maryland, I think."

"Did you have to pay for a parking permit for your contractor's car?"

"Don't recall that. But I don't recall much these days. Mostly it's a blessing."

"Thank you so much, Ms. Pope."

"My advice, never pay a penny up front. Wait until all the banging and sawing and hammering's done."

After disconnecting, I tapped on a number listed among my recent outgoing calls.

Archie Baxter was still manning his desk. Made me wonder about the man's home situation.

Baxter listened to my update without interrupting.

"What is it you want now?"

"Might the parking permit have been issued to Willie Pope but for a vehicle belonging to her contractor?"

"That's possible."

"Would the contractor's name be in your records?"

"You're thinking he or one of his employees could be the owner of the yellow Camry."

"Or was."

"Hold on," he said, sighing. I'm sure he thought I was a bit around the bend for so doggedly trying to thank a stranger.

Seconds later he was back.

"I have it," he said, a plaintive note in his voice suggesting hope that this would be my last request.

Jotting the name, I thanked Baxter, disconnected, and thumbed another number.

Deery didn't pick up.

Did the man ever answer his phone?

Burgos was equally unavailable.

It's Saturday night, Brennan. Other people have lives.

Peeved, I left a voice mail for each.

CHAPTER 24

I was on a church pew beside an elderly woman wearing enough bracelets
to stock a Macy's jewelry counter. Rhinestone-studded glasses. A red wig.

*The woman leaned close to whisper to me. Her breath felt hot and moist
on my ear.*

I didn't like it and shushed her.

*When the woman drew back, a tiny stained-glass window shimmered off
each of her bejeweled lenses. The wig hitched sideways revealing a hairless
pink scalp.*

*The woman raised a blue-veined hand. In apology? Disapproval?
Supplication?*

The bangles clinked loudly.

The minister, an Asian woman, whipped around and pointed at me.

"She is not what she seems."

I tried to ask what that meant. My mouth wouldn't work.

*In a gallery above, an organ began a litany composed of a single repet-
itive note.*

Shrill. Too shrill.

My lids flew up.

As I reached for my mobile, the screen shifted from a message
announcing an incoming call to one indicating that I'd missed it.

Ryan?

Crap!

I checked my voice mail.

Nothing.

I checked my list of recent callers.

Unknown number.

Disappointment shot through me, tinged with hurt. It hadn't been Ryan.

Maybe the no-show lady, as I'd dubbed her? Had she phoned to explain her absence? To try to talk me into another meet-up?

The indifferent screen offered nothing except the date and time, 8:47 a.m.

Early-morning gray oozed through the window behind my bed. The sky appeared to be considering options.

I'd had another dream. This was getting ridiculous.

But I remembered this one. At least the final fragment.

And I understood the subliminal message.

The meaning of the *psst* at Willie Pope's house.

While I'd been asleep, my id had cracked the enigma of the Asian woman in the poop with Norbert Mirek.

From far off, I heard the muted bonging of church bells beckoning the faithful.

It was Sunday. My second in DC.

I wanted justice for the subcellar vic. But I also wanted to get back to Birdie. To Charlotte.

To Montreal?

My emails yielded nothing of interest.

Not so my text list. Comprised of two words and an emoji, the most recent had arrived just past midnight.

Let it go!

The three-word missive was accompanied by a cartoon-styled human skull with large black eye sockets.

I didn't recognize the number from which the text had been sent. Was it meant for someone else? Was it a joke? A mistake?

A threat?

I tried entering the digits. Got a message that the line was no longer functioning.

I knew that anonymous texting could be done using a third-party service—an app, a website, or a VoIP, a voice over internet protocol. I understood that such services could strip out an originating number and substitute another random one.

But who would do that? And why?

Feeling uneasy, I vowed to mention the text to Deery.

Antsy knowing that nothing would happen until Monday, I dressed, did a quick *toilette*, and clumped downstairs.

The kitchen was empty. Perhaps Lan was turning the pages of a hymnal somewhere?

Someone had made coffee. Mentally thanking them, I helped myself and added cream. Was carrying the mug to my room when my iPhone again exploded with the opening guitar riff from AC/DC's "Back in Black."

Jarring, I know. But I'd grown tired of Jelly Roll and the link had popped up when I'd searched with the keywords "DC" and "ring-tone."

I double-stepped the last two treads, and grabbed the device so quickly I slopped coffee onto my tee.

The screen now happily provided a name. One that surprised me. And proved me wrong.

"Lizzie. I'm impressed you're working on the Lord's Day," I said, plucking tissues to blot the stain splattered across my belly.

"Until the big guy sends me a sugar daddy, that's how I roll."

"Seriously?"

"No." Throaty chuckle. "It's a dreary morning so I figured I'd do some paperwork catch-up. The office is blissfully quiet. Why do you always sound out of breath?"

"Did you send me a text last night?" I asked, ignoring her question.

"No. Why?"

"You received the samples?"

"The package was waiting when I arrived. That's why I'm calling."

"Did you look at them?"

"A quick glance."

"Will you be able to extract usable DNA?"

"The bone quality is shit."

That didn't sound promising.

"But it's doable?"

"We'll see." Not exactly a promise.

"I really appreciate your bumping my case to the front of the queue." A request I'd not made explicitly but had implied in the accompanying note. "I've been stuck in DC far longer than I'd planned."

"People pay big bucks to visit our nation's capital."

"No kidding. Half the country was here last weekend."

"Get your ass out and take in an exhibit. I like the bonsai museum."

"That's a real thing?"

"Hell, yeah. One of their bitsy little trees dates to 1625 and survived the Hiroshima bombing."

"Your lab has a genetic genealogist on staff, right?"

"It does."

"Is she fast?"

"He's lightning itself," she answered, correcting me on the gender. We disconnected.

I changed my top, then, inspired by the knowledge that some people did work on weekends, I phoned the ME's office in Charlotte.

Dr. Nguyen was not one of those people. I left a voice mail.

Breakthrough on the Mirek case. Call me.

Next, I tried Deery.

To my amazement, he answered.

"Deery."

"It's Temperance Brennan."

"I know."

Stupid. Of course, he had caller ID.

"Sorry to bother you on a weekend, but—"

"It's what you do."

"I have a name for the owner of the yellow Camry."

"The vehicle you claim was present at both fire sites."

"It *was* present."

"Uh-huh."

I managed to unclamp my jaw.

"Should I be speaking with Burgos instead?"

Deery sighed heavily through his nose.

"What is it you want me to do?"

"Perhaps you could verify the car's ownership."

"How did you get this name?"

I told him about the construction work done at Pope's home. About the Montgomery County parking decal requirements.

"Give it to me," he said quietly.

"Ronan Stoll. He owns or works for an outfit called Safe and Sound Home Repairs and Renovations."

Deery grunted and disconnected.

To my shock, Deery rang back twenty minutes later.

"Not sure why I'm sharing this with you."

"Because I found the lead."

I waited out a round of background sounds different from those on our earlier call. Sharp footfalls suggested Deery was striding along concrete. The *shoosh* of hydraulic brakes suggested a bus.

"Ronan Stoll is co-owner of Safe and Sound, along with a brother, Roy, same last name. Same DOB: 12/12/83. The outfit is small time, mostly just the two, and has an address on T Street Northeast. As of last March, Ronan still owned the Camry."

"Does either have a sheet?"

"Parking tickets for both, some moving violations, a DWI for Roy back in 2008. Otherwise, the pair are clean as choirboys."

"Anything else?"

"Roy was married briefly to a woman named Georgia Daughtler. That went south in 2012. No kids. Currently, the brothers share a rental on Willard Street in Northwest DC."

"Worth a follow-up," I said.

Deery didn't agree or disagree.

I debated telling him about my experience at the Einstein Memorial. What the hell? The woman had blown me off.

Deery listened and drew air through his nose. Then,

"What the devil goes on in your brain?"

Figuring the question was rhetorical, I didn't respond.

"You do understand that you're not a cop?"

More nothing.

"Do you have any sense of how reckless your behavior was?"

"Meeting a woman in broad daylight in a public place?" Way too defensive.

"Let me recap. Some dodgy female drops a dime and asks for a face-to-face, so you gallivant off."

"I do not gallivant," I snapped.

"I'll rethink the verb."

"And the woman did not sound dodgy." She did. And failed to show up.

Another pause, longer, Deery's nasal inhalations filling the gap.

"I'll speak to the brothers Stoll later today."

"Dropping in unannounced on a Sunday. That's smart. Catch them off guard. What time?"

"You're not seriously suggesting I take you along?"

"I most seriously am."

"Now why would I do that?"

"Because I discovered their link to the fires."

"Possible link."

A very, very long pause. Then,

"I talked to a colleague in Charlotte about you."

"And who would that be?"

"A detective named Erskine Slidell."

"Retired detective." Largely true. Though Skinny still did the occasional case for the CMPD. Note to self: Update Skinny regarding Norbert Mirek.

"Detective Slidell has an interesting take on you."

"Does he." Glacial.

"Where are you staying?"

I gave him Doyle's address.

"Be ready at four."

"I'll—"

Beep. Beep. Beep.

Dead air.

I realized I hadn't mentioned the anonymous text.

Admit it, Brennan. You avoided the topic knowing Deery's reaction.

The light through the window was filling out and growing cheerier. It seemed the sun had decided to take charge.

I watched the room brighten while considering the two cops with whom I was forced to interact. Slidell frequently. Deery currently.

I reached two conclusions.

While Skinny had the edge in terms of overall loutishness, Deery had marginally better manners and a superior command of language.

Neither would top my list of candidates for sharing hugs and warm cookies.

Nguyen returned my call at eleven.

"Are you still in DC?" she asked.

"I am. Has something come up that you need me in Charlotte?"

"No, no. I played your voice mail about Norbert Mirek. I must admit, I'm intrigued."

"Bluestein's report threw me for a while."

"Finding such hair in the fecal matter was definitely odd."

"Finding human hair at all. Every photo submitted showed that Mirek was bald as a cue ball. It finally dawned on me"—I didn't mention that my epiphany came from visiting Willie Pope and the subsequent dream—"maybe the old man wore a toupee."

"Many of which are made of Asian female hair."

"Exactly. The nephew—"

"Halsey Banks."

"Yes." Impressed Nguyen remembered the name. "Banks confirmed that his uncle had purchased and begun wearing a hairpiece six months before his disappearance. He opined that the thing was donkey-ass ugly. His descriptor."

"Well done, Tempe."

"Thanks."

I downed the last of my coffee, now unappealingly tepid.

Checked the time. Noon. Four hours until Deery's arrival.

I got my ass out to go see Griesser's bitsy little trees.

CHAPTER 25

It was going on six when Deery pulled up and blasted his horn. I hurried out the big front door and slid into the passenger seat of his black Dodge Durango.

And nearly gagged.

The SUV's interior smelled of perspiration, drugstore aftershave, and cheap hair gel. A Febreze odor fighter was trying its best, but the syrupy overlay only made matters worse.

I switched to drawing air through my mouth. Wondered fleetingly if the noxious mix could be the source of Deery's nasal issues.

Deery mumbled a halfhearted apology but offered no explanation for being two hours late. I merely nodded.

Deery waited until I'd secured my belt, then carefully repositioned the gear selector, double-checking visually to be certain he'd shifted into drive. Satisfied that all was well, he gently pressed one giant shoe down on the gas. The Durango crept forward, slow and steady as a barge being dragged through a lock.

Though the view was unobstructed at the end of the drive and showed not a single vehicle on Chain Bridge Road, Deery made a full stop. Looking left then right then left again, he cautiously made the turn.

My grandmother was in good standing with the DMV until her ninety-first birthday. Even when her eyesight began to fail and she gave up her license, the old gal never drove this timidly.

Totally focused on the road, Deery made no attempt at conversation.

Suited me. I concentrated on keeping the contents of my stomach where they belonged.

The sun was preparing for its daily adieu, promising, but not yet delivering those golden tones so passionately sought by Monet. As we blistered along at thirty miles an hour, I watched a feebly bronzed capital roll by outside my window.

Nebraska Avenue. Ward Circle. Massachusetts Avenue. We were turning from Florida onto U Street when I stole my first sideways glance.

Deery's tie hung loose, and a sweat crescent darkened the pit I could see. Today the neckwear was carrot, the shirt periwinkle blue. No jacket. Black framed Ray-Bans rested low on his nose.

I noted that, in keeping with his feet, the man's hands were extraordinarily large for his frame. And tense. His knuckles bulged yellow-white in their death grip on the wheel. His chest rose and fell in steady waves as he inhaled through his mouth and exhaled through his nose.

A calming yogic exercise? Postnasal drip?

Whatever the reason for the judiciously paced breathing, it was clear that the man was stressed. Not wishing to elevate his level of anxiety, I kept silent.

Sunday traffic was light. Twenty minutes after leaving Doyle's house we were turning from 17th Street onto Willard.

A long twenty minutes. My brain had responded to the cloying atmosphere by setting up a metronome pounding in my frontal lobe.

Deery pulled to the curb at the far end of the block. Cut the engine. Checked the side and rearview mirrors. Leaned back, hands still clutching the wheel.

Apparently, we'd be doing some surveillance before approaching the Stoll brothers. An activity as exciting as watching dust settle.

I surveyed my surroundings.

Willard was as polychromatic as the street that had hosted the second Foggy Bottom fire. Multihued two- and three-story brick town houses ran along each side. Desert tan. Butter yellow. Royal blue. Lots of gray and white.

A two-part staircase connected each building with a glaringly bright red brick sidewalk. One set of treads rose to a painted front door, another wound down and sideways into a concrete well. Curtained windows at ground level suggested basement units.

There were no real yards, just a few reasonably happy-looking flower beds. Trees and shrubs rose from rectangular dirt patches spaced at intervals along the walks.

My impression: the street was a tad shabby—rust-stained paint here, a broken railing there—but had the vibe of a place whose residents liked it that way.

We'd been there a good ten minutes when I took a stab at conversation.

"The Stolls live in the yellow building three up from the alley, right?"

Deery's absorption must have been total. Or he'd forgotten I was there. The sound of my voice seemed to startle him.

"What?" Ray-Bans whipping toward me. Fingers momentarily tightening, then relaxing their grip.

"Their building is the yellow one at midblock?"

"Yes."

"Do you know if they're home?"

"I do not." With a brusqueness suggesting that I should zip it?

Five more minutes dragged by.

"Are we in Dupont Circle or Adams Morgan?" I asked, my limited knowledge of DC geography based on a quick perusal of one of Doyle's maps.

"AdMo."

An elderly man walked an elderly poodle past the Durango. The man was stooped, the poodle obese.

A woman exited a building near the 18th Street end of the block, crossed to a red Mini Cooper, and drove off.

A kid on a bike wove lazy figure eights up the center of the pavement, blue-and-yellow jersey proclaiming his loyalty to Golden State and his appreciation of number thirty.

Bored, I googled for a player ID. Stephen Curry.

Beside me, Deery breathed with painstaking precision.

I checked the time. Seven-ten.

A moment later I was the one startled by an unsolicited comment.

"AdMo was once the place to go."

When Deery didn't elaborate, I asked, "Not anymore?"

"Same venues there. Just less lively these days."

Two complete sentences. Stunned by Deery's loquaciousness, I ventured another question. Not really caring, but trying to avoid death by boredom.

"Where's the action now?"

"The Wharf, the Navy Yard."

I was surprised Deery knew that, but not by his answer. I'd dined there with Doyle and Zanetti, ergo the area had to be hip.

Did anyone say "hip" anymore?

Another long pause, then I tried again.

"Is property expensive in this part of the district?"

"Yes."

"That odd combination of downmarket feeling and upmarket price."

Deery didn't acknowledge my witticism. I soldiered on.

"The Stoll brothers must do well enou—"

"They live in a cellar."

"Yes, but—"

A silencing hand lifted.

I glanced at Deery. His eyes were narrowed, his attention focused on the rearview mirror.

I quelled the urge to swivel my head.

A beat.

Two.

A car passed close to the Durango.

Electricity slammed through me.

The car was a piss-yellow Toyota Camry.

I could tell little about the silhouette at the wheel. Tall, probably male. Wearing a brimmed cap. The passenger seat was empty.

Barely breathing, I followed the Camry's progress.

The car crawled the block, its taillights flashing fitfully. Suddenly the driver shot forward and braked. A six-point maneuver got him into the space vacated by the Mini Cooper.

A man climbed out.

Sunglasses covered his eyes—standard drugstore issue. A Washington Nationals cap covered his head.

After locking the Camry, the man walked in our direction, a grease-stained brown bag cradled in his left arm.

"That's one of the Stolls?" I asked.

Either Deery didn't know, or he didn't bother to answer.

I put Possibly Stoll's height at six feet, his weight at slightly less than Birdie's. His tee—perhaps the ugliest I'd ever seen—was plum with two chartreuse parrots wing-draping each other. Below the tee, neatly pressed khaki shorts, sandals, and white socks pulled up to mid-calf.

As expected, Possibly Stoll headed for the yellow building. A series of muted metallic thuds came through my window as he clumped down the stairs.

A door opened. Slammed.

I waited for a signal from Deery. A directive. An admonition to remain silent. Got the usual nothing.

Somewhere out of sight, a dog yapped, high and whiny. A car engine turned over.

Another five minutes passed.

Just as I feared my eyes might bleed from the tedium, Deery spoke.

"You say nothing."

"Got it."

"We do this by—"

"The book."

One lifted eyebrow. Then Deery hit the door handle with his left elbow, swung his legs sideways, and levered himself out of the Durango.

Wordlessly, I did the same.

The sun was sinking below the horizon now, banding the pavement and the lawns along Willard with skeletal versions of trees and utility poles. A soft breeze had kicked up, causing the elongated shadows to shift and heave.

The yapping dog? The undulating gloom? The potentially threatening text? No idea what sent a chill running down my spine.

Refusing to grant credence to the strange sense of foreboding, I fell into step behind Deery. Who gave no indication he knew I was following.

Up the red-brick sidewalk. Down the rusted metal staircase.

There was a small window to our left. A trio of utility meters jutted from the brick beside its frame. An algae-green door lay straight ahead. On it, rusty digits identified the unit as 4B.

Flexing his right elbow to bring that hand to gun level, Deery reached out with his left thumb and pressed the bell.

Inside the unit, a buzzer sounded.

No one appeared or called out.

We waited, both of us spring-loaded and logging details.

The air in the well was moldy and dank, the window at my shoulder almost opaque with years of accreted gunk. Maybe decades.

Through the grimy glass I could see two potted cacti. What looked like a rubber snake. A figurine in a cowboy hat, sex indeterminate.

I was eyeballing the statue when, beyond the succulents, I caught a flicker of pink. There, then gone.

"Someone's home," I whispered, excited. Knew instantly the response my comment would elicit.

"I know."

"These apartments usually have back entrances." Defensive. Why was I constantly self-justifying with this jerk?

Sighing, Deery went another round with his thumb, this one longer and more insistent.

The buzzing was followed by a clamorous silence.

Head wagging, Deery curled his fingers and banged hard with the meaty side of his fist. "Police! I know you're in there."

Up the block, the invisible pooch began yapping again. Another dog joined in, this one more a baritone.

The duet was going well when a voice came through the door, high and reedy.

"You're at the wrong address. We're good, here."

"Roy Stoll?"

"Who wants to know?"

"Detective Merle Deery, Metropolitan PD."

"What do you want?"

"A moment of your time."

"Your car isn't official. How do I know you're really police?"

"Open up and I'll present credentials."

"I do that, you're not legit, I could be in trouble."

Possibly Stoll had a point.

"Detective Deery can hold his badge up to the window so you can view it," I said.

A brief silence suggested Possibly Stoll was thinking about that.

Seconds later, knuckles rapped the inside of the glass.

Deery scowled at me.

I scowled back.

Deery raised his shield.

Possibly Stoll took his time, either studying the info or deciding on a course of action.

"Think he's phoning the station?" I asked, voice low.

Deery lifted one shoulder.

"Maybe talking to his brother?"

"Maybe flossing his teeth?"

Though snarky, at least it was a response.

We waited, the tense hunch of Deery's shoulders radiating his displeasure. I wasn't sure whether it was Stoll or me who was darkening his mood.

And I didn't care. It was past eight. I was hungry and tired and wanted to get on with the interview.

"Phone off?" Deery asked without looking at me.

I pulled the thing out and flipped the mute button.

As I did so, a lock snicked, and a deadbolt slid sideways.

The green door swung inward.

Possibly Stoll was no longer wearing the ugly parrot tee.

CHAPTER 26

Possibly Stoll had changed to moss-green shorts and a lilac-and-teal Hawaiian shirt featuring Roy Rogers saddled up on Trigger. Up close, his scrawny limbs brought to mind old black-and-white photos of death camp survivors.

Deery's opener was typically curt.

"Roy Stoll?"

Before the man could react, his exact duplicate appeared at his side, this version still sporting the ugly parrot tee. He, too, looked like he lived on nothing but celery. The cap and shades were gone, revealing hazel eyes flecked with gold and sandy hair fast losing ground to pasty white scalp. Features identical to those of the man to his right.

"My, my. What brings Johnny Law to our humble abode?"

"I assume you are Roy Stoll?" Deery tried again.

"You know what they say about that?" The man's lips lifted into a smile showcasing remarkably small teeth. "Assume makes an *ass* out of *u* and *me*," he explained, emphasizing the breakdown in case the joke wasn't clear.

Deery's face never changed.

"I'm a detective with the—"

"Yes, sir. We saw your badge."

"Am I speaking to Roy Stoll?"

"You are, indeed. And this is my brother—"

"—Ronan Stoll." Hawaiian shirt.

"What in hell could the police possibly want—"

"—with us?"

They were twins. I got it. But their manner of finishing each other's sentences was somewhat disconcerting.

"Perhaps this matter is best handled inside," Deery suggested, sotto voce.

"My brother and I have nothing—"

"—to hide."

"Your neighbors. Your choice."

A quick sideways glance, then Roy stepped back. Brushing past Ronan, my nose took in a tsunami of something relying heavily on sage.

The brothers led us down a short hall, then left into a somewhat feminine version of a man cave. Faux cowhide rug. Faux maroon leather sofa. Dual recliners facing a billion-inch flat-screen TV.

A laminate bar ran the room's rear wall, looking like a piece straight off an Amazon truck. A Bud Light sign hung above it, buzzing softly. A mini fridge sat behind it. Four matching stools bellied up to its front, each outfitted with a lavender vinyl seat.

"Por favor." Roy arced a hand toward the couch.

"Make yourselves comfortable," Ronan added.

Deery and I circled a coffee table—a hippo supporting a tinted glass oval on its back—to sit where directed.

Ronan settled into a recliner and tucked one scarecrow leg under his bum.

"Nice place," I lied.

"It's home." Ronan smiled broadly. Same undersized dentition.

Deery's eyes met mine, narrowed in warning.

I nodded, acknowledging my earlier commitment to total silence.

Roy remained standing, arms crossed on his chest.

"Please sit down, sir," Deery said.

"I'm happ—"

"Sit. Down." Steely.

"Do you have a warrant, Detective Deery?"

"Do I need a warrant, Mr. Stoll?"

"Just comply," Ronan whined. "I have things to do."

Eyes rolling like synchronized pinballs, Roy sat.

"Have you an objection to my recording this conversation? For accuracy. For your protection as well as mine."

"Of course not," Ronan said.

Roy looked dubious but didn't object.

While Deery set up his phone, I assessed my surroundings.

The room was tinted blue by the neon beer sign, giving it a watery, *Twenty Thousand Leagues Under the Sea* vibe. The air smelled of fried food. I guessed the takeout Roy had been carrying in the bag.

The unit was larger than its humble exterior suggested, probably occupying the building's entire footprint. A narrow hall ran backward from the man cave to end in a kitchen at the rear. Checkerboard linoleum and harvest gold appliances suggested a love of sixties design. Or a lack of updating.

I counted five doors along the corridor, assumed they led to bedrooms and baths. Maybe closets. A study or library seemed unlikely.

The walls were hung with what I guessed were family photos. From where I sat, I could only see those on the left. One was a professional portrait. Three were amateur shots, enlarged, matted, and framed.

The portrait resembled those for which Gran had posed in her youth. Sepia-toned, it showed a woman seated in a high-backed chair, hair in a complicated updo, hands placed one atop the other in her lap.

The Kodak moments were in color and had a theme. Each showed the same woman at varying ages, with two identical boys at her sides. In the nearest photo, the boys were seven or eight and had on matching sweaters and bow ties. In the next, they were preteens wearing plaid open-collared shirts. In the third, they were young men, probably in their twenties, and finally dressing themselves. One had long hair and wore a Foo Fighters tee. The other was in a buzz-cut and Izod polo.

"May I ask about the lady?"

Roy's voice brought me back.

"Accompanying me is Dr. Temperance Brennan," Deery replied, giving zero reason for my presence.

"A dick and a doc. Catchy. You should pitch it to one of those true crime shows."

Apparently, Roy considered himself quite the humorist.

"Do you feel my presence here is related to a crime, Mr. Stoll?" Deery's face showed not the slightest trace of amusement.

"You're a policeman."

"Omygod!" Ronan angled forward, spine arced, a red patch spreading across each of his cheeks. "Is this about the break-in at Joyce and Clive Zamzow's condo? We heard that their home was totally trashed. I was terrified. What if we'd been targeted instead? We could have been killed!"

"Their condo was not *totally trashed.*" Roy's mocking tone was clearly meant to deride his brother. "And the detective who interviewed us said the Zamzows were burglarized because they were out of town. We were *not* out of town."

"You aren't always right, you know." Ronan slumped back in his chair, all cocked chin and affronted scowl.

The brothers weren't always in sync, I thought. Made sense. Even twins must disagree at times.

Deery waited out the bickering, then, "I'm engaged in an arson investigation." Calculatedly offering no further detail.

"Can't help you with that. There's been no scuttlebutt about a fire around here," Roy said. Then to Ronan, "Have you heard anything?"

"What am I, gossip central?"

"There's no call to be snappy," Roy snapped.

"The fire was in Foggy Bottom," Deery offered, watching carefully for a reaction. As did I.

The brothers exchanged puzzled looks.

"Foggy Bottom is way out of our—"

"—price range. What has this got to do with us, detective?"

"I'm VCB, sir."

"I'm Sagittarius." Roy pantomimed waggling a cigar, Groucho style.

"VCB is the department's violent crimes bureau."

"I didn't think you were referencing a Vacuum Circuit Breaker." Roy chuckled at his own wit. "That's a gizmo we install—"

"People perished, Mr. Stoll."

"Ohhh," said Roy, drawing out the word in what seemed like mock anguish. "Forgive my tactlessness. I am truly sorry," he said, sounding not sorry at all. "But we know nothing about buildings burning down in—"

"—Foggy Bottom. Please excuse my brother. Occasionally, Roy's comedic timing is less than ideal."

The brothers kept their eyes on their laps. Maybe their genitals.

The beer sign buzzed.

Seconds ticked by.

Ronan shifted from one skinny buttock to the other. Laced his fingers atop the lilac-and-teal horse and its rider.

Roy picked nonexistent lint from the parrot tee.

Roy cracked first.

"It's tragic that people died," he said. "Of course, it is. But my brother and I are simple contractors. We fix things."

"You drive a yellow Toyota Camry. Is that correct, sir?" Deery employed another tactic, the quick segue.

"Yes." Roy sounded genuinely puzzled. "But, meaning no disrespect, so do thousands of other people."

"Your vehicle was spotted near the fire scene."

"What? When?"

"The morning of May twenty-four."

"Not our car." Roy wagged his head so hard I feared an eyeball might fly from a socket. "No way."

"Your Camry has a parking decal on its left rear window and a bumper sticker saying 'I brake for aliens'?"

"What? What?" Simultaneous.

"And there's this." Deery pulled a copy of the photo taken at the second fire location from his pocket and laid it on the unfortunate coffee table.

Ronan sprang from his lounger, snatched it up and looked at the print.

"Let me see that." Roy curled impatient fingers.

Winging the pic to his brother, Ronan dropped back into his chair.

"Where was this photo taken?" Roy asked.

Deery told him.

Roy studied the image a very long time. Trying to recall why his car was at that place on that date? Buying time to construct a cover story?

"Look. Detective. We own a business that operates in DC, Maryland,

and Virginia. We move around, our vehicles move around. Occasionally I allow a friend or employee to drive the Camry. What can I say?" Spreading upturned "what can I say" palms.

Roy and Ronan gazed at us across the fake fur and fake hide, faces innocent as those of scouts selling cookies.

"Can you think of any reason your vehicle was in that area at that time?"

"Maybe we were working a job near there?" Roy looked to Ronan for help.

Ronan shrugged.

"We don't bring our work calendar home with us, but I'd be happy to check," Roy said.

"Do that."

"First thing tomorrow morning."

"Where is your business located, Mr. Stoll?"

"T Street. It's no big deal, just a small garage in the back of a very large building. But it's perfectly situated for our little operation and we've been there for years. We keep some tools, our books, a work van there."

"Let's try an easier one, now. Where were you on the *evening* of Thursday, May twenty-second? *After* work hours?"

"Seriously?" Nervous chuckle. "I hardly remember where I was last night."

Not a twitch of a reaction from Deery.

Again, Roy turned to his brother, brows, hands, and shoulders raised in entreaty.

Eyes performing another theatrical roll, Ronan pulled a smartphone from a breast pocket of his shirt. Lips pursed, he scrolled with one skeletal finger, presumably checking his calendar app.

"Roanoke, Virginia."

"You're saying you were out of town, sir?"

"From late afternoon that Wednesday until midmorning the following Friday."

"Can someone corroborate that?"

"Our grandmother."

"You went on a road trip to Roanoke with your granny?" Skeptical.

"Our grandmother wished to visit her sister. We took her."

"Did you drive there in your Camry?"

"We did not. We felt the Camry would be uncomfortable, so we borrowed a cousin's SUV. They're roomier, you know."

"Where was the Camry?"

"We left it with my cousin."

A beat, then,

"Perhaps you'll have better recall concerning the evening of May twenty-eighth. Last Wednesday."

"That's easy," Roy said. "My brother and I have dinner every Wednesday with our grandmother."

"You two are very good to your granny."

"Is that a question, detective?" Ronan's tone now held all the warmth of a walk-in cooler.

"Our mother died when we were kids," Roy offered, hoping to ease the escalating tension.

"Uh-huh. During what hours were you at your grandmother's home?"

"We usually arrive at six," Roy said. "GrammaSue always opens some excellent wine, and it's a long drive out to Mount Airy, so we usually spend the night."

"You did so on that occasion?"

"We did."

"Your grandmother's name, please?"

"Susan Jane Lipsey." Roy flashed one of his tiny tooth smiles. "The old dear is eighty-eight years old but still goes by Susie. We call her GrammaSue."

"Ms. Lipsey can corroborate that you were with her for the entire night on both the twenty-second and the twenty-eighth of May?"

"It's *Mrs.*" Ronan sniffed and recrossed his legs. "GrammaSue hates being called Ms. Detests the whole concept of hiding one's marital status."

"I'll need *Mrs.* Lipsey's contact information. And that of the cousin who lent you the SUV. And the address of your garage."

Deery dug a Bic and small spiral from a hip pocket and extended them to Roy.

While Roy scribbled, I compared the brothers. Spotted not the tiniest feature to distinguish one from the other.

"Please don't take offense, detective." Roy returned the pen and notebook with an apologetic grin. "My twin can be overly protective when it comes to our grandmother."

His twin raised one offended brow.

I understood Ronan taking offense. But giving Deery the benefit of the doubt, I assumed his use of the term "granny" was meant to bait.

But had he noticed? Deery was a skilled interrogator. Was he an equally good listener?

I couldn't wait to leave. To be alone so I could ask him.

Still, I kept my face totally neutral.

"None taken." Deery rose, pocketed his phone and other belongings, and placed a card on the hippo.

"If you think of anything further, call that number."

I knew there was no way that would happen.

Ronan walked us to the door.

Back in the Durango, Deery was his usual taciturn self.

Before he could start the engine, I said, "You caught it, right?"

"Caught what?" Deery's eyes were on me now.

"Caught that the bastards are lying."

CHAPTER 27

Explain."

"Let me rephrase. I think the brothers know more than they're saying."

"Concerning the fires."

"There you have it."

Deery cocked a questioning brow.

"Roy referred to buildings burning down. How did he know there was more than one? Your use of the singular was brilliant."

Deery neither confirmed nor denied it had been intentional. "Why would they lie?"

"I have no idea." I considered mentioning the peculiar text. Decided it wasn't a good time. "Now what?"

"Most would have missed that," Deery mumbled.

Omygod. Was that a compliment?

"GrammaSue is their alibi," I said, buoyed by what I chose to interpret as positive feedback. "It's time to visit Granny."

"The woman is eighty-eight and most likely asleep."

"Good point. So where do we go from here?"

"You go home."

"What?"

Deery placed a large foot on the brake pedal, pushed the ignition button, then carefully shifted into gear. Judiciously applying pressure to the gas, he eased the Durango out onto Willard.

Knowing argument would be futile, I leaned back in my seat, formulating a plan.

The house was lit like a discount mall at Christmas.

I smelled nothing to indicate action at the stove. Remembered that Lan had Sundays off.

"Ivy?" I called out.

No response.

Dropping my purse on the sideboard, I headed for the kitchen, hoping to find the makings for a sandwich.

A pink paper had been folded in half and taped to the fridge. My name was written on the front flap.

The wording was disjointed, suggesting a message typed in great haste.

> Tempe:
> Sorry. Rushed. Tried to call, no answer.
>   Urgent assignment. Flying to West Virginia STAT. Kid in a mine shaft. Whole country losing its shit.
>   Hate to ask. Can you look after the chinch?
>   Food and instructions by cage in my bathroom. Zanetti OOT with client until Wednesday. (Plus, freaking allergies!)
>   Forever in your debt.
>   Will call if I have signal out in Deliverance Land.
> (If I never return, take the Blahnik pumps.)
>   Ivy

I retrieved my phone and checked for missed calls.

Yep. Two from Ivy.

Crap. A chinchilla?

Every time I thought I might be able to boogie for Charlotte something else came up.

Seriously, Brennan? Leave and abandon your commitment to four murder victims? Miss the opportunity to work with Chuckle Berry Deery?

Ivy had maintained her sense of humor. I vowed to do the same.

Chastised by yet another suck-it-up-girl pep talk, I dug deli meat and cheese from the SubZero and slapped some of each between two slices of bread. After adding mustard and pickles, I parked my creation on a plate and climbed to my room.

Hating to dine alone, I grabbed the remote, clicked on the TV, and scrolled to my old reliable, CNN. The regulars were there, "going straight to the source for the best reporting on the day's biggest stories."

The most current of which involved coverage of Ivy's mine-shaft kid. As I tuned in, the on-scene journalist was speaking directly into the camera, backdropped by dark forest and large equipment lit by powerful floods. Behind him, rescue personnel milled and called to each other under the unnatural illumination.

The man was reporting, probably for the umpteenth time, that a fourteen-year-old boy had fallen into an abandoned coal mine in Marshall County, West Virginia, at approximately four o'clock the previous afternoon. Looking grim, he stated that the shaft was more than five thousand feet deep, that the mine had been closed since 1956, and that the entrance had never been capped. Authorities were uncertain how far down the boy was or the extent of his injuries.

Concluding with the update that there was no update, he handed over to the anchor, a young Black woman looking equally grim. The woman was introducing a representative from the West Virginia Office of Abandoned Mine Lands & Reclamation when my mobile buzz-vibrated.

The name displayed was a shocker.

"Detective Deery," I answered.

"They *are* being untruthful."

"The Stolls?"

"Ronan claimed that he and Roy were in Roanoke, Virginia, from twenty-one through twenty-three May."

"Dates bracketing the first Foggy Bottom fire."

"Earlier in that conversation, Roy reminded his brother that they'd been at home when the Zamzow condo was robbed. I pulled the file. The Zamzow B and E took place on May twenty-two."

"So where were they? DC or Roanoke?"

"They claimed Granny could verify their story."

"We need to talk to Susan Lipsey."

I waited out a ration of nasal breathing. I couldn't tell if Deery was irritated or undecided.

"I caught Roy's slip about multiple fires," I reminded him.

"Seven sharp," he said.

"I'll be ready."

After disconnecting, I went in search of Chuck, thoughts of sharp teeth and zoonotic diseases damping my enthusiasm.

Ivy's room was at the back of the house. Like mine, directly above, its square footage equaled that of a high school gym.

Unlike mine, the décor leaned toward girly romantic. The palette was pink, dusty rose, and lilac. Lots of candles. Lots of ruffle-edged pillows. A flouncy bed skirt.

An enormous painting hung above the white-lacquered headboard, an impressionist angel with wings spread, violin tucked under her chin. I wondered if the work was by Anne Neilson.

The bath was off to the left. Not wishing to intrude on Ivy's privacy, I beelined to it.

Chuck's cage was a split-level affair, with each elevation having platforms of mesh, wood, or plastic. The upper portion, apparently meant for sleeping, had corrugated tubing, a hollowed-out tree trunk, and hammocks hanging from the bars. The lower portion, designed for exercise and dining, had a workout wheel, more tubing, and a boatload of toys. A food dispenser and water bottle hung from one side.

Blue plastic ramps provided access from top to bottom.

Chuck was one pampered rodent.

But where the hell was he?

Drawing close, I spotted the creature burrowed into a mound of torn newspaper on the uppermost level. He remained where he was, observing my every move with large, dark eyes.

I had to admit that, with his velvety gray fur and big rounded ears, Chuck was one cute little mammal. I guessed his weight at maybe two pounds, his length at a little over a foot—ten inches of animal and four inches of tail.

Other than the fact that they came from the Andes, I knew zip about chinchillas. Should I speak to him? In English? Spanish? Quechuan? Out of luck on that last one, buddy.

I noted that the food and water dispensers were empty.

Chuck watched as I filled them, motionless amid his shredded *Post*.

"You good now?" I asked, turning to leave.

Chuck gave what could only be described as a bark.

Surprised, I pivoted back.

"You want company?"

Chuck flicked his tail, eyes never leaving my face.

I dragged a chair over to his cage and we discussed recent events. The Foggy Bottom fires. The tiny subcellar lady. The four upstairs DOAs. Deery. The Stoll brothers. The upcoming interview with Susan Lipsey. The broken icemaker that had rendered my home uninhabitable.

"I think the twins lied," I said, testing how it sounded with the rodent.

Chuck's whiskers twitched.

"Exactly. Why would they do that?"

I described my quarrel with Ryan and the ensuing period of non-communication. Calculated. Seven days, now.

"Am I being childish? Is he?"

Chuck rendered no opinion.

"Should I be angry? Worried?"

If Chuck had a view, he kept it to himself. The chinch wasn't much of a talker.

But he was a helluva listener.

It was past ten by the time I got back to my room. Knowing the next day would start early, I brushed my teeth, did a few other basics, and climbed into bed.

A green dot on the icon indicated a newly arrived text. Clicking on the app, I was surprised to see another unfamiliar number.

With some trepidation, I opened the message.

Dead serious. Drop it!

Below that decidedly unfriendly directive was the same ominous skull emoji.

As before, I tried entering the digits. As before, the number came up as a nonfunctioning line.

WTF?

Was someone threatening me? Ordering me to back off from my investigation? My investigation of what? The Foggy Bottom property? The four fire victims? The subcellar lady in the burlap bag?

This time I vowed to let Deery know.

Somewhat unnerved, my brain would have nothing to do with sleep.

Twenty minutes of sheet-twisting and pillow-punching, then I sat up and turned on the light.

As always, the house was absolutely still.

My book lay on the bedside table. Opening to the page I'd dog-eared—yeah, shoot me—I tried to focus on the story.

My brain would have nothing to do with fiction, either.

My eyes roved the room.

Ivy's triaged photocopies still lined one wall.

Why not? Reading about gangsters beat agitated staring into the dark.

Throwing off the covers, I crossed and sat down on the zebra carpet. As with the novel, I began where I'd left off.

Further perusal of the articles gave me a better sense of how the Warrings shifted from illegal booze to illegal numbers, which they called the commission brokerage business. And of the scale of their success. According to many reports, the brothers were earning millions annually and, as early as 1936, were employing more than fifty people.

Gun battles were a favorite topic of several publications. One colorful series described how six members of the Warring operation, including Rags, were convicted of assault with intent to kill in the shooting of a rival bootlegger.

Most coverage made it clear that, as it was for Al Capone, the IRS was the Warrings' biggest problem. In 1938, the brothers were indicted for conspiring to hide a big chunk of change on their tax returns. Based on the sample of coverage that Ivy had printed, it seemed their trial filled the front pages of every DC paper for almost a year. The proceedings ended in a hung jury.

In 1939, five days into a second trial, Emmitt was accused of bribing both a juror and a US marshal and ended up serving twenty-six months for criminal contempt. Finally, well into a third trial, all three brothers pled guilty.

Did the Warrings' legal woes negatively impact business? Not a chance. By the late forties the boys were raking in at least seven mil annually.

Though of moderate historic interest, accounts of the Warrings' battles with the IRS hardly set my heart racing. *One more story*, I told myself. Then I'd have another go at sleep.

Hoping for variety, I shifted to a different stack.

The item I pulled had appeared in the society section of a paper whose name was deleted in the photocopy process. A wedding announcement comprising seven column inches and a small photo, it was headlined LIPSEY-STOLL.

Coincidence?

Maybe one. But both names?

I read the piece with growing excitement.

The marriage had taken place on August 15, 1982, in Silver Spring, Maryland. Listed were the bride and groom, along with the parents and grandparents on both sides.

Pulse high-stepping, I dialed Lizzie Griesser.

Despite the late hour she was happy to provide a quick tutorial.

I reached for my laptop.

CHAPTER 28

The Durango rolled up precisely at seven.

"Good morning, detective." The day promised to be sunny. I vowed that I would be, too.

Half nodding, Deery hooked a thumb toward two cups bearing the little green Starbucks logo.

"I've made a breakthrough," I said, wiggling the closest coffee free of its center console holder.

"As have I."

Though bursting to share my news, I let Deery go first.

"A judge granted a warrant allowing me access to W-C Commerce." The man came as close to effusive as I believe he was capable.

"The holding company that owns the two Foggy Bottom properties that were torched."

"W-C stands for Warring-Clock."

That surprised me. I thought the second initial would turn out to represent Warring's associate, Bill Cady.

I lifted the small flap on the cup's plastic lid and took a tentative sip. Flinched as the scalding liquid touched my lip.

Clock. Where had I heard that name?

Before my brain could cough up an answer, Deery provided one.

"Amon Clock was a Warring henchman who went by the nickname Alarm."

"Yes! Alarm Clock dated a woman named Doris Gardner." Disparate data bytes were toggling in my brain. "Gardner was killed during a shoot-out between Clock and a rival bootlegger."

"Mmm." Dismissive? "The relevant fact is that the sole living partner in W-C Commerce is Lloyd Emmitt Warring."

"Lew. The man gunned down in his driveway last week."

"The fires. The shooting. It's become clear that someone is targeting the Warrings. What remains *unclear* is the reason. When I get to the why, I will get to the who."

"I may have made a breakthrough with regard to motive."

Deery regarded me with a face locked into skeptical angles.

"Doris Gardner died in 1944, leaving behind two daughters, Susan, age eight, and Sally, age six. In 1954, Susan Gardner married a man named Roger Lipsey. In 1961, the Lipseys had a daughter, Marilyn. Marilyn Lipsey married a man named Fenton Stoll and, in 1983, gave birth to your favorite twins, Roy and Ronan."

"You know this how?"

I told him about the Lipsey-Stoll wedding announcement and my subsequent online research. One brow lifted slightly. In surprise? Approval?

"Doris is the great-grandmother of Ronan and Roy." Deery grasped the link right away.

"Yes."

"The twins who maintain a rather casual relationship with the truth."

"Yes."

"Susan Lipsey is their grandmother."

"And their alibi."

"Are you suggesting the arson and the drive-by are connected to Doris Gardner's murder eighty years ago?"

"I'm suggesting they could be."

"In your scenario, who is the doer?"

I shrugged. Who knows?

A moment of silence, then Deery's eyes went needle thin. "I'm looking forward to our little talk with GrammaSue."

Our?

Don't read too much into that, Brennan.

Deery did his measured walk-through to get the car moving. Then we were off to Mount Airy.

Knowing that the drive would take forever with Detective Dragass at the wheel, I pulled out my cellphone to pass the time. A bit of googling produced several interesting factoids.

Mount Airy, Maryland, lies roughly sixty miles north of DC and thirty-five miles west of Baltimore. Its main street—not surprisingly called Main Street—straddles the Carroll and Frederick County lines. The town has a population just under ten thousand. The little burg exists due to its elevation.

Explanation. In 1830, when the B&O Railroad was attempting to connect the cities of Baltimore and Frederick, engineers concluded that a nearby ridge was too high for trains to navigate. The lines were laid two miles to the south and, as a result, Mount Airy was born. The town's name had something to do with cold wind chilling a brakeman's ears.

By looping through a warren of sites and message boards, I got the sense that entering the twenty-first century wasn't a popular idea with many Mount Airy residents. Nevertheless, all the usual players were present—Walmart, Safeway, TJMaxx. You get the picture. Keep my burg quaint but assure me discount pickles and sandals.

We'd just crossed into Maryland when my mobile buzzed in my hand.

"Dr. Thacker," I answered, seeing the name on caller ID. "How can I help you?"

"I got tox results back on the four Foggy Bottom DOAs. Thought you might be interested."

"Definitely." I meant it. But I was also suspicious of Thacker's real motive for calling. Did she have additional cases in need of external review? A desire for written reports on the files I'd already read?

"I'll keep this brief. Hill was clean. Not so much as an aspirin."

"The young Canadian woman."

"Yes. Green and Star both had traces of coke and high blood alcohol levels. El-Aman had alcohol and Xanax on board."

"Wasn't el-Aman Muslim?"

"When the cat's away, as the saying goes."

"No wonder they all slept through the fire."

"All except Hill."

"Right." Thacker had allowed me to listen to a recording of the girl's desperate 911 call. It still broke my heart to imagine the terror of her last moments.

"Unless there's something else you need, I'll be releasing the bodies today," Thacker said.

"The families will be pleased."

"Anything more on the subcellar remains?"

"I'm waiting for a call back from a colleague in Virginia."

"The genetic genealogist?"

"Yes."

"Here's hoping that doesn't blow too big a hole in my budget."

"Thanks for the update," I said.

Though I knew Deery had been listening—stilled movement, lowered breathing—he kept his eyes on the road, his questions to himself.

The address Roy provided took us to an elm- and poplar-shaded block two turns off Main Street and not far from Mount Airy's small downtown area. A mix of old brick bungalows and older one- and two-story frame houses lined both sides. An auto repair shop took up part of the far end on the southeast corner.

Deery pulled to the curb beside a cop's old tried-and-true. A fire hydrant.

The sun was beaming, the day growing warm. Only a few bits of gray fluff marred an otherwise flawless blue sky.

So why the cold prickle spreading across my skin?

Apprehension? Déjà vu?

Ignoring this most recent of my hindbrain's curious alerts, I focused on Susan Lipsey's home.

It was another Victorian, similar to the one that had burned in Foggy Bottom. Same fish-scale shingled roof. Same recessed and spindled second-story niches. Same high-peaked gables. Same round corner tower topped with turret and finial. The color scheme here was mustard and brown.

A wide front porch stretched the breadth of the first floor, ending in a roofed gazebo on the far right. Through leaf-plastered screening, I saw stacked lawn furniture and a collection of empty terra-cotta pots.

I followed Deery up a walkway bordered by thick, thistly bushes and climbed a balustraded staircase to a glossy brown front door. The buzzer made a tinny bleating sound when encouraged by Deery's thumb. No bonging church bells for GrammaSue.

A very short wait, then a muted voice, deep and raspy, posed the anticipated question.

"Who's there?"

"Police, Mrs. Lipsey. Please open up."

To my surprise, a dead bolt *shicked*, the lever handle dived, and the door swung in on its chain.

The woman was tall and, despite her advanced years, well-muscled in a loose, fleshy way. Her hair was snowy, her skin so pale it seemed almost translucent. She had no brows or lashes, but several long white hairs corkscrewed from her corrugated upper lip.

A shapeless apricot housecoat draped her large frame, flattering as a hospital gown on a corpse. A pocket in a side hem bulged with a collection of items whose purpose I could only imagine. Phone? Keys? Inhaler? Stanley Cup?

Crimson polish added color to the woman's nails. Neon blue and orange HOKAs added inches to her already impressive height.

"ID?" she demanded through the narrow space she'd created.

Deery badged her.

The woman read the shield, smoke drifting across her face from an unfiltered Camel squeezed between the knobby fingers of one blue-veined hand. After mumbling words I didn't catch, she closed the gap, disengaged the chain, and opened the door wide.

"You are Mrs. Susan Lipsey?" Deery asked.

"Not sure that's your business." Defiant.

Deery's face went stony.

"The boys said you'd be comin' to grill me." Though red-rimmed and watery, Lipsey's eyes were the same gold-flecked hazel as those of her grandsons.

"May we come in?" Deery asked.

"I got a choice?" Welcoming as a straight-arm.

"No."

"You carryin' any airborne viruses I can catch? Covid? RSV?"

"No, ma'am."

"At my age, you gotta be careful."

"Of course."

Lipsey dropped then crushed her Camel with one well-cushioned heel, then bent to scoop the butt into her palm. Taking one backward step, she indicated that we could enter.

I noted that she didn't question my role. Assumed my presence had been part of the boys' heads-up.

The air inside smelled of decades of fried food. Of laundry left too long in a washer.

Just beyond the door, a three-panel gilt-framed mirror leaned at a cockeyed angle against a baseboard, either fallen from a wall or waiting to be hung. While passing, I caught triptych snapshots of myself. White jeans. Chambray shirt. OluKai sandals. Anxious face.

The décor was a gloomy affair, all somber wallpapers, carpets, and drapes. Heavy brass fixtures overhead, dark hardwoods underfoot, here and there covered by a threadbare area rug. I knew that signs of wear could indicate carpets with history and value. These sad puppies just looked old.

Pocket treasures clanking and rustling, sneakers squeaking like an athlete's crossing a gym, Lipsey led us down a hall to a solarium pooching out from the rear of the first floor. The small sunroom had top-to-bottom windows on three sides, a cathedral ceiling, a black-and-white tile floor. A jungle of vegetation waterfalled from hanging baskets and blossomed from freestanding pots.

Deery and I dropped into wicker armchairs, once white, now dead fish gray, the pattern on their cushions faded and unrecognizable. Lipsey sat on the matching sofa.

I've picked up certain competencies over the years. Horticulture and gardening are not among them. I could identify philodendra, pothos, and Boston ferns, all species I'd killed in the course of my lifetime. The remaining flora was a mystery to me.

Early-morning sunlight filtered gently through the grime-coated glass. The air carried a pleasant earthy scent.

Until Lipsey dug her pack of Camels from the pocket jumble, slid a book of matches from beneath the cellophane, and lit up. The acrid mix of nicotine, carbon monoxide, and tar soon overrode the aromas of greenery and moist soil.

"May I record our conversation?" Deery asked, waggling his phone.

"You're assumin' we'll have one."

"Is that consent, Mrs. Lipsey?"

No response.

"Ma'am?"

Eyes hard, the old woman quipped, "You tell me."

Though in her late eighties, it was clear that Susan Lipsey wouldn't be short-listing herself for a retirement home anytime soon.

Deery glared at the old woman.

Lipsey glared back.

As per Deery's directive, I continued to hold my tongue.

For a very long moment, silence filled the small space, punctured only by Lipsey's wheezy breathing and a rhythmic ticking.

Tic.

Tic.

Tic.

My eyes ran a quick circuit. Noted water dripping from a hanging fern into a plastic container below.

Tic.

Tic

Tic.

"May I begin, ma'am?" Deery engaged the recorder on his phone.

Lipsey raised the Camel's burning tip upright. Eyes crimped, she watched the red glow nibble tobacco and paper.

"I'm here about a fire that took place in the Foggy Bottom area of Washington, DC," Deery began, voice flat.

Lipsey took a deep drag. Exhaled slowly. Focused on the pale gray cone she'd sent into the air.

Why the hostility? I wondered. Did the old woman's animosity stem from a general distrust of law enforcement? Or, like her grandsons, was Susan Lipsey hiding something?

"When?" she asked, rheumy eyes fixed on the cloud disintegrating in front of her face.

"When what?" Like the smoke, Deery's patience was disappearing fast.

"When do you know when you've had enough? Done enough?"

"I'm sorry, ma'am. I don't understand."

"Is it just before you succeed? Just after?"

"I'd like—" Deery started.

"Ask me. It's right before the reaper takes to eyeballing your ass. And lately, I feel his crosshairs on mine."

Lipsey flicked the remains of her cigarette toward the fern's catch basin. The butt hit the water with a soft *hiss*.

"So. It's your lucky day, detective. I'm gonna give it to you straight."

What followed shocked me to the core.

CHAPTER 29

In looking back, I'm never certain of the exact sequence of events that morning.

But I'll never forget that old woman's voice.

"It wasn't that I didn't get my fair share in life," she began. "I didn't get crapola."

Deery said nothing.

"After Ma died, we were on our own."

"You and Sally."

"No. Me and Eleanor Roosevelt."

"I understand relatives took you in," Deery said, ignoring Lipsey's sarcasm.

"You talkin' Aunt Laura and Uncle Clarence? Nice job pokin' down that rat hole. If you've done proper detecting, *detective*, you know they weren't no kin at all."

"Seems an act of kindness to assume responsibility for two young girls."

"Kindness. Yeah. We can go with that."

The rheumy eyes clouded with something unreadable. Then it was gone.

Sadness?

Resentment?

Hatred?

"I been on my own since Jesus did his little Lazarus act."

"What happened to your guardians?"

I was certain Deery had researched the couple. Assumed he was trying to push Lipsey toward some edge.

"Dead when I was sixteen."

"Your sister, Sally?"

"Dead."

"Your daughter, Marilyn?"

"Bad heart. Never made it to forty."

"Your husband?"

"Roger?" Lipsey laughed, a wet, braying sound. Until the laugh turned into a coughing fit. Digging a tissue from her pocket, she blew her nose loudly.

"That peckerhead reached his high-water mark when he learned not to shit his diapers."

"Where's Roger now?"

"No freakin' clue."

"You have your grandsons."

"Don't you dare talk about my grandsons." Suddenly cold and tire-iron hard. "And, for the record, Ma didn't just up and die. She was *murdered.*"

"Doris ran with a rough crowd."

"The world's a rough place."

"Not everyone chooses to hang with gangsters."

The withered lips compressed so tightly their edges blanched. A flush spread over the pale cheeks.

"My mother didn't deserve to die." Lipsey's glare—aimed at Deery—had gone fierce enough to break bones.

Deery responded with his favorite. Silence.

Unlike most interviewees, Lipsey didn't fall for the ploy.

Tic.

Tic.

Tic.

Other than the slow cascade of drops, the only sound was Lipsey's breathing, wheezy through nostrils thick with white hairs.

Tic

Tic.

Tic.

I risked an oblique glance toward Deery.

His eyes never let go of Lipsey.

Tic.

Tic.

Tic.

I swallowed. Inhaled. Swallowed again.

The silence grew long.

Deery finally broke it.

"Your mother was with Amon Clock the day she was killed. Clock was an associate of the Warring brothers."

"Pond scum. All of them."

"When you and your sister were orphaned, Clock never reached out to help," Deery guessed.

"The spineless toady always did the Warrings' bidding."

"A member of the Warring family ordered Clock not to help with your upbringing?"

"You got it."

"Do you know that for a fact?" Deery asked.

"I know for a fact that those people are egotistical, vindictive bastards, always thinking they're better than me and my kin and never missing a chance to stick it to us."

"So you're out for revenge," Deery deduced further. "It's been eighty years. Why now?"

"You're damn right it's been eighty years. Eighty years of torment and humiliation."

Deery opened his mouth to follow up, but Lipsey was on a roll.

"When my daughter got sick, she couldn't get the right medical care because the Warrings took away our insurance. When my husband's business was going under, we found out it was because the Warrings had cut a sweeter deal with the main supplier and left the business high and dry. When my grandsons went to the new school in town, the Warring boys were there to make sure they were taunted."

I shot a quick look at Deery, wondering what he was thinking. Lipsey's litany of Warring offenses seemed almost cartoonishly cruel. My mind spun with a half dozen questions related to why Lipsey hadn't long before packed up her family and herself and moved a thousand miles away. Inwardly, I sighed. No matter how bad it is, sometimes people just prefer to dig in and seethe.

"So you set fire to the Foggy Bottom properties and had Lew Warring shot."

"You've got nothing points to me."

"You didn't do it yourself," Deery said. "You used your grandsons."

Tic.

Tic.

Tic.

A sucking noise overrode the dripping as Lipsey took another long drag. I noticed that the hand holding the cigarette was trembling.

The tension in the room was thick enough to roast in a pan.

Lipsey's gaze crawled to me.

I looked deep into the hazel eyes. Saw nothing behind them. No anger. No joy. No buzz that comes with the thrill of engagement. They were empty, like those of a lizard sunning on a mudbank.

Tic.

Tic.

Tic.

Lipsey lifted one hand to rub at her forehead. A distraction, as she slid the other sideways across her lap.

Too late, I realized what was happening.

Before I could warn Deery, the old woman drew an object from the five-and-dime collection in her dress pocket.

My heart kicked into high gear.

Clutched in the gnarled fingers was a .38 Special snub-nosed revolver. A pink lady. Identical to the one my sister, Harry, owned.

The muzzle was pointed at the center of my chest.

Cold fear slithered into my gut.

Head motionless, I slid my eyes sideways.

Deery's gaze remained fixed on Lipsey, his expression neutral.

"You don't want to do that," he said, voice low and steady.

"Says who?"

"You know the consequences."

"I'm eighty-eight."

"Who would look out for Roy and Ronan?"

"Didn't I say never mention my grandsons?" Harsh as a buzz saw.

"You did."

"Yet I hear their names comin' off your cop tongue!" A vein throbbed in her forehead.

It was as if a spigot had suddenly been turned. The spike from rational to manic was shocking. And terrifying.

And very familiar.

All her adult life my mother suffered from a condition that held her captive to seismic and unpredictable mood swings. The name of the disorder changed over the years, but the mercurial pattern never loosened its grip. Recognizing that Lipsey was exhibiting similar symptoms, fueled by an additional underbelly of paranoia, I knew argument was pointless.

Not fully appreciating the level of Lipsey's mental instability, Deery continued to press.

"I don't—"

Eyes filled with murderous rage, Lipsey swung the gun toward the detective and pulled the trigger. The sound ricocheting off glass and tile was deafening.

The bullet entered Deery's chest, sending a spray of blood into the air. Letting loose a low groan, he slumped sideways onto the sofa.

Before I could reach out, his body slid from the threadbare cushion. His head hit the floor with a sickening crack.

Adrenaline shot through me so fast my mind short-circuited. Still, some lucid faction of neurons did the math.

It would take me six steps to reach Lipsey. I'd have to grab her hand, maybe break it, and wrestle the gun free. Plenty of time for the old hag to empty a round into my sternum.

I remained frozen in place.

It was a good call. In a nanosecond the pink lady was again leveled on me.

Placing her free hand on one knee, Lipsey pushed to her sportyingly shod feet.

I held motionless, now looking up at the pink-cloaked two-inch barrel. Beside my right ankle, spittle dribbled from a corner of Deery's mouth. A crimson stream oozed from below his torso.

"Now what?" I asked quietly.

"Now I blow your bony ass to kingdom come." Waving the pistol back and forth in front of my face.

"Before you do that, may I tell you a curious thing to come out of the Foggy Bottom fire?"

I knew that six inches from my right foot, Deery had a spare strapped to his ankle. I wanted to distract Lipsey so I could make a grab for his piece.

"Four people got killed," she said. "That sucks, but it was never my intent. Life is timing."

"We recovered five bodies," I said.

"Yeah?" Curious, despite herself.

I told her about the tiny subcellar lady. She listened, arthritic grip tightening and loosening on the handle of the .38.

"So who the hell is she?"

"I'm not sure."

"How'd she end up in a burlap bag in a basement?"

"Her skull was fractured, and her jaw was broken." Lowering my voice to a conspiratorial whisper. "She was murdered." I didn't really know that, but hoped the melodrama would draw Lipsey in.

"Why the bloody hell are you telling me this?"

"I think the killer was a member of the Foggy Bottom Gang." Another lie for survival.

"One of the Warrings?"

I nodded, grim.

Tic.

Tic.

Shush.

Tic.

Movement behind me?

My expression held, giving no indication that I was totally focused on listening.

My ears picked up nothing but dripping, erratic now.

Had I imagined the sound?

Lipsey took a step left, then right, gun steady on my chest, reptile eyes glued to mine. Then she centered herself in front of me.

"You're making this up," she said.

"I'm not."

"Why's this old-timey murder your concern?"

"I'm a scientist. I'm looking for the truth."

Shush.

"You're full of crap." One bony finger slid from the pistol's handle to curl around the trigger.

"I'm not," I said. "You despise the Foggy Bottom Gang for what they did to your mother. I despise them for what they did to that small, defenseless woman."

Shush.

Lipsey caught it this time. Her gaze went over my shoulder.

A good moment to make a grab for the gun?

No, the neurons screamed. She's nuts but alert. Ready to fire.

I heard a short high squeak behind me. A rubber sole scraping?

Lipsey's chin jerked up. "Roy?"

"It's Ronan."

"What the hell are you doing here, boy?" Clearly, Lipsey was not a welcome-them-with-open-arms-any-time kind of granny. "I didn't invite you today."

"Why are you pointing a gun at that lady?" Ronan's voice was quivery.

From where he stood, Ronan couldn't see my face. Or the detective bleeding out at my feet.

"That's none of your business," Lipsey snapped.

"Are you having one of your spells, GrammaSue? Did you forget to take your meds?"

"Snake oil. I don't need that crap."

"Why are you agitated?"

"You know why. Those bloodsuckers struck again."

"It's all right. We'll find another place to rent space."

"You and Roy have put your hearts and souls into your business. You've worked out of that place for decades. That bastard bought the building just so he could evict you. So he could drive more nails into our coffins."

"We don't know that's the case."

I heard Ronan's cautious footfalls as he circled the couch. His sharp gulp of air upon seeing Deery.

"Jesus Christ! GrammaSue. Did you shoot this guy?"

"No. The man from UNCLE showed up and capped him for me."

Ronan stared at his grandmother, mind working through a labyrinth of twisted possibilities. A very long moment of shocked horror, then he stepped toward the old woman, one hand extended.

"Give me the gun, GrammaSue."

"Why?"

"I'll finish this for you."

My gut went cold—cold, terrified, and empty.

"Not a chance. You don't have the bubbies for it."

"Hand it over, GrammaSue."

"Back off."

Ronan lunged, grabbed her elbow, and shot that arm upward into the tendrils of a hanging plant. Making a noise somewhere between a snarl and a hiss, the old woman threw her shoulders forward and down. Ronan curled over her bent torso, attempting to wrench the gun from her grasp.

Before I could react, a second explosion shattered the stillness.

Lipsey collapsed, pistol still clutched in her hand.

Squatting, Ronan gently pried the weapon from his grandmother's lifeless fingers.

He held almost a full minute, back and shoulders softly convulsing in tremors. Then he rose on shaky legs.

Tears running down his cheeks, he swiveled to face me, the .38 clutched in his right hand.

My diaphragm clenched in panic.

CHAPTER 30

Two fitful nights of dark, convoluted dreams. A man's lifeless form sending red Rorschach blossoms onto grimy black-and-white tile. An old woman crumpling like an unstrung puppet. A skinny man running hard beyond pollution-smudged glass. Grim-faced EMTs. Rolling gurneys. Ambulances and police cruisers flashing red-blue. Red-blue. Red-blue.

Two anxious days of checking my phone. Lunging for the thing every time it rang.

Finally, the calls I nervously awaited. Good news on two fronts.

Deery was out of danger. Lipsey would survive.

A bullet had entered each in the fleshy part of the upper chest, hooked a turn at the clavicle, and exited near the base of the neck. Neither projectile had struck a major vessel.

Weird parallels, but some significant differences. Deery's trajectory was front to back, his wound superficial. Lipsey's path was back to front and deeper, resulting in more extensive damage.

Good news on three fronts, actually.

Ryan called the night of the events in Lipsey's greenhouse. Asleep in my bed at Ivy's house—thanks to an ER doc's pharmaceuticals and the silencer on my phone—I failed to answer.

I listened to Ryan's message the following morning.

Tempe, you won't believe what an idiot I am. I was so fâché that you canceled on me, I tagged along last minute on a fishing trip to Lac Mabille with a couple of SQ buddies. When I finally cooled down, we were so far off the grid there was no signal and the plane didn't return for five days. Je suis désolé, ma chérie. I'm back in Montreal. Call me. S'il vous plaît.

His frenzied bilingual sincerity brought tears to my eyes.

Or maybe that was due to an Ambien hangover.

Whatever.

I'd phoned Ryan as fast as my fingers could tap the digits. We'd had a sappy it-was-my-fault-no-it-was-my-fault conversation. He'd described his flight to Goose Bay, his subsequent hydroplane landing on the lake, the eighty-four trout they'd caught. Those parts sounded like fun. The blackflies and mosquitoes, not so much.

Unsure how current Ryan was, I'd recounted all the developments of the past two weeks. The Foggy Bottom fires. The four upstairs vics. The yellow Camry leading to the Stoll brothers. Susan Lipsey's rant implying that, as part of her vendetta against the Warrings, she'd directed her grandsons to torch the buildings and carry out the drive-by. Ronan Stoll accidentally shooting his grandmother in the greenhouse.

Ryan listened without interrupting or indicating that he already knew some of what I was telling him. When I'd finished, he cursed in complicated Québecois, as expected. Asked if I was truly unhurt, as expected. I said I was fine.

A long moment, then Ryan queried my progress on the tiny sub-cellar lady. The odd segue surprised me. A quick change-up to allow him to quash his anger at learning that I'd been in danger? I admitted that, sadly, I'd learned nothing more about her identity or manner of death.

"Why now?" he asked after a pause.

"Why now what?" Ryan had lost me.

"Lipsey's mother was killed eighty years ago. What set her off now?"

"According to Ronan—"

"The grandson."

"Yes. According to him, Lipsey has held a lifelong grudge. He and his brother were raised on anti-Warring vitriol and he himself is convinced the Warrings had a vendetta against their family. Three weeks ago, he and Roy got an eviction notice because their landlord had sold the building that houses their business. Relocation meant they'd take a disastrous financial hit."

"Let me guess. Lew Warring bought the property to add to his W-C portfolio."

"Bingo. Roy or Ronan shared the bad news with Grandma, who is bipolar and had recently gone off her meds. She snapped. The twins had been brainwashed sufficiently and were angry enough about having to move that they went along with her scheme for revenge. But only in part. Thinking the Foggy Bottom buildings were empty, they agreed to set the fires, planning to cause only minor damage."

"They killed Lew Warring?"

"Ronan says they meant to merely scare Warring and then lie to the old lady. Something went wrong, and their target ended up dead."

"Do you think the Warrings actually did repeatedly harm Lipsey and her family? Did Lew actually buy that building specifically to evict the twins? Or was it all paranoia?"

"We'll probably never know. But Lipsey believed it and managed to persuade her grandsons."

Ryan asked if I was still in Washington. I told him that I was, and apologized because I had to stay until Ivy returned or the chinch was retrieved. The latter required some explanation.

I asked Ryan if he'd ever been to the bonsai museum. He replied in the negative. Saying that was a serious breach in his personal development, I suggested he meet me in DC.

I said I'd call Ivy for an update on her ETA as soon as we'd disconnected and offered to book us into a romantic hotel. He explained that he was committed to helping clean his share of the four-score fish but promised to fly to DC on Friday.

So.

First things first. Clearing my getaway date.

Ivy answered quickly.

"Tempe. Lucky girl." In the background, the same grinding machinery and shouted commands.

"Why so?" I asked.

"You're in the middle of the action and I'm stuck in West goddam Virginia."

"Isn't the rescue going well?"

The story was still national news. To date the kid had been down in the mine for four days. Packets of food and water were being lowered to him. Blankets. A first aid kit. A two-way radio that the kid was using to communicate with those up top.

"A team is drilling a parallel shaft, but one thing after another keeps going wrong."

"The boy seems in good spirits."

"He is. But his parents are in serious need of controlled substances. What's up?"

"I'm wondering when Chuck's owner will be coming to collect him."

A long moment passed. A moment I guessed Ivy was using to structure an unpopular response.

"I was going to ring you about that."

I waited, apprehensive.

"My friend's father—the friend who owns Chuck—has taken a turn for the worse. The doctors think this could be it."

"That was fast."

"Cancer is a mean bastard."

"It is."

"She's worried about Chuck but doesn't know exactly when she'll get home."

"What about Ben?"

"I'd ask him, of course, but he's out of town for the rest of the week. And a chinchilla really would trigger his allergies."

"When will *you* be back?"

"Here's the thing. The network liked my on-site reporting, so they've asked me to do a series on abandoned mines, the hazards they pose to the environment, to public safety, that angle. Did you know there are over forty-eight thousand abandoned coal mines in the US?"

"I didn't." A sinking feeling was overtaking me.

"This could be my big break, Tempe."

Where had I heard that before?

"Ryan is flying to DC to join me the day after tomorrow," I said. "We'd like—"

"Of course!" Chirpy as a sparrow in a sprinkler. "You're both welcome to stay at my house for as long as you like."

"Perhaps you could find—"

"Words can't express how much I appreciate this. Chuck texted this morning to tell me he adores you. Said that in his fantasy life he'd live with you always."

"How's that work, what with the tiny claws and all?"

"He uses gloves with touch-screen tips."

"Uh-huh." Rolling my eyes, though no one could see.

"You'll need to buy more food. I owe you, girl."

"You do."

Sibley Memorial Hospital has been serving the sick and injured in our nation's capital since 1890. Staff and patients from those early days would be gobsmacked at the size of the complex today.

A multi-pavilioned, red brick and glass Goliath, Sibley sprawls above the intersection of MacArthur Boulevard and Loughboro Road, in Northwest DC, not far from the American University campus. The parking garage is the size of an airport terminal.

I pulled in shortly after eleven. Found a spot after circling upward so high I feared a nosebleed. Sharing an elevator with an obese woman holding an unruly toddler, two nuns, and a kid trying—with limited success—to control a bouquet of balloons, I descended, crossed to the portico-shaded walkway, and entered the main building.

The tiled lobby gleamed with an enthusiasm equal to that at the ME's office. People waited in gray vinyl chairs, drinking soda, slumping, or fidgeting impatiently. Signs routed patrons to the cafeteria, gift shop, business office, and myriad medical departments. Pediatrics. Urology. Radiology. Oncology.

An information counter faced the glass doors through which I'd entered. The receptionist, an elderly woman wearing lipstick the color of a baboon's butt, offered a smile whose brightness rivaled that of the flooring.

I gave her Deery's name.

As her fingers worked a keyboard the smile dissolved.

"I'm so sorry, miss, but that patient is cleared for visits only by family and police officials." Looking genuinely regretful.

"Oh, no." Feigning devastation. "May I have these sent up to him?"

Raising the nosegay of daisies and tulips I'd purchased for such a possibility.

"Of course. Let me have them."

Baboon Lips reached out and I handed the flowers to her.

I stepped away, then turned back as if suddenly struck by an afterthought. As I hoped, she'd written a room number on a Post-it and stuck it to the florist's green outer wrapper.

Room 716.

Exiting the elevator on the seventh floor, I needed no direction. Halfway down the corridor, past a station occupied by nurses and orderlies indifferent to my presence, a uniformed cop sat on a folding chair reading a copy of that day's *Post*.

I walked toward him, my reflection winking in the small rectangular windows of at least a dozen closed doors. Hearing heels clicking his way, the cop turned his head, then pushed to his feet. His name tag said F. Rassmussen.

After checking my ID, F. Rassmussen pulled out his phone, scrolled, then looked up puzzled.

"You're not on my list, ma'am." Tone neither friendly nor unfriendly.

"Seriously? It must be a mistake. They gave me his room number downstairs at reception." A stretch, but close.

"You're family?"

"Mm."

One long, dubious look, then F. Rassmussen nodded and stepped aside.

"Leave it ajar."

Half expecting a "don't try anything funny" follow-up, I opened the door and went into the room.

Deery was propped up in bed dozing. A bulky construction of gauze and tape wrapped one side of his neck, forcing his head left at an awkward angle. A needle infused liquids into a vein in one wrist.

Not wanting to wake him, I settled into the single visitor chair. Scrolled through recent emails and texts on my mobile.

Every now and then I glanced up to watch lines jump their erratic zigzag patterns on a machine monitoring Deery's vitals. Oversized hands and feet aside, he wasn't a large man. But somehow his body looked smaller than normal. Shrunken. Maybe it was an illusion created by the cast-off glow of the screen.

Time passed.

Muted hospital sounds drifted in through the cracked door. A gurney or cart rattling by in the hall. An elevator bonging its arrival. A speaker paging a code or a name.

Inside the room, just Deery's steady breathing and the soft pinging of the sensors.

"What time is it?"

"Almost noon." His words startled me. "How are you feeling?"

"Fit as a fiddle. Weren't but a scratch."

"I'm glad to hear that. When can you leave?"

"Waiting on paperwork. They don't release me by three, I'm pulling a runner."

"Mm."

"Raise me up more." Twirling a finger at the controls clipped to the bed rail.

"Are you sure? Maybe I should call a nurs—"

"Raise it."

I did.

When fully elevated, Deery gestured that I drag my chair closer to him. I did that, too.

"So Granny was driving the train." Deery's voice was strong, but his mouth moved stiffly.

"She was."

"Where is the old bat?" he asked, obviously referring to Lipsey.

"One floor up. The docs say she'll make it. The ambulances brought you both here because the hospital in Mount Airy was pushed to its limits with the victims of a multi-vehicle crash."

"And the scumbucket grandsons?" Harsh for Deery, who rarely cussed.

"Still in the wind. Their pictures are everywhere and there's a BOLO out on the Camry. It shouldn't take long to net them."

Deery nodded.

I was about to elaborate when the door swung wide, and a nurse pushed a cart into the room. On seeing me, she tensed.

"How did you get in here?"

Having no good response, I said nothing.

"This patient is only cleared for authorized visitors." Face obsidian hard. "Out with you, now."

"Of course."

I stood.

"I'm here 'cause I'm a cop," Deery barked to my retreating back. "Not cause the wound is bad."

Back in my car, I did a Google search for nearby pet stores. Found many, including Doggy Style, The Big Bad Woof, and Howl to the Chief. Struck out repeatedly when I called to inquire about chinchilla chow.

With one exception. The place wasn't exactly around the corner, but at least Chuck wouldn't go hungry. Punching the address into my navigation system, I headed toward 7th Street.

Twenty minutes after leaving Sibley Memorial I pulled to the curb outside of a Petco. I'd just shifted into park when my eyes registered a scene that kicked my pulse up a notch.

Sweet Jesus on a pancake.

Was I mistaken?

CHAPTER 31

I stared, making sure I wasn't wrong.

I wasn't.

Was I?

Ben Zanetti—maybe Ben Zanetti?—was striding down the walk skirting the west side of the Petco, a Wizards cap on his head, a hefty package cradled in his left arm. Clinging to his right arm was a woman who couldn't possibly have closed out her twenties. A woman whose sense of style leaned toward "look at me."

The woman's hair was bleached platinum, shag cut, and dyed flamingo pink at the tips. Her arms were inked from the wrist to the point where each disappeared into the sleeve of a tee declaring, *Let me pour you a tall glass of get over it.* The ear I could see was loaded with enough metal to open a hardware store. A touch of whimsy that blended nicely with the eyebrow ring.

A bee blundered against my windshield. Danced across the glass, either stunned or confused. Gathered itself and flew off.

My recovery wasn't happening that fast.

Realizing that I'd been holding my breath, I let the air out slowly.

I watched Maybe Zanetti and Pink Tips cross to an ancient Ford Focus with a sombrero-wearing mouse dangling from the rearview mirror. Using his remote key to open the trunk, Zanetti leaned forward to toss in the parcel.

Pink Tips caressed his bent back and spoke words I couldn't make out.

Shrugging off her gesture, Maybe Zanetti straightened. Though the cap's bill kept his upper face in shadow, a taut twist of one corner of his mouth suggested a scowl.

Pink Tips reached up to stroke his cheek.

Maybe Zanetti batted away her wrist.

I needed no audio to know she barked *"fuck you."*

Flipping a two-finger bird, Pink Tips stomped to the passenger-side door, yanked it open, and threw herself into the seat. Slamming the trunk, Maybe Zanetti pivoted, body tense as a coiled spring. His shadowed gaze swept the asphalt and the vehicles surrounding the Focus. Hesitated a moment on mine.

A wave of queasiness rose up into my throat.

Had he recognized my Mazda? Seen me?

Wordlessly, Maybe Zanetti folded his very long legs behind the wheel and cranked the car's engine.

I watched the battered Ford gun from its spot, leaves and pebbles spitting from its badly worn tires.

Shock jockeyed with confusion.

Was the man in the cap really Ivy's fiancé? Ben Zanetti drove a Range Rover, not a Ford. And he'd told Ivy he'd be away from DC all week.

The curly black hair. The six-foot-six frame. It had to be Zanetti.

And the body language was unmistakable. Zanetti and Pink Tips were quarreling, but her gesture made it clear they were more than just friends.

Anger surged up from my chest and pounded in my temples.

The bastard was two-timing Ivy with a pierced and bleached bimbo half his age.

Closing my eyes, I did a full minute of yogic breathing.

In. Out. In. Out.

Images of Ivy and Zanetti together did slow somersaults across my mind: snuggling in a single lounger while watching late-night TV, frying eggs and bacon at the stove, laughing at peas spilled on the kitchen floor.

All the way home I debated what to do.

Tell Ivy that the love of her life was a deceitful son of a bitch? Keep quiet and hope she discovered his cheating on her own?

I liked neither option.

The house was still as a church on a Tuesday morning.

No Lan.

No Zanetti.

Chuck was busy doing whatever it was he did with his shredded newspaper. He abandoned the project when I appeared and set his chow on the floor by his cage.

"Do I tell her?" I asked.

His whiskers did something probably meaningful to him.

"You're right. But what if the guy wasn't Zanetti?"

One furry ear flicked. The rodent equivalent of lifting an "I'd be careful" brow?

To take my mind off thoughts of kicking Zanetti's nads into his brainpan, I climbed to my room, got online, selected the Tripadvisor icon in my bookmarks, and entered the keywords "inns," "lodges," and "Washington DC." Found nothing that appealed to me.

My heart just wasn't in it. I'd planned to ask Ivy for suggestions about romantic getaways in the area, but now that didn't feel right.

I fidgeted, antsy. Swiveled in my chair, wondering what to do with my empty afternoon.

My gaze fell on the sorted and stacked photocopies provided by Ivy. Some read, others not.

I'd heard nothing from Lizzie Griesser. Hesitated to call her again. Might one of the articles shed light on the name or fate of the tiny subcellar lady?

In for a penny.

Before turning to the old news stories, I fired off a text to Katy. Queried the state of the floors at my town house. Birdie's disposition. Her knowledge of romantic spots near DC.

She replied within minutes.

Cat sulky.

Floors delayed. Occupancy still a no-go.

Salamander Resort, Middleburg, Virginia.

I googled the hotel, then linked over to the website. The place looked perfect. A two-night stay might require me to sell a major organ, but what the hell. Ryan and I badly needed some romance. He'd arrive in two days and stay with me at Ivy's. Once I knew the date that Chuck and I would part ways, I'd book us in.

I spent the rest of the day and well into the evening reading about the Warring brothers and the colorful exploits of the Foggy Bottom Gang. Juicy stuff, but uninformative regarding the subcellar remains.

At six, I spoke with Ryan for almost an hour. Considered telling him what I'd seen at the Petco. Decided that might qualify as gossip and didn't. Besides, he knew neither Ivy nor Zanetti.

At ten, I zapped a frozen pizza for dinner.

While eating, I watched a *West Wing* rerun—I *was* in DC—then Colbert.

I fell asleep just past one.

It was getting to be routine.

Startled awake by a buzzing on the bedside table, I reached out and scrabbled for my mobile.

The screen told me it was 4:24 a.m. And that the caller was Jada Thacker.

"Are you a fan of *Groundhog Day*?" she asked cryptically.

"What?" Brain still too sleep-fogged to pick up on the reference.

"Bill Murray? Reliving the same day over and over?"

"It's four in the morning and you're asking for a movie review?"

"Another fire's going gangbusters in Foggy Bottom."

That snapped my mind into focus.

"Any fatalities?" I asked.

"One DOA is rolling toward the morgue as we speak."

"Holy sweet Jesus," I said, and thought of the four corpses that had lain on my table.

"Yeah."

"Arson?"

"Looks that way."

Ice solidified in my chest.

"Susan Lipsey is still hospitalized and not allowed any form of communication," I said, puzzled.

"She is."

"Where are the Stoll twins?"

"Still in the wind."

"Would they . . . ?"

I let the question hang unanswered. Thacker didn't try.

"What do you want me to do?" I asked.

"Go back to sleep. I'm calling to make sure you're still in DC."

"I am," I said.

Shitballs, I thought.

Morning dawned with a fine drizzle spattering the leaves outside my window. The sky, a melancholy gray, was threatening to ratchet things up into full-on rain.

First off, I checked my phone. Was shocked to see that I'd slept until nine-thirty.

Understandable. I hadn't fallen asleep again until after five. And—except for the muted drops beyond the glass—as usual there wasn't a sound in the house.

Propping myself up in bed, I scrolled through my latest emails and texts. Ads. Credit card offers. Facebook notices. Found nothing from Thacker.

Pulling on sweats, I brushed my hair and teeth, then dialed the ME's office. Thacker was busy doing an autopsy. The receptionist assured me my call would be returned as quickly as possible.

Four hours later it was. I was at Ivy's mile-wide kitchen island, making a salami sandwich and looking out over the soggy grounds.

"Thanks for making yourself available," Thacker said. "But we won't be needing your help on this one."

"You've IDed the vic?"

"No. But we will. The DOA is female, probably white, probably in her twenties. She was badly burned, but we managed to lift prints and observe a carnival of body details."

"Death was due to smoke inhalation?" I asked.

"I'm still working on that." Did Thacker sound uneasy? Or merely tired?

A brief hum of empty air. Then she asked, "Do you remember Sergeant Burgos?"

"Fireman Frolicsome."

"That's the guy. Laugh a minute. Anyway, Burgos is also heading the team handling this investigation and, with some *urging* from yours truly, he shared a few very early observations. As you know, the two other buildings that were torched belonged to the same holding company."

"W-C Commerce," I said.

"So does this third one."

"Are you serious?"

"Not something I'd kid about. Which explains why this fire was discovered so quickly. You know Merle Deery, right? The homicide detective that Susan Lipsey shot?"

"I do."

"While investigating the first fire deaths, Deery discovered that a few other Foggy Bottom properties also belong to W-C. And that one building was standing empty. Crafty cop that he is, he ordered eyes on those places. Nothing steady, just a unit cruising by now and then."

Way to go, Merle, I thought.

"Why was the building vacant?" I asked.

"It had just gone on the market."

Deep down, yet another soft ping in my subconscious.

"Here's another curious twist," Thacker continued. "Burgos says this was arson, but the MO was totally different from the previous two. And quite creative. The doer doused a pan of kitty litter with gasoline. Then he went outside to disconnect a line supplying propane to a clothes dryer. Returning inside, he disconnected the appliance end of that line. After tossing a match into the litter, he went back outside, reconnected the gas line, and opened the valve. Ka-boom! Sound familiar?"

"The same MO as in one of the files you asked me to review."

"Yes, ma'am," she said.

"Do you think this fire is connected to your earlier case?"

"*Anything's* possible," she answered. "But it's unlikely. That homicide involved a kid killing his granny."

"Doesn't sound like a copycat," I agreed.

"At least not a very wily one."

"What was the DOA doing in an empty house?" I asked.

"Who the hell knows. By the way, this latest hasn't hit the news yet. Not that there's been much interest. Those who've contacted my office agreed to hold off until the vic's next of kin have been notified."

We disconnected.

I sat a long time, listening to the brush of wind in the branches outside. To the rhythmic tapping of raindrops on glass.

Troubled, but oblivious as to the cause.

Until the front door opened, and heavy boots clomped my way.

CHAPTER 32

Zanetti smiled at me from the doorway, all Hollywood hair and amber eyes.

"Tempe. What an awesome surprise. Though I knew you were stuck here on chinch duty."

"Hey, Ben." Voice totally neutral.

"I was on my way home but thought you might want a break from the little guy."

"Aren't you allergic?"

"I am. But what's a little sneezing and itching if I can score points with my sweetie. Also, my Wi-Fi's out and I need to use Ivy's computer for some work stuff."

Zanetti crossed the kitchen, placed a bag on the island, and perched on the stool next to mine. Legs outstretched in faded extra-long jeans, he leaned back, elbows on the marble or quartzite or whatever the stone was.

"You are in luck, Madame." Nodding solemnly at the bag. "I am the bearer of treasure from the Old Line State."

I just looked at him, face blank, brain racing through a memory-based facial comparison. Nose. Ears. Cheekbones. Jawline. *Was* this the same man I'd seen at the Petco?

"That bag contains nothing less than steamed blue crabs from Cantler's," he declared.

I raised questioning brows.

"Jimmy Cantler's Riverside Inn?" He waited for recognition to leap across my face, but I wasn't cooperating. The brows stayed up.

"You know *not* of these delicacies?" he asked, feigning shocked disbelief.

I wagged my head no.

"You are in for a treat. I did my usual and bought far too much for one person."

"Sorry, but I just made myself—"

"One never refuses bounty from Cantler's."

"What if one is allergic to seafood?"

"Is one?"

"No."

"Excellent." Crow's-feet crinkling at the corners of his eyes. "Would you like a beer?"

"Water, please."

"Evian?"

"Tap. I'm opposed to the concept of single-use plastic bottles."

"I admire such conviction."

Zanetti went to the fridge to get a Sam Adams for himself. To the sink to fill a tumbler for me.

The kitchen was slowly yielding to an irresistible aroma. The scent of seaweed and salt water and the things that live in it was sending an olfactory cue straight to the appetite center deep in my gray matter.

What the hell. The guy had blue crabs. I'd eat with him, figure out the Petco sighting later.

Returning to the island, Zanetti said, "I drove these bad boys all the way down from Annapolis. My Rover's going to smell like a fish market for months. Do you know if Ivy has shell crackers and picks?"

As I searched drawers, Zanetti pulled items from the bag. Paper plates and napkins. Lidded pots containing butter and vinegar. A grease-stained brown paper bundle.

I lay tools beside each plate. Unwrapping the bundle, he centered a crustacean on mine.

For a moment we focused on cracking and digging.

Sweet Christ on a pickle. Cantler's knew how to do crab.

Zanetti chatted as we ate, relaxed and self-assured. Not the demeanor of a man whose dinner partner had just caught him cheating on his fiancée.

Was I wrong? Did Zanetti have a doppelgänger who frequented strip malls with tattooed bimbos? Or had I been right, but escaped detection among the parked cars?

Zanetti wasn't the brightest squirrel climbing the tree. I knew that. But would he go all alpha gorilla if I let on that I'd seen him? If he guessed that I was probing to confirm my suspicion?

What the flip. I owed it to Ivy.

"These came from Annapolis?" I asked, casual as hell.

"Yes, ma'am."

"Ivy said you'd be out of town this week. You were in Maryland?" Zanetti nodded.

"Someplace nice?"

Zanetti snorted. "Flintstone, a toad's turd of a place crapped between the Tussey and Warrior Mountains."

"You must have finished earlier than you expected." Hoping the fine citizens of Flintstone never learned of Zanetti's crude remark.

"Yeah."

"A big sale?"

"Big enough."

"Good for you."

Blotting butter from his lips, Zanetti switched the focus to me. "I hear there were developments in your case while I was incommunicado in Hooterville."

"Sorry?" I hadn't a clue what he meant.

"More arson in Foggy Bottom."

"Right." Surprised. Thacker said there was a blackout on coverage until the DOA's next of kin had been notified. Had some go-getter journalist ignored the agreement and reported on the blaze anyway? Or had word spread via the net? It was impossible to keep a gag on social media.

"Super-weird MO like that. All three blazes have to be linked."

"What do you mean?" I asked.

"Nothing. It's just a crazy-ass way to start a fire. Anyone die in this new one?"

"I can't discuss an open investigation." Cool as frost in February.

Zanetti gave me a vaguely offended look, like maybe I'd failed to reciprocate in the sharing of confidences.

When we'd devoured the last crab, I helped clean up the mess. Zanetti watched as I made myself a mug of chamomile tea and walked from the room, fervently hoping he'd complete his online business quickly and leave.

Upstairs, I cleaned Chuck's cage, then filled his water and food dispensers. Thinking he might like to bathe, I filled a shallow tray with chinchilla dust, a product recommended to me by a clerk at the Petco.

The chinch regarded me with what I took to be appreciation.

"You're on your own with the bath, little guy," I said. "I'm not going to groom you." The packaging stated that brushing was recommended post-*toilette*.

Three-fifty-five.

Feeling jittery and trapped, I debated what to do with the rest of the afternoon.

Rain was falling with gusto now, and the sky had darkened to an even more pessimistic gray. Unable to bear the thought of my already damp boots, and not wanting to slog through the downpour in sneakers or sandals, I decided to hunker in and spend more time with Ivy's photocopies.

Not a sound drifted in from elsewhere in the house.

Still, I couldn't concentrate.

It wasn't just the feeling of being corralled. Something else was bugging me. What? Why were my nerves on edge? Thacker's call? The third fire? The Zanetti-bimbo sighting? Maybe Zanetti. The two anonymous texts? My failure to tell Derry about them?

Focus, Brennan. Find some crumb that will shed light on the subcellar lady.

A couple of hours later I was taking a break from skimming newsprint, checking email, when the sound of movement caused me to look up. Not really a sound, more a change in the air.

Zanetti was standing at my open door, a steaming mug in his right hand, tea bag label hanging over one side.

"I'm an asshole," he said.

"Sorry?"

"Asking about a case. That was way out of line."

I didn't disagree.

"I brought a peace offering." He raised the mug. "Figured your tea would be gone by now. Or stone cold. Seems like a chamomile kind of day."

I uncrossed my ankles and stood. Again, my legs tingled from the sudden change in orientation, from the new responsibility of holding me upright.

Zanetti crossed to me and offered the mug. I accepted it, slid the string along the rim, and took a small sip.

"Brewed with a little help from Twinings," he said, smiling.

I smiled back.

Wondered.

Again.

Could this man really be a player and ten yards deep in denial?

Zanetti tipped his head to read the headline topping the story I'd just laid down. "You're interested in the Warrings?" he asked.

"Mm."

"Bad dudes in their day. No surprise they made enemies."

"What do you mean?"

"Nothing at all." Giving a nothing-at-all shrug. "I'll let you get back to it."

With that he was gone.

I took up the article I'd set aside but found my concentration had grown even poorer than earlier. My conversation with Zanetti kept looping like software at an ATM.

Why? What was I uneasy about? The man was a successful realtor. Ivy's boyfriend. Ivy was no dummy. Surely, she'd vetted the guy.

Still.

Was it because Zanetti knew about the most recent fire? About the way it was set? Because he questioned my interest in the Warrings? Because he was in DC and not away as he'd told Ivy?

Because he was a goddam cheater?

I pictured Zanetti with his pierced and tattooed companion.

Inexplicably, a comment made by Jada Thacker channeled into my thoughts.

Ping.

Impossible.

Still.

I hesitated, then dialed DC's chief medical examiner.

Thacker took my call and provided the information I sought, never questioning my reason for needing it.

No way, Brennan. You're overreaching because you don't like the guy.

Then why the red flags from my id?

I booted my laptop and opened a series of case files. Logging over to Zillow.com, I entered an address. Then another. And another.

Lightbulb moment.

Bloody hell!

Body details. Kitty litter. A man at a Petco. A real-estate listing.

I sat back, heart pumping fast and hard.

To calm myself, I drank more tea, now meltwater cold.

Still, I was thirsty. Desperately thirsty.

What's going on? I don't feel right.

Craving something cold and fizzy, I took the mug and descended to the kitchen. Was at the fridge when a noise at my back startled me.

I whipped around.

Something deep in my brain gave a sideways lurch.

CHAPTER 33

My skin felt strange. As if moths, maybe spiders were crawling over my body.

My thoughts were beginning to coalesce like sludge in a pond.

Zanetti said nothing. But I'm also good at that game. I said nothing. Silence filled the space between us.

Zanetti stood motionless, one hand on the door frame, the other behind him and out of sight.

The air crackled with tension. Or was I imagining hostility that didn't exist?

"Forget something?" I asked.

No response.

The mug slipped from my grasp and hit the tile with a sharp crack.

Disjointed memories flashed in my brain, slides in some cerebral power point delirium.

A chinchilla.

A face obscured by a Wizards cap.

Tattooed arms.

A Victorian building in sooty ruin.

Charred corpses.

Body bags rolling on gurneys.

My stomach roiled and I tasted bile in my mouth.

Zanetti's face had become a blurry mask.

I smelled danger, dark and quick as a viper's tongue.

Get it together, Brennan!

I blinked, struggling to bring the world back into focus.

How had I gotten to the kitchen?

Had I brought my phone?

I dropped my right hand from the fridge door, keeping my arm close to my body in hopes of detecting a hard bulge in one pocket.

Felt nothing.

My thoughts were a swirling vortex circling one question.

Where was my mobile?

Dizzy, I raised my left hand to cover my face as I ran my eyes over the room. Countertops. Stove. Sink. Table.

Zanetti in the doorway.

No phone.

Ivy's words slammed home from our initial tour of the house.

Think! Where was the damn thing?

Beside the sink. A short six feet away. But how to get to it without setting him off?

Buy time.

I drew a series of deep breaths.

My mind was still spinning, but more slowly now, thanks to the oxygen intake. Images and voices were rearranging and connecting with soft little clicks.

I inhaled again. Moved my hips slightly, seeming only to shift my weight, but inching a few steps to my right.

"You screwed up, Ben." It was hard to talk, the words seeming to take forever navigating from my mind to my tongue.

"How's that?"

"Who was she?"

"Who was who?"

"The third fire didn't burn long enough or hot enough for your plan to work." My voice felt thick, my words slurry.

"What are you talking about?"

"Jada Thacker said the most recent victim didn't die in the fire," I said, carefully forming each word. "No smoke in her lungs or trachea, that sort of thing."

Some emotion rippled across Zanetti's face, but he said nothing.

"Thacker said the vic would be easy to ID based on body details. I just phoned to ask what she meant."

I swallowed, fighting down a new wave of nausea. Inched another small step.

"She was referring to tattoos and piercings. I saw you and your friend at the Petco."

"What's your point? That I was dancing with someone besides my ball-and-chain fiancée?"

"I had to wonder why you'd go to a pet store, you being so allergic to animals."

Zanetti's jaw muscles clenched, relaxed.

"I might not have put it all together, but you tipped me with your 'super weird' comment." Hooking shaky air quotes. "You got that wrong, too."

Adrenaline was pumping through me now, muscling out whatever Zanetti had put in the tea. I feigned dizziness and, imperceptibly, eased another few inches toward my goal.

"You overheard Ivy and me discussing kitty litter and gasoline, thought we were talking about the MO for the earlier Foggy Bottom arsons. You used the trick to make the third blaze look like the work of the same person."

"You're fucking nuts."

"What you didn't know, being out in 'Hooterville'"—more air quotes—"was that a suspect was already in custody for the first two arsons."

"This is all lunatic speculation." Though concern now wrinkled his brow.

"Is it?"

"You've got nothing to tie me to any fire." Firm, but with an undercurrent of intense feeling growing in his voice. "Or to any fricasseed chick."

"The property was on the market, Ben. Listed with your firm. You knew that W-C held title. You had the keys. The entrance code. Whatever."

"That could be true of a dozen other realtors."

"The dead woman was a poster child for tattooing and piercing.

The ME says she'll have her IDed by day's end." Not exactly Thacker's words, but close enough.

Sweat was now dampening the black curls at Zanetti's hairline.

If you don't set him off, this doesn't have to get violent.

Good advice from my frontal lobe. I ignored it. I'd made it across the room and was now close enough.

"Sound like anyone you know, Ben?"

"You're batshit crazy."

Maybe it was the drug-laced chamomile. Or the adrenaline rush. Maybe outrage at the way Zanetti had obviously been playing Ivy, whose wealth had likely kept him close. Maybe it was the false confidence I felt from having managed to reach and push the panic button. Ignoring the cerebral warnings, now at Defcon 1, I pressed even harder.

"Are you familiar with the big three in cop lingo, Ben?" Still brain-clouded, I had to think for a second to recall what they were: "Motive, means, and . . . opportunity? You . . . you're rock solid on the last two. But for the life of me I can't figure out *why* you killed her."

No response. Just a hot amber sizzle that sent electricity fizzing through my chest, down my arms, and out into my palms.

"You're batshit crazy," he repeated.

I must have kept talking, but I couldn't remember most of what I laid out. Warnings about the risk of physical harm during a takedown by cops? About the hazards of prison? The needle? Eternal damnation?

I was going full throttle when Zanetti straightened, bringing the hidden arm into view.

For the second time in three days, I was staring down the barrel of a handgun pointed at my face. This one was a big-ass Ruger 5.7 semi-automatic.

"You're dead, lady."

The amber eyes flicked to the gun's inspection port, checking for a live round.

What happened next is a kaleidoscopic montage of whirling colors and figures and voices and sounds.

"Down!" A barked command.

As I dropped, Zanetti's gun hand flew up.

"Who the fu—!"

Before hitting the floor, I caught a flash of a cylindrical object arrowing toward Zanetti's skull. A rolling pin? A baton? It was all too fast to register. All I really understood was that Zanetti's massive upper torso was lurching sideways.

Head covered with both arms, I listened to scuffling, cursing, gagging, and panting. The thud of flesh and bones slamming tile.

Finally, quiet.

I held in place for what seemed an eon but was probably less than a minute.

Then I mustered the courage to look up.

Zanetti was lying prone, arms above his head like a teller on a bank floor during a heist. Two uniformed cops hovered over him, one clutching his baton, both with hair in disarray and breathing hard.

A third cop stood just inside the door, weapon drawn and trained on the big man's chest.

CHAPTER 34

I t was another warm and balmy southern night.

The distant woods had gone a deep wooly gray. Closer in, wooden fences threw looping shadows around acres of paddock and lawn.

Now and then, an owl hooted, a horse whinnied. Otherwise, the only sound was the industrious chirping of crickets.

Ryan and I were relaxing on the balcony of our suite. Sipping café au laits and watching the last rays of a butterscotch sunset yield to night.

"Recovering" might be a more accurate term than relaxing. Tennis. Horseback riding. Hiking. Swimming. Winery touring. Except for the three spa sessions, our schedule had not been leisurely.

Katy had nailed it. Given the stress of the previous weeks, the Salamander Resort was exactly what Ryan and I needed.

We'd talked frequently about the events in DC. Especially as new intel trickled in. We'd be doing something unrelated—croquet, chess, dining, reading—when one of us would make a comment or ask a question.

That happened now.

"I've forgotten," Ryan said. "Who was the last DOA?"

"Raelynn Krassle."

"Zanetti's pierced and inked twenty-something?"

"Yes."

"He killed her because—?"

"Krassle wanted to be more than just a sometime diversion," I replied. "When Zanetti refused to make a bigger commitment, she threatened to phone Ivy."

"Getting busted cheating hardly seems like a motive for murder. On the other hand, preserving the chance to marry into a fortune would be strong incentive."

"Zanetti claims Krassle's death was accidental. That she did it to herself."

"How's that work, her weighing at least a hundred pounds less than him?"

"Zanetti says they argued, and Krassle got physical. To avoid a full-out battle, he pried loose from her grip, shoved her against a wall, and stormed off. When he returned, Krassle was still lying where she'd fallen, cold and not breathing."

"So, conscientious citizen that he is, Zanetti bundled her body off to an empty Foggy Bottom property that he'd listed, dumped it inside, and lit the place up."

"Mistakenly thinking the kitty litter and gasoline MO would point to whoever had torched the other two houses. And unaware that Susan Lipsey had already taken the fall for those arsons."

"*Sacrebleu.*" I heard Ryan wag his head in disbelief. As he had upon first learning of Zanetti's confession.

"I got a call from Deery while you were recovering from your little mishap with Trigger," I said, offering a small grin.

Ryan's lounger creaked as he shifted to face me.

"I did not fall off that horse."

"You could have fooled me. And Trigger."

"Her name was Baby Doll."

I bit back every witty quip that suggested itself.

"How's your hip?"

"The sauna helped," he said sheepishly.

"And the Advil."

"And that. Have you heard from any next of kin of the four upstairs fire vics?"

"Skylar Hill's husband phoned Thacker."

"Alvon Finrock."

I nodded. "To Thacker's surprise, Finrock was reasonably polite. He grudgingly thanked her for expediting the transfer of Skylar's remains to Canada for burial."

"What was the deal with Jawaad el-Aman's old man claiming to have a rendezvous that didn't exist?"

"Turned out the bank was wrong. Or at least uninformed. El-Aman senior was, in fact, scheduled for a sit-down with two of his financial planners. Wanting confidentiality, he'd requested that the meeting be off the books."

"Nice job hitting that panic button, champ," Ryan said.

"Thank God Ivy had briefed me on those."

"I'm surprised Zanetti wasn't watching for that."

"Ivy hadn't told him about the security system."

"Why not?" Ryan sounded surprised.

"When I asked her she said she wasn't sure."

We fell silent, watching night snap down like a lid on a trunk. The chirping had gone fortissimo, the ensemble working toward the evening's crescendo.

"Crickets make noise by rubbing their wings together," I said. "The males have a scraper on one wing which they draw across little pegs on the other."

"Why?"

"To attract females."

"And you know this how?"

"I googled cricket behavior."

"Of course, you did." Ryan was now a disembodied voice in the dark. "And the cricket ladies just sit back and enjoy the performance?"

"Presumably."

"Zanetti should have stuck to a similar approach with Ivy," Ryan said.

"Instead, he killed Krassle. He couldn't risk losing the meal ticket that Ivy represented."

"Wasn't Zanetti a hotshot realtor raking in big bucks?"

"That's what Ivy thought. But Deery interviewed several of Zanetti's colleagues. According to them, the guy wasn't earning enough to cover the rent on his office."

"How's Ivy doing?" I heard Ryan reach out to take a sip of his coffee. Return the delicate cup to its delicate saucer with a soft *clink*.

"She's devastated, but tough. Her podcast and a never-ending chain of breaking news will keep her busy for now."

"And she has Chuck."

"Apparently that's become a permanent arrangement."

"I like Chuck," Ryan said. "The chinch is ambitious."

"Ditto Ivy."

"They'll definitely go places," Ryan agreed.

"As will Zanetti. For a very long time. He's been charged with first-degree murder, attempted murder, kidnapping, arson, mayhem, I forget everything the DA listed."

"Was it Zanetti who sent you the two threatening texts?"

"You ready for this?" I couldn't help but smile. "It was Halsey Banks."

"Who?"

"Halsey Banks is Norbert Mirek's nephew."

"The guy whose bones you dug out of the animal poop?"

"Very good, sir. I'm surprised you remember that."

"Why did Banks try to intimidate you?"

"He didn't. He just wanted me to stop working on his uncle's case because he feared an exorbitant bill for my services."

We were quiet for maybe four or five minutes. Like mine, Ryan's thoughts drifted. But in a different direction.

"Have you learned the identity of your no-show caller?"

It took a moment to unfold the question.

"The woman who ghosted me at the Einstein Memorial? Deery cracked that nut. Her name is Georgia Daughtler."

"Why did she phone you?"

"Daughtler is Roy Stoll's former wife, and feels less than kindly toward her ex. She hoped to cause him trouble but got cold feet and decided to back off."

"How did Daughtler get your name and contact information?"

"She works as a secretary in the law office that represents the W-C

Commerce holding company. When Ivy called there, doing her journalist on the prowl thing, somehow my name came up."

More of the buoyant wing-scraping sonata. Another soft clink of
china. Then Ryan asked,

"What's happening with Susan Lipsey?"

"When discharged from the hospital, she'll face four counts of
first-degree murder, two counts of attempted murder, two counts of
arson, and a slew of others charges I don't recall."

"Tweedle Dum and Tweedle Dee?"

I shot Ryan a look of faux disapproval. "The Stoll twins may be the
most curious aspect of all this. Clearly, Lipsey is not well, but that a pair
of forty-something men would carry out their grandmother's felonious
plans seems a stretch. Roy is apparently the badder apple—lucky for
me since it was Ronan who showed up when Lipsey was on the verge
of putting a bullet in my chest. We're only just discovering all the ways
the Warrings seem to have preyed on Lipsey and her brood over the
decades, but there's quite a history there that's coming to light."

"You'd think that eighty years would have been long enough for the
feud to burn out," Ryan said.

"Weirdly, it seemed to burn brighter every year. From the Foggy Bottom Gang, via Amon Clock and his ill-fated girlfriend, Doris Gardner,
through Gardner's daughter, Susan Lipsey, right down to her grandsons,
Roy and Ronan."

Ryan shook his head, let the silence linger for a moment, then asked:
"Have you managed to ID the little subcellar gal?"

"Sadly, no. And prospects don't look good. Lizzie's lab couldn't
extract usable DNA."

Ryan reached over and took my hand. "You'll figure it out."

Maybe, I thought.

Just maybe.

EPILOGUE

Four months later

Call it a character flaw or whatever. I'm obsessed with mysteries that I'm unable to solve. Cannot let them go.

Ivy's three hundred photocopies went with me to Charlotte. I won't say I spent all my free time working through them that summer and fall, but I spent many hours with those smeary, smudgy pages.

In mid-October when the days were growing cool, the nights almost crisp, and the hardwoods were considering a split from their leaves, I made my first breakthrough. At the bottom of the second to last stack.

The article had appeared in the *Washington Post* on February 19, 1943. Nothing lengthy, only six column inches.

POLICE SEEK 7 MISSING PERSONS

Police in Washington are seeking information relating to seven persons who have disappeared. Relatives and friends are inquiring for them.

Anyone knowing of the whereabouts of the following should communicate with Sergeant Arthur Gunders at the Cathedral Heights station on Idaho Avenue.

A list followed that brief bit of text.

The fourth entry caught my attention.

Ruby Berle Dockeray, age twenty-five, had been reported missing by her sister. Ruby was last seen thirteen months earlier outside a home in the Foggy Bottom neighborhood.

The address was that of the first fire.

Hot damn!

I had a name.

Ruby Berle Dockeray.

Suspecting the effort was probably futile, I phoned the Cathedral Heights station. Sergeant Arthur Gunders had retired in 1972. Died in 1984.

I asked if Ruby Dockeray was ever found. Response: An MP case from 1943? Are you serious?

Undeterred, I pressed harder. Was told that if a file that old still existed—an extremely remote possibility—it might be in the district's archives.

A very lengthy and somewhat confusing conversation with the archivist revealed that, prior to DC home rule, the National Archives would have set the records management requirements for police reports in the district. Unfortunately, the gentleman had no knowledge of retention regulations back in 1943 but felt they were probably like those of 1979, the earliest with which he *was* familiar. As of 1979, a missing person report had to be kept at the local department for two years, then transferred to the Federal Records Center for ten. After that, it would be destroyed. He felt chances were slim to none that a 1943 missing person file would still exist.

Discouraged, I phoned Ivy. She was delighted to help—in exchange for a promise of exclusivity should a newsworthy scoop emerge. I suspect she was envisioning a human-interest piece that would win her a Pulitzer or some other journalism prize.

While awaiting Ivy's feedback, I started my own digging.

Googling the name "Ruby Berle Dockeray" and "1943" yielded nothing but the original *Post* story about the seven MPs. Substituting "1918," the year of Ruby's birth, was another dead end.

I turned back to Ivy's photocopies and spent weeks rereading every one in my spare time. Found no mention of Ruby Berle Dockeray. Not surprising. Ivy had focused on coverage of the Warrings and the Foggy Bottom Gang.

I'd had luck with the *Post*, so, after ponying up the fee for a half-year plan, I wasted an additional month troweling through the newspaper's online archives.

Births. Marriages. Obituaries. Arrests. Divorces.

Nada.

Like a rat working a maze, I buzzed through cyber-loop after cyber-loop, hoping for pay dirt.

More nada.

Frustrated, I decided to try another angle.

Ruby Berle Dockeray was last seen at the Foggy Bottom house. As of 1942, the house belonged to W-C Commerce. W-C was a holding company established by Emmitt Warring and Amon Clock.

I'd already read Ivy's articles generated by a search using the keyword "Warring," so I went with the name Amon Clock.

Though fewer in number, an abundance of links popped up.

A big chunk of that autumn's reading was devoted to those sites. Katy thought I was obsessed. Maybe I was.

Eventually, I stumbled across the picture.

The Washington Times. May 4, 1937. Page four, below a continuation of front-page coverage of the Hindenburg disaster. A suspect had been cited for holding the largest cache of illegal liquor in DC since the repeal of Prohibition four years earlier.

A group photo accompanied the article. Two men, one the suspect, a woman, and a child. The foursome was standing in bright sunlight on the National Mall. A banner in the background announced the first National Boy Scout Jamboree.

Names ran below the image. The "child" in the middle was Ruby Berle Dockeray.

It took less than a minute to establish that the jamboree had taken place in June of 1937. I did the math. Ruby was nineteen at the time the pic was snapped. Fully adult, but small.

As I studied the faces with a handheld lens—each surprisingly sharp for an image that old—odd thoughts began fluttering in my head, frail and ill-formed, like ghost moths circling a porch bulb. Eventually, disparate bytes collided, leading to a pair of irrefutable conclusions.

The subcellar victim was, in fact, Ruby Berle Dockeray.

The constellation of features barely discernible on her mummified and decomposing corpse—the low nasal bridge, prominent forehead, thin, silky hair, and extremely short stature—suggested a disorder known as Laron syndrome.

Laron syndrome is a condition that occurs when the body is unable to utilize growth hormone. Reduced muscle strength and endurance are additional symptoms frequently seen.

I'm not the overly emotional type. But I'd felt a tremendous sadness as an imagined scene surged up in my brain. A tiny woman, perhaps weak and vulnerable, succumbing to blows hard enough to fracture her skull and jaw.

As the archivist had predicted, Ivy struck out in her search for an MP report on Ruby Berle Dockeray. The young woman had simply vanished.

I took solace in knowing that, more than eight decades after Ruby's disappearance, I'd helped with the recovery and identification of her remains. Sadly, her sister was long dead. And Deery was unable to locate a single living relative with whom to share the news.

Ruby was laid to rest in Congressional Cemetery in Southeast DC, a graveyard older than Arlington. I was there. Deery. A preacher. A few of the kind church ladies who attend the burials of those lacking kin.

It was a crisp winter day, the wind grabbing our scarves and hems and sending them dancing. Carrying the scent of dead leaves, fresh-turned grass, and moist soil swirling among the headstones around us.

Watching the simple casket inch down into the grave, I wondered about Ruby's view of her neighbors in death. Supreme court justices, cabinet members, senators, representatives, at least one vice president.

Somehow, I think she'd have approved of the company she'd be keeping.

Ruby's time, place, and manner of death remain mysteries. There seems to be no way to determine her final path to the dismal non-grave below the Foggy Bottom house.

Technically, then, Ruby's file is still open.

I hope someday her whole truth will be known.

ACKNOWLEDGMENTS

As usual, this book was made better and more accurate by the input of others.

I owe thanks to Detective Michael Pavero, IAAI-CFI, MIAAI, Crime Scene Technician, ATF Arson/Explosives Task Force, MPDC Homicide Branch, and to Vito Maggiolo, Public Information Officer, DC Fire and EMS Department.

Much of my knowledge of the Warring brothers came from a single volume: *The Foggy Bottom Gang: The Story of the Warring Brothers of Washington, DC* by Leo Warring (Parafine Press: Cleveland, 2020).

I am grateful on multiple levels to my daughter, Kerry Reichs, a longtime resident of Washington, DC. For rides to and from the airport. For a lovely soft bed on the third floor of her home. For endless driving tours of our nation's capital. For millions of insider tips on life in the district.

A heartfelt thanks goes out to my editors: Rick Horgan in the US, Brittany Lavery in Canada, Katherine Armstrong in the UK, and Anthea Bariamis in Australia. You guys rock!

I appreciate the support of Deneen Howell, my legal representative at Williams and Connolly, LLP. Way to go keeping me legit and lawful!

Melissa Fish was always there to check details and facts. And to set me straight on backstory from earlier Temperance Brennan novels.

Paul Reichs offered constructive editorial advice.

Turk and Roy kept me company and buoyed my spirits when I felt sad missing Skinny.

I want to recognize all those who work so very hard on my behalf.

At home in the US, Nan Graham, Ashley Gilliam, Zoe Cole, Jaya Miceli, Brian Belfiglio, Abigail Novak, Brianna Yamashita, Sophie Guimaraes, and Katie Rizzo. North of the border, Nicole Winstanley, Lisa Wray, Jasmine Elliott, Kaitlyn Lonnee, and Rebecca Snoddon. On the other side of the pond, Ian Chapman, Suzanne Baboneau, Harriett Collins, Rich Vlietstra, Polly Osborn, Maddie Allen, Dominic Brendon, Rich Hawton, and Mathew Watterson. Down Under, Dan Ruffino, Elissa Baillie, Fleur Hamilton, Gabby Oberman, Kate Charlton, and Kiara Codemo.

Thanks to Ervin Serrano for the wonderful jacket. Big hugs to Kevin Hanson for his support across so many books.

There are scores of others too numerous to name. If I failed to mention you, I apologize. Your constant support and occasional ribbing are appreciated!

I send my love to all of Tempe's loyal followers. You are the reason I write these books! I hope to see hordes of you at this year's signings and other live events.

Please continue to visit my website (KathyReichs.com), like me on Facebook (@kathyreichsbooks), and follow me on Instagram (@kathyreichs) and X (@kathyreichs).

If this book contains errors, they are my fault.